ALSO BY DENNIS KOLLER

Be Sure to Read His Powerful
Debut Novel *The Oath*.

To Janet + Jason

KISSED BY THE SNOW

A ROB KINCAID NOVEL

Enjoy. You are The best neighbors in creation. We love you.

Dennis

Dennis Koller

Pen Books
California

Pen Books
A Division of Pen Communication
Pleasant Hill, California

This book is a work of fiction. Names, characters, places, and incidents either are products of the author's imagination or are used fictitiously. Any resemblance to actual events or locales or persons, living or dead, is entirely coincidental.

First Pen Books paperback edition September 2014

For information about special discounts for bulk purchases, please visit denniskoller.com

Cover Design by Will Jackson at wdjacksoncovers@gmail.com

Manufactured in the United States of America

ISBN-13: 9780692286951

ISBN-10: 0692286950

To Sarah:
Whose inspiration and
prodding never allowed
me to abandon the dream.

ACKNOWLEDGMENTS

The writing and publication of a book requires many hands:
My thanks to:

My sons, Rob, John and Joe, whose nuanced critiques made this a much better novel.

Clyde Matsumoto, my editor, whose careful attention to detail found my every inconsistency.

Dave Almeida, who I taught in high school and who ended up teaching the teacher a thing or three or four about life in a war zone.

1

MONDAY
SAN FRANCISCO

Hartmann drummed his fingers on the desk, glancing quickly at the clock hanging on the opposite wall. Eight-eleven. "Come on. Come on," he shouted into the empty room. "Answer the god damn phone."

"Federal Aviation Administration. Phil Cruz speaking," the voice said.

About F-ing time, he started to say, but then caught himself. "Mr. Cruz?" he said with as much self-restraint as he could muster "This is Special Agent William Hartmann. FBI out of San Francisco. Our Deputy Director gave me your name. He said you were the only FAA person on the west coast who could change the flight path of a plane already airborne. I need you to do that immediately."

"Sir, I can't do that unless ..."

"I'm sorry to interrupt, Mr. Cruz, but there's no time for *I can't do that*. You've got to get that plane back on the ground. There's a bomb on board.

2

Walt Kincaid awakened that misty Monday morning and squinted at the large red numbers on the clock radio beside his bed. Four forty-five am. He toyed with the idea of turning over and squeezing in an extra thirty-five minutes of sleep before the alarm sounded, but the adrenaline already coursing through his body told him that further sleep was not an option.

He rolled on his back, propped his pillows behind his head and stared at the ceiling. He would take an eight am flight from San Francisco to San Diego's Lindbergh Field where a driver would take him to Naval Special Warfare Command in Coronado. It was there that Kincaid and NSWC's commanding officer would put the finishing touches on Operation *Snow Plow*, the work authored by Walt and his secret FBI Task Force 64.

He got up and walked to the kitchen, putting his coffee in the microwave. The only thing that nagged him about *Snow Plow* was that, when fully operational, a number of innocent people were going to die. He had tried to rationalize away his concern by telling himself that they were in a war, and in war there were always going to be civilian casualties. Couldn't be helped. Collateral damage. His Jesuit professors at Georgetown would have told him that what he was planning was evil. But they were, he had decided, wrong. The ends *do* justify the means.

On the way to the shower, Walt stopped to look at his reflection in the full-length mirror located to the left of the bathroom door. What he saw was a sixty-seven year old FBI agent of medium height with a sagging face and a full head of wavy hair almost completely free of gray, thanks mostly to the hair coloring he had been using every six weeks for the past ten years. He hated getting old. He wasn't going to give in to the aging process just like he hadn't given in to the prostate cancer he was diagnosed with fifteen years ago. This was just who he was ... and had always been.

That attitude hadn't made him an easy person to live with. He realized that now. At times, and more frequently now since he was so close to mandatory retirement age, he regretted having such a hard-nosed personality. Especially with his close relationships. It had cost him his wife, and, to a certain extent, his son.

His wife had divorced him twenty years ago. She died ten years later of breast cancer. No matter what he did, he couldn't make amends to her. But Rob, his son, was a different story. He could still reconcile with him. Rob had gone into the military after high school and became a Navy SEAL. While they corresponded occasionally, they hadn't seen each other much over the past fifteen years or so.

With retirement looming, and *Snow Plow* promising to be a lasting testimony to his FBI career, he had begun to think how great it would be if Rob could come back home. He had left the SEALs a year ago and opened a

"Security Agency" that contracted with the Department of Defense and the Department of Justice, offering his "special talents" for jobs that may not pass Congressional oversight if they were carried out by the military.

The firm, headquartered in Virginia Beach, could just as well be HQ'd in San Francisco. He had written Rob a letter to that effect almost a month ago but hadn't heard back from him yet. If he could actually speak to Rob, he would tell him he was a different person than the one he knew fifteen years ago. Loneliness, it seemed, had trumped his tough guy persona.

Walt dried off and quickly dressed. Before leaving, he went into the spare bedroom as he did every morning, and knelt on the kneeler placed in front of a statue of Our Lady of Guadeloupe. It was a mini-shrine Betty had put up. Crossing himself, he said a quick prayer for the success of *Snow Plow* ... and Rob's safe return home.

=

Walt Kincaid arrived at San Francisco International at seven twenty-five and boarded Flight Five-Sixty to San Diego. At exactly eight-oh-two, the big plane rolled down the runway and glided gracefully into a crystal blue sky.

A few minutes later, the plane banked gently left and headed over the West Bay hills. Over the intercom, the pilot's calm voice told him that they were just now passing through eleven thousand feet on their way to a cruising altitude of thirty-six thousand feet, and that the high in San Diego was expected to be seventy-three degrees.

Walt sat back in his seat, and looked at his watch. It was eight-twelve. He closed his eyes in the hope of catching a quick nap before his flight reached San Diego.

=

Two men stood on a ridge in the West Bay hills and watched the big plane make the turn that would bring it almost directly overhead. They had parked their non-descript car in one of the many regional parks that dotted the landscape of the coastal hills running from San Francisco to Santa Cruz, and then hiked to the ridge just as dawn was breaking. Both wore black North Face parkas to ward off the cold, drippy mist that rolled off the Pacific Ocean that time of morning, and black ball caps with the red logo of San Jose's professional soccer team.

As the plane passed overhead, one of them pulled a stopwatch from his jacket pocket. "Are you ready?" he said in a thick Mexican accent.

"Si," his partner said, already keying a string of numbers into his iPhone.

=

Cruz had pulled up the flight on his computer screen. "Five-Sixty had wheels up at eight-zero-three," he told Hartmann. "It just now cleared the coastline over Pacifica. I've alerted the pilot to return." He paused. Hartmann could hear a few faint clicks of Cruz' keyboard. "He got the message," Cruz said. "The plane is beginning its turn back now. How much time do we have?"

Hartmann looked at his watch. It was eight-four-teen. "I wish I knew," he answered.

—

The plane had just started its wide arching turn back toward the airport when the man with the iPhone tapped the "Call" button. The seven-thirty-seven shuddered violently and then erupted in a massive orange and crimson ball of flame, scattering pieces of Walter Kincaid and one hundred eighteen other poor souls over four square miles of the blue Pacific below.

When Hartmann heard Cruz whisper, "Oh, shit," he knew they had run out of time.

—

An hour after Flight Five-Sixty went down, a white van bearing the name *Expert House Cleaning Service* pulled into Walt Kincaid's driveway.

Witnesses said there were two men in the van, and that both got out and went into the house. They all agreed they were wearing blue overalls and carrying what looked to be large laundry bags. It was in those "what looked to be large laundry bags" that the two *Expert House Cleaning Service*'s "cleaners" carried out the contents of Walt's wall safe, the flash disc containing his *Snow Plow* file, the hard drive from his computer and the contents of the top two drawers of his filing cabinet.

3

Tom McGuire had just finished getting dressed when he heard a faint explosion. Even though he couldn't tell how far away it was, he knew it had to be big because a few seconds later his house trembled slightly as the blast's shock wave rippled over it. It reminded him of the explosion and fire that occurred in San Bruno a few years back, caused by the eruption of a utility company gas line. Thirty-five people died in that explosion. He had been a cop for so long, his first reaction was to call the office. Which he did.

"Homicide. Inspector Murray speaking."

"Inspector Murray. This is Inspector McGuire calling."

"Sorry, sir. I can't tie up a line on someone I don't know." He paused. "Come to think of it, I did know a Tom McGuire once. Used to be my partner in Homicide, but he quit a while back. Haven't heard from him in years."

"He didn't quit," replied McGuire with a laugh. "Retired. And it was only twenty-eight days ago."

"Must just *seem* like forever," Murray responded, and then said, "Mac, it's damn good to hear from you, man. How have you been? Really, it seems like forever ago."

"Yeah, for me too, Bill. I haven't been in contact because I thought it best just to stay out of your hair for a while. Let you adjust. How are things there? You get a new partner yet?"

"Nah. They're still interviewing. At least that's what they tell me."

"Some things never change, do they?" McGuire said. "Hey, we will get together soon, I promise. Tell everyone I said hi. One of the reasons I called, though, was because I heard a big explosion about ten minutes ago. South of me. You have anything on that?"

"Yeah, we do. Main switchboard has been going crazy. Mostly eyewitnesses. Or so they say. You remember how that goes."

"I do indeed."

"The word is a plane blew up. Commercial. Out of SFO. Turn on TV. If that's the case, it'll be all over the news."

"Thanks, Bill. I'll wait for an hour or so. After they get it sorted out. Right now it will all be rumor and innuendo. If you hear anything definite, give me a shout, okay?"

"You bet, Mac. Hey ... really. Drop on down here sometime. All the guys ask about you. Wondering what you are up to."

"I will, Bill. You have my word. Give my best to the guys."

McGuire hung up and walked back to the bedroom. He had been a SFPD homicide inspector just shy of thirty years. He had told everyone he was *retiring,* but it was just a way he had to "save face." A way not to have to tell long-time friends and teammates that he was "quitting" on them. The truth of the matter was if he hadn't been personally recruited by Rob Kincaid, the son of his best friend and who, as a kid, had practically been part of his family, he would still be a cop.

Robert Kincaid had opened what he euphemistically called a *Security Agency* after he himself had retired from a distinguished career as a Navy SEAL. Rob told him that his *Agency*, which already had contracts with the Department of Defense and the Department of Justice, could use a fellow like him to run its "Law Enforcement" division, working primarily with the DOJ. *More money and less stress* was how Kincaid described the job in his recruiting pitch. He also said he was thinking seriously of moving his headquarters to San Francisco. McGuire was sixty-four years old and a year away from mandatory retirement age anyway. How could he refuse?

4

MONDAY
HINDU KUSH, PAKISTAN

Half a world away, as the sun was retreating behind the high peaks of the Hindu Kush, Robert Kincaid, Wolf Rosen and JJ Johnson squatted behind Chris Fuller and watched the infrared images being transmitted by the "Bird" back to the iPad in Fuller's lap. The *Bird* was the *RQ-11 Raven*, a hand-launched, battery-operated, propeller driven drone. Fuller was using what looked like an old-fashioned joystick to control its flight.

Radiating on the screen were the heat signatures of two sentries stationed half a mile from where Kincaid and his Red Squadron operators were quietly sitting in the evening twilight. They were thirty klicks inside Pakistan. It was 2050 hours.

"Doesn't look like these two guys are going to give us any problem, Rob," whispered Fuller over his shoulder. "They're not expecting us, that's for sure. Shootin' the shit with each other. Smoking. Just sittin' there waiting to die."

"Anything else moving around?" Kincaid asked.

"Nothing. Means their friends are all indoors. Hopefully asleep."

Kincaid and his team knew these mountains. Before retiring a year ago to form Red Squadron Security Agency, they had spent two years together in Afghanistan as members of the Naval Special Warfare Development Group or DEVGRU. That's what they are called now. In the old days, before all the unwanted notoriety they received from taking down Osama bin Laden, they were known simply as SEAL Team Six, the smallest, most elite special operations force on the planet.

Red Squadron had been hired by the CIA to capture a "high-value target" (HVT) taking up residence in a small village compound in the tribal area of northwest Pakistan. The usual drill would have been to send in a Predator drone to rain Hellfire missiles down on the dumb bastard, but for some reason they wanted this guy alive. Active duty SEAL operators at Jalalabad were stretched too thin to handle the mission, so the CIA turned to Kincaid's group to do the snatch job.

Two hours before, Kincaid and his men had been dropped out of the belly of a CH-47 *Chinook* helicopter behind a mountain ridge four klicks from the compound. They climbed up the mountainside for an hour before finding the goat trail that would lead them to their destination. Another half-hour of climbing and Kincaid's GPS showed the compound to be half a klick away.

It was no secret why militant groups had been fond of this terrain for centuries. High peaks and narrow valleys made it virtually impenetrable. It was *bandit country*. For the bandits, it was perfect. For Kincaid and his men? They honestly didn't give a shit. As far as they were concerned, this could be the moon. The bandits were still going to die.

Scheduled extraction was 2330 hours. *A little over two and a half hours from now*, Kincaid thought as he looked at his watch. *We haven't got much time.*

Aerial photos showed the compound to consist of a central building and two small cabins. Drones had confirmed there were twenty-three bandits in that compound, including the HVT. The central building was where they all slept, making Kincaid's mission much easier. The two smaller cabins were used for making IED's. They were also instructed to blow the two cabins before they left.

"Okay. We're calling the *Bird* home. Any questions?"

"You still want me and the 417 as lookout on that ledge above the village, L-T?" asked JJ Johnson. Johnson and Rosen, out of habit, still referred to Kincaid by his former military rank of Lieutenant.

"Roger that," Kincaid answered. Johnson's HK 417 was the team's Squad Automatic Weapon (SAW) of choice. Hand held. No tripod needed. It fired the equivalent of a .308 cartridge; big enough to bring a man down and keep him down. They all knew that the best-case scenario would be for Johnson not to have to go *hot*. But they were a seasoned group that knew the three basic rules of combat: if the shit hit the fan, keep shooting, keep moving, and keep communicating. No matter what, they had each other's backs. The four of them had fought and bled together for a long time.

"It's *Go* time," Kincaid said. "Let's move out."

Rosen, who they called Wolfman, moved to point. Right before the path spilled into the village, he raised his right hand in a fist. They stopped. Rosen moved to his left and was gone for just over a minute before four faint clicks from his HK MP7 were heard.

Except for Johnson, they all carried the MP7. Everyone agreed it was the perfect weapon for close-quarter combat: small and compact. When equipped with the 556K suppressor, which they also carried, the only sound heard when the weapon fired was a faint metallic click. It allowed them the luxury to shoot some-body in one room and not wake his buddy in the next.

The weapon's one disadvantage was that it fired a very small cartridge. Not much bigger than a varmint round. When they shot someone, most of the time they had to shoot them twice, sometimes even three times, to put them down. Rosen had done his job well. Two guys, four clicks. Perfect.

"Sentries down," Kincaid whispered in the micro-phone attached to his earbud. "From now on, take it slow and quiet. It's show time." Kincaid felt his senses come fully alive and alert. The adrenaline rush before combat was like no other drug on earth.

While Johnson took his position on the village over-look, the others moved to the front door of the main building. Not knowing the configuration of the interior of the structure, they all put their MP7s on full-auto. They tried the front door handle. It was unlocked. Quietly they eased it open.

They each breathed a sigh of relief. The door didn't open into a big sleeping area as they had been antici-pating, but instead to a small foyer. There was a sentry guarding it. Fortunately, the sentry was asleep. He paid for that mistake with his life. As the man came awake, Rosen quickly pushed his selector switch to single-shot mode and fired. *Click-Click*. One down.

Kincaid quickly surveyed the surroundings. There was a large hall off the foyer, and three doors off the hall, all closed. He crept to the door on the far left wall. It opened inward, right to left. Kneeling between Fuller and Rosen, Kincaid reached in and slowly turned the handle. They had practiced this maneuver a hundred times. Rosen stood on Kincaid's right. His responsibility was to enter the room and face right, clearing out all opposition on that side of the room. Once the door was fully open, Fuller's responsibility was to clear everything directly to the front.

The door squeaked when opened, but fortunately not loud enough to disturb the inhabitants inside. Six guys. All were asleep. Four racked out in the two bunk beds in the right side of the room, and two on the floor directly in front of the door. Their weapons were by their sides.

Rosen entered first. He quickly surveyed the room and used a hand signal to assure the other two there was no immediate threat. Kincaid stood, and from the doorway determined none of the sleeping men was the HVT. They had come here to take only one prisoner, and that one prisoner was not in this room. Twelve clicks and three fresh magazines later, they were in front of the second door.

It was a bigger room. Eight fighters. None of them the HVT. They shot them all, changed magazines, and moved to the third room. Just as they started to open that door, Johnson's HK 417 went hot, its roar echoing down the valley.

Shit, Kincaid thought. *Say goodbye to surprise*. He kicked open the door and stood in the frame, firing at anything that moved. There were a lot of bad guys in that room, and a few already had their weapons in hand and were firing blindly back. Kincaid saw one with a rocket- propelled grenade strapped to his back climbing out the window. He quickly knelt in the doorway and walked half a magazine into the poor bastard, from ass to neck. As the fighter fell through the window, his RPG launcher got stuck in the frame. One of Kincaid's MP7 rounds had hit the rocket, igniting its propellant. Sparks and flames shot out the back. The fighter died there, hanging out the window, looking like a human sparkler.

As the return fire became more intense, Kincaid, Rosen and Fuller were forced to flatten themselves against the hallway wall on either side of the door. *Screw this*, Kincaid thought. One thing experience had taught him was that a gunfight in close quarters against an enemy with numerical superiority almost never ended well. He grabbed a grenade from his vest, pulled the pin, and lobbed it into the room.

"Frag out," he yelled.

The grenade exploded and the shooting from inside the room immediately ceased. Once the smoke and dust cleared, Kincaid cautiously peeked around the door-frame. Blood and body parts coated the floor and walls.

The HVT the CIA sent them after was most certainly in this room, and was now most certainly dead. *The CIA is going to have a shit-fit,* Kincaid thought. *Never hire us again. But screw 'em. It was either them or us.*

"Hey, guys. Take a look at this," Kincaid said, pointing to the guy hanging out the window. "The dude the CIA wanted was the prick trying to escape with the RPG on his back."

"Better take his picture," Fuller said as he handed Kincaid the camera he carried for situations like this. "The CIA is gonna be pissed we didn't take him alive. Might as well show them their guy died as an enemy combatant."

The three quickly checked the bodies in all the rooms, collected anything of intelligence value, and left.

Once outside, Kincaid keyed his mic. "Clear here, JJ. What the hell made you go hot?"

"CIA's intel was bad. L-T. We had bandits in the two cabins. They were coming over to the main building. Had to take them out. Now we got about seven bandits on the hill to our left. Making their way down here."

"Roger that, JJ." Kincaid told Fuller and Rosen to set the explosive charges in the two cabins with twelve-minute delays. He did the same in the large house.

Finished, he glanced at his watch. "Let's giddy-up," he said into the mic. "We're running out of time."

They were half a mile up the goat trail when the explosives went off. A large fireball illuminated the mountainside around them.

At 2350 hours they were aboard the *Chinook* heading back to Jalalabad. Kincaid asked the crew chief to call ahead and tell HQ that the HVT wasn't secured. A few minutes later the crew chief handed him a headset. "For you, Sir," he said.

"Mr. Kincaid? This is Ensign Michael Dowling. Sir, please stay on the radio. Major Cavanaugh wants a word with you." Cavanaugh was the commander of the Special Forces forward base at J-bad.

Shit, he thought. *The bastards can't even wait until I get back to base before reaming my ass out over the loss of their god-dammed target.*

But Kincaid was wrong. This phone call had nothing to do with the HVT.

"Rob? This is Bob Cavanaugh. I just received word from Admiral Thompson at Joint Special Operations Command. He wanted you to know he is bringing Red Squadron home immediately. I'll fill you in with as much as I know when you land."

5

MONDAY
SAN FRANCISCO

Just as Johnson's HK 417 was going hot on the mountaintop in Pakistan, Tom McGuire was sitting on the edge of his bed patting the ass of his wife Michele, inviting her to go with him to Mollie's for donuts.

"What time is it?" she asked, stifling a yawn.

"Doesn't matter, baby," he replied. "Just get that cute little ass of yours out of bed. Me, the day, and Mollie's donuts are waiting for you."

"If we keep going to Mollie's everyday like we have been, this cute little ass is going to be the size of this pillow," she said, rolling over toward him while tucking said pillow between her knees. "It's not good having you out of a job. You're going to get fat. And I'm going to be as big as a house."

"I'm not fat," McGuire said, laying his head on the bed next to hers. "And I'm not out of work. Just between jobs."

He looked into Michele's two large blue eyes. It had been four years since he met her on a case that ended, unfortunately, in the assassination of the man who was the Governor of California. She was a stunning Irish girl, twenty years his junior. Why and how she fell for him was one of those unsolvable mysteries of human interaction. But he wasn't searching for any answers. He considered himself the most content, as well as the luckiest, man on the planet.

"Well, since you made that clear," she said with a smile, "I guess I'll get up and go with you."

Thirty minutes later they were standing in line at Mollie's Donut Queen. A long line. That's because Mollie's had the reputation of making the best donuts in all of San Francisco. If you took a poll of those in line, you would find every neighborhood in the city represented, as well as a few tourists.

Even at that, McGuire was a little annoyed. Waiting in lines, especially long lines, had a way of driving his "annoyance meter" into the red zone. He found that the older he got, the crankier he became. Mostly about these little things. He wasn't proud of it. Had even tried to fight it, but knew it was a losing battle. Standing in line never seemed to bother Michele. That's what twenty years age difference meant.

They had just gotten through the line and were trying to find an empty table when McGuire's cell phone's vibration tickled his left nipple. His "annoyance meter" sprang to life again. He was just old enough to hate cell phones. They found you wherever you were. Reluctantly, he gave the tray to Michele and answered the call.

It was Murray. "Sorry to bother you, Mac. If it weren't important, I wouldn't have called. You know that explosion? Well, it *was* an airplane. Apparently it just exploded. Lots of speculation about a bomb. Possibly terrorist. Homeland Security is all over it."

"Shit," McGuire responded. "Is the department being dragged into it?"

"No. At least not at the moment. It's just that the FAA sent us the passenger list. To see if we had any active investigations going on with any of the known passengers."

"And?"

"We don't." He paused. "That's not why I called. Sorry to be the one having to tell you this, Mac. Walt Kincaid's name was on the manifest. I know you guys were tight. Thought you'd want to know."

"Fuck," McGuire whispered. "Thanks for telling me." He walked to the back where Michele had finally found an empty table. "Bad news, baby. Don't sit. Let's take the donuts home. I've got a phone call to make."

6

McGuire explained to Michele what had happened to Walt Kincaid, and as soon as he was in the car, he called Rob's cell number. It rang and finally went to voice mail. He hung up. He wasn't about to leave the news of Walt on Rob's voice mail. Next he tried his office in Virginia. A young woman answered and told him that Rob was on assignment and couldn't be reached. She did say, however, that he called in everyday at seven in the morning eastern time, which would be four in the afternoon where he was.

McGuire made a mental note to tell Kincaid that if he wanted anonymity, he had better instruct his secretary not to be giving out information like she did. There was a nine-hour time difference between Afghanistan and the east coast. It wouldn't take a genius to figure out where he was. "That time won't work for me," he said. "I have to get in touch with him immediately."

"I'm sorry, I just don't know how to contact Rob. All I can do is give you numbers of people who might know." She gave him six phone numbers.

Four phone calls and an hour later, he was speaking to Admiral Roy Thompson, Deputy Director of JSOC. It hadn't been easy. McGuire was convinced that it had been his liberal use of the name *Red Squadron Security* that finally got him connected.

Besides being Deputy Director of JSOC, and a primary contractor of Red Squadron's services, Admiral Thompson was also Rob's friend and SEAL Team Six mentor. When McGuire called, he was about to go into a meeting with the president, so didn't have much time to talk. After hearing what McGuire had to say, Thompson promised he would get word to Rob as quickly as possible. As he was being escorted into the White House Situation Room, he had called Major Cavanaugh in Jalalabad asking him to set up a secure line where Thompson could speak with Kincaid.

7

MONDAY
JALALABAD, AFGHANISTAN

An hour after they had returned to base, Kincaid and his team were seated in Cavanaugh's office wondering what the hell was so important that the Deputy Director of JSOC wanted to talk to them on a secure phone line. The team had been issued headsets so they could listen in on the conversation between Kincaid and Thompson. All wondered if the call had to do with that damn HVT they killed. Two cups of coffee, and thirty minutes later, the phone in Cavanaugh's office rang. They were about to get their answer.

"Rob? This is Admiral Thompson. It's been a while."

"Indeed, it has, sir," Kincaid responded.

Rob Kincaid had known Thompson for more than ten years. He was a legend in the Teams. A former member of SEAL Team Six, and commander of SEAL Team Three, Thompson had been awarded the Navy Cross for gallantry in the Battle of Mogadishu in nineteen ninety-three, where he took four bullets saving a squad of fellow

SEALs trapped on the upper floor of an apartment complex in the middle of the city.

He was a mentor to Kincaid as well as a personal friend. Thompson had been the person most instrumental in getting Kincaid accepted into the SEAL Team Six training program.

"How'd your mission go last night?"

Kincaid gave him a brief description, including the part about not getting the CIA's *High Value Target* out alive.

"Well, don't worry about the CIA. You did what you had to do to protect you and your men. Shit happens.

"But that has nothing to do as to why I am calling you. I'm afraid I have some bad news. I don't know any other way to tell you than straight out. This morning, at 0830 California time, your father was killed in an airplane explosion over San Francisco."

"Oh, shit," Kincaid said softly, closing his eyes and pushing back into his chair. His team sat straight up in their seats. Fuller reached over and put his hand on Kincaid's thigh.

"I know how you must feel," Thompson continued. "We've been through a lot together, Rob, so you know how much this pains me to tell you. The cause of the explosion was a bomb. A bomb placed on board on the order of a man named Victor Lopez, head of Mexico's largest drug cartel, the *Tormenta*s. Your father was the target of that bomb. One hundred eighteen other people died with him."

Kincaid bit on the inside of his cheek, and took a deep breath. There was a long silence before he uttered a barely audible, "Fuck."

"Are you there with your team?" Thomson asked, shifting gears.

"I am," Kincaid replied.

"Listening?"

"Yes, sir. They are."

"Good. There's a shit-load of things happening here. I just got out of a meeting with the president. Red Squadron was brought up in our conversation. Particularly as it related to your father and the drug cartels." He paused, and then asked, "Did your father ever talk to you about the plan of his named *Snow Plow*?"

Kincaid looked up at the ceiling, thinking. "Yes, sir. He did mention it once. Long ago, though. Not much more than he was working on something that in his view would be a game-changer in our war against the drug cartels. That was all. No details."

"*Snow Plow* was, and is, a highly classified operation. Even I don't know all the details. One of the details I do know, however, was it called for the United States to send Special Ops troops into Mexico to eliminate the cartel leadership."

"Shit," Johnson blurted out.

"But before you get too excited, the president just nixed that idea. Just now. In the meeting I had with him. He was afraid of the political fallout. Personally, that's where I think Red Squadron might just fit in, and why I want you and your team to meet with me at 0900 on Thursday at Naval Special Warfare Command in Coronado. Can you be there?"

Kincaid looked at his people. They all nodded in the affirmative. "We can, sir."

"Good," came the reply. "I'll see you there."

"Before you go, sir," Kincaid said. "How did you know the bomb was planted by this Victor Lopez?"

"The president told me," Thompson said. "He had been briefed by the Director of the FBI who had himself been told by one of his agents in San Francisco. A man named Hartmann. A member of your father's Task Force 64." There followed a silence, and then Thompson said, "Anything else?"

Kincaid looked around the room. "Doesn't seem to be, sir."

"We'll talk about all this when I see you on Thursday. In the meantime, I've asked Major Cavanaugh to arrange transportation to get you and your team back to the States. See you in California."

Not quite knowing what to say, they all sat in silence after Thompson disconnected. Rob had his head bowed, picking imaginary dirt off the legs of his combat fatigues. Finally Rosen spoke. "L-T, this is really shitty. We all feel for you. Is there anything we can do?" Fuller and JJ leant their voice in agreement. "If you're going back home, I'd be happy to come with you. Keep you company. I'm sure these guys would, too."

"Thanks, Wolfman. Thanks, you guys. I'll be okay. Just a little hard to digest right now. I'll go back to San Francisco. They'll be plenty for me to do there. I'll just see you at NSWC on Thursday, okay? After that, who knows what they'll ask us to do." He stopped and looked over at them. "I know one thing, though. By killing my father, Victor Lopez signed his own death warrant. As far as I'm concerned, he's a dead man walking."

8

MONDAY
SAN FRANCISCO

About the time Kincaid was preparing to leave J-bad, Special Agent Bill Hartmann was entering his favorite North Beach restaurant for an early dinner. He was immediately escorted to a private dining area in the back corner of the restaurant. With him were the other three members of Task Force 64: Agents Brian Jackson, Michael Gray, and Pete Garcia.

Hartmann came here often enough that management was only too eager to give him the VIP treatment. For him, VIP treatment meant that he and his guests were left alone after having eaten their meal so they could converse in private. Privacy this night was of utmost importance.

When dinner was done, Hartmann ordered two bottles of wine. Once they had been delivered, and the wait staff had finished cleaning up and gone, he called for attention. "We're here to discuss the president's decision today *not to allow* Spec Op troops into Mexico to eliminate the cartels, once and for all."

"He's a fucking coward," Agent Gray said, shaking his head in disbelief.

"We can say that until we are blue in the face," said Hartmann, "but it won't get us anywhere. We have to talk now about how we are going to move *Snow Plow* forward."

"Yeah? And how exactly are we supposed to do that, Bill," Gray continued, "when that cowardly, pissant prick of a president won't do anything even when one of his own guys gets blasted out of the sky by a bunch of foreign druggies? I still can't believe he did exactly zip about Kincaid."

"Kincaid's on us," said Garcia. "We miscalculated the president's reaction to his death. I sure as hell hope Walt didn't die in vain. That would be a real shame."

"For him and for us," Hartmann said. "So, let's regroup. We all know that operation *Snow Plow* is the last chance this country will have to win the drug war. We've got to get it operational. How do we do that?"

"Let's start with the president," Garcia said. "The whole operation depended on him saying *yes*. How do we convince him?"

"We thought Walt's death would convince the son-of-a-bitch," Gray said.

"It didn't, so let's forget about that for now and move on," Garcia continued.

Gray wouldn't let it go. Turning to Hartmann, he asked, "Did the Director tell you what the president's objections were?"

"For one, he said almost everyone in the room was in favor of the deployment, except the Secretary of State."

"That bitch? Shit! How come I'm not surprised?" said Jackson. "What was her objection this time?"

"Same as always," Hartmann said. "Says she's concerned about the *legality* of the operation. Sending US troops into a county *uninvited*."

"Where does she come up with that shit?" asked Gray, shaking his head again. "Hasn't anyone explained to her that Pakistan didn't exactly invite us in when we went after bin Laden? Or Iraq? Or Afghanistan? Come on. Let's stop kidding ourselves. She and the president are really only concerned about the political fallout if we get caught down there with our pants around our ankles."

"I agree with Mike," said Jackson. "I say it's time to raise the ante. It's our only chance. I'm in favor of going to phase two of *Snow Plow*. It's really the only thing we have left. And frankly, if it doesn't work, *Snow Plow* wasn't going to work anyway."

"Walt's son, Robert, is coming home," Hartmann interrupted, switching topics.

"Where the hell did that come from, Bill?" Gray said. "What's that got to do with the success of *Snow Plow*?"

"Not sure at the moment, but just worried about possible complications."

"Complications? I'm not tracking," Garcia said.

"You know he's a former SEAL. ST6, as a matter of fact. What if he comes back here full of questions about his father's death? Right in the middle of us rolling out phase two earlier than we expected. That's what I meant about *complications*."

"On the other hand," Garcia said, pouring himself another glass of wine, "Lopez is the real guy we have to worry about. I'm guessing Lopez' scalp is something the young Kincaid would like on his mantle."

"Good point, Pete," said Jackson, taking Garcia's lead and also pouring himself another glass of wine. "Lopez knows too much."

"But now that you bring it up, Bill," Gray said, "I'm seeing what you mean about him being a threat. Maybe we can get the Mexican's to kill him, too. I'd be in favor of that if it would push our asshole president to get off his butt and do what he needs to do."

Hartmann looked around the table. "For the record," he said, "I'm opposed to harming Walt's son. But if something should happen to him, make sure I know nothing about it."

"Understood," Gray said. "Now let's get back to the important thing ... phase two."

Hartmann nodded. "If we bring phase two on-line, we have to be very careful how it gets rolled out. Without Walt, I question whether we have the capabilities and abilities to make it work."

"Walt's gone," said Gray. "And I, for one, am glad. He was becoming a hindrance to us. And phase two was just the part he was becoming squirrely about. God dammit, Bill. He was the guy who thought it up, and then he started to have pangs of conscience? Give me a break. Casualties? Well, hell ya. In war there are always casualties. Can't be helped."

"I know what you are saying, Mike, but my question had to do with whether we have the capabilities to carry it off. Do we? Let's see a show of hands." The verdict was unanimous. "Okay. How quickly can we become operational?"

"We have the product ready to go," Garcia said. "We can get it into the distribution channels almost immediately. If we started tomorrow, first signs of illness would appear by late Thursday or early Friday. If we followed Walt's original distribution plan, Tuesday would be the biggest day, then it would slowly start to taper off."

"Let's get at it, then, gentlemen," said Hartmann. "I guess I won't be expecting you at the office tomorrow." He laughed.

"One last thing, Bill," said Gray. "What about Lopez?"

"What do you mean, *what about Lopez*?"

"You know ... how are we going to get rid of him? He knows too much."

"We don't have to worry. That's what we have the military for. Once the president grabs hold of the cojones we are going to give him, Lopez will be dead within the week."

"Amen to that," said Jackson. "The guy's a real prick. I wouldn't mind being in on his kill."

They sat in silence for a few moments, and then Hartmann stood and raised his glass, "One for Walt. No matter what you think of him, he got us this far. We owe him." He paused. "To Walt Kincaid. Long live Walt Kincaid." Everyone raised his glass but Mike Gray.

9

An hour after learning about his father, Rob Kincaid and his team were on their way home. Cavanaugh had secured a chopper to take them to Kabul and had virtually hijacked an Air Force *C-38 Courier* to take them all from there to Ft. Bragg. After a four-hour layover in Madrid, the plane was scheduled to arrive at Bragg a little before 1400.

From there, Fuller, Rosen and Johnson had made arrangements to take a military air shuttle from Bragg to Oceana Naval Air Station in Virginia Beach where they could easily get a ride to their homes. Kincaid had made a similar military air shuttle arrangement, but his was to take him to Dulles International, where he had booked himself on a non-stop American flight to San Francisco International. His ETA was 2100 hours. He had spoken to McGuire from Madrid, and McGuire had insisted on picking him up at the airport.

By the time Kincaid was at Dulles boarding his flight to San Francisco, phase two of *Snow Plow* had been operational for seven hours.

=

Nine thousand six hundred miles and thirty-one hours later, Kincaid got his first in-person view of the new span of the San Francisco Bay Bridge. He was still living at home when a section of the old bridge collapsed in the Loma Prieta earthquake in nineteen eighty-nine. He thought back to that day. He was at Candlestick Park that early evening with his dad, mom and his dad's best friend Tom McGuire, who Rob still affectionately called Uncle Mac, for game three of the World Series between the San Francisco Giants and the Oakland A's when the quake struck. Except for the Giants losing that Series to the A's in four games, those were good years. Happy years. Ones he remembered fondly. He didn't know it at the time, but there weren't many of those left. A few short years later his family was in shambles. His mom divorced his dad, which put a real strain on Rob's relationship with his father. Rob was already in the Navy by then, stationed in San Diego. His mom moved there to be closer to him. She died a few short years after he was accepted into SEAL Team Six. Because of his continual deployments over the intervening years, his relationship with his father never had a chance to repair itself. Looking at the Bridge now, he reflected on how much he had missed in those years. Especially now that his dad had been taken from him.

==

Sleeping on airplanes had never been a problem for Kincaid, so he was a little surprised that on this trip he slept only in fits and starts. Truth was, every time he closed his eyes, all he saw was his dad's plane exploding. He hadn't allowed himself to go there. So sometime over the Atlantic Ocean, he rummaged through his duffle and pulled out an envelope with his name neatly written across the front. It had arrived in Afghanistan last week after a circuitous two-week journey through the Navy's FPO system. He removed the letter from the envelope, opened it and stared at his dad's handwriting. But as he read it, he still had a hard time imaging his father had written it. Its tone was so ... he had a hard time describing it ... so *soft*. That was the only word that came to him ... *soft*. The father he had known was anything but *soft*. When he first read the letter, he thought it might have been a hoax.

The father that Rob had known had been one tough son-of-a-bitch. As a young man, Walt had spent three tours of duty in the jungles of Vietnam as part of the First Air Cavalry Division. He was with Lieutenant Colonel Hal Moore's First Battalion, Seventh Cavalry Regiment in the Battle of the Ia Drang Valley early in the war. Moore had written a book about that battle. In it, Walt Kincaid was mentioned four times for his extraordinary valor under fire. His three tours had produced a drawer full of medals. While he never bragged about them publicly, Rob had caught his father any number of times with that drawer open, lovingly touching those medals.

But Rob was painfully aware that the characteristics that made his dad a brave soldier undoubtedly were the same characteristics that made him a demanding father and, it turned out, a remote husband. Growing up in the Kincaid household as the first-born son was not for the faint of heart. Especially after his older sister died in a car accident caused by some asshole high on methamphetamines. It was the start of his dad's obsession with drugs, and with that obsession came even higher expectations for Rob, the only surviving child of Walt and Betty Kincaid. And a male child, at that. Over the years, he and his father had butted heads like two Rocky Mountain Big Horn sheep in rut.

It wasn't until he became a SEAL years later that he put his upbringing in perspective and came to a restive peace with his father's behavior. As a junior and senior in high school, he had been an All-City baseball player. Good enough to be drafted in the tenth round by the Chicago Cubs. At first, he was proud of the fact that someone thought him good enough to even be drafted. But when contract time came along, it turned out they weren't going to be all that generous. He started to see himself stuck forever in some little town in Iowa or South Carolina. He decided if he was going to give his life to something, he wanted it to be something important.

Even after all the bullshit he had gone through with his father, he still came out the man his father had wanted him to be. Someone willing to work hard to make a difference in the world. To be the best at what he did. And to be the best, his dad had taught him you had to test yourself against the best. As Walt's son, he carried inside him the desire to be the best of the best. The apple had not fallen far from the tree.

But underneath it all, Rob knew the real tension in their relationship came from the way Rob perceived how his dad had treated his mother. She was a good woman, and a good mother. And a good wife, at least from what he could see. Thinking back, he now realized it all started to unravel when his dad was diagnosed with prostate cancer. Walt's own father had died of prostate cancer, and it was like he wasn't going to let that happen to him. Like everything else in his life, Walt was not going down without a fight. The fight turned out to be within himself. Growing older. Getting prostate cancer was an old man's disease. It was telling him that he had to come to terms with his own mortality. That was never going to happen to Walt Kincaid. He was never going to give in to growing old.

＝

But the letter he held in his hand was not written by *that* father. This letter was written by someone who *had* grown old. By a man approaching his sixty-eighth birthday. Written by a father who was asking the only *family* he had left to come home to him. To essentially settle down, get married and give him grandchildren.

Rob pocketed the letter and looked out the window into the inky darkness. For the first time in years he realized how much he loved his father. How much he owed him. And he was struck by the irony of it all. That he *was* coming home, just as his father had asked.

But now, shit ... it was too damn late.

10

TUESDAY
SAN FRANCISCO

Fifteen minutes after the plane touched down, Rob was in baggage claim giving Tom McGuire a bear hug. "Uncle Mac! God, it's good to see you again."

"And you too, Robbie. Sorry about the circumstances, though. Walt was a good man. I loved him like a brother."

"Thanks, Uncle Mac. I appreciate it. My dad loved you, too." He stepped back, appraising McGuire up and down. "You haven't changed a bit since the last time I saw you. What? Fifteen years ago? What magic elixir have you been drinking?"

"Ha. That magic elixir, boy-o, is named Michele," McGuire replied. "It's what happens when you marry a woman twenty years younger than you. She keeps me young ... and I keep her old." He laughed at his little joke.

Kincaid smiled politely, and said, "Good for you, Uncle Mac. Can't wait to meet her. Now that you've agreed to work with me, I'll bet I'll be seeing a lot of her."

"That you will," he replied. "Speaking of which, she invited you over for dinner tonight if you aren't too tired. Michele is a great cook. I'd take her up on it if I were you."

"Thanks, Uncle Mac," Kincaid said, grabbing his duffle off the carousel and carrying it over to a chair. "Hold on, I have to check something." He felt through the bag, and apparently satisfied, zipped it back up. "Sorry about that. I packed quickly out of Afghanistan. Not knowing if I'd be taking any commercial flights, I packed my Sig 9mm. At Dulles, I had to get special permission before they would allow the duffle with the gun on board. Certain government personnel get a pass. My Department of Defense credentials got me through. Just think, you'll be getting a pass just like this as soon as I get you to sign on the bottom line."

"Don't know how I ever functioned without one of those special passes," Mac responded with a smile.

"Anyway, about coming over tonight," Kincaid continued. "Would Michele be offended if I took a rain check on her kind invitation? I wouldn't be very good company tonight, I'm afraid. Been on airplanes for better part of two days now. I feel and smell like shit."

"Of course you can," Mac said leading Kincaid down to the parking garage. "Oh, before I forget, let me give you these keys." He reached in his pocket and passed Kincaid two keys on a chain that had a little flashlight on it. "One is for the front door of your house, and the other is the key to the desk in Walt's office. I was guessing you might not have a key to the house."

"You guessed right. I was going to go wake up old man Popovich next door. I know, at least when I was growing up, Popovich had a key. For emergencies."

"I have one because I'm the executor of Walt's estate." He paused, looking around the parking garage for his car. He found it two rows over. As they walked toward it, he said, "About a year ago, your dad dropped by my house and out of the blue asked if I would be the executor of his estate. I resisted. It sounded so ghoulish. Besides, I was convinced that he would outlive me by years." McGuire fastened his seatbelt, turned to Rob and said, "I was sadly wrong. But I want you to know, I would have given anything to have been right."

11

They arrived at the house twenty minutes later. "Come on in for a drink, Uncle Mac? I'm feeling just a little bit strange. Would you mind at least coming inside with me as I re-introduce myself to this place?"

"Of course not, Rob. It would be a pleasure."

Both men walked into the house together. "I know my dad kept a lot of liquor in the cabinet above the kitchen sink for when he had meetings at the house," Rob said. "Don't know what he has in there, if anything. Why don't you just find something good and pour us a glass while I go up to my old room and dump the duffle."

"The kitchen is where he kept the rotgut. I know where he kept the good stuff. For close friends like me." McGuire smiled. "In the bottom drawer of the desk in the office. Get that key I gave you and throw it to me, okay? Many a night your father and I would sit in his office shooting the shit until the wee hours with a bucket of ice and the bottle of Jameson's he kept in the bottom right hand drawer. I'll get two glasses and the ice from the kitchen and meet you in the office. How's that sound?"

"See you in a minute," Rob said as he walked up the stairs and entered his old room. First thing he did was put the duffle down and take out the Sig p226. It had been broken into three pieces as required by the TSA. He reassembled it, grabbed a magazine, checked that it had a full load, slammed it home and jacked a round into the chamber. Not that he expected anything, but he had been taught early on in SEAL training that you never wanted to come to a gunfight with an unloaded weapon. For them, having an empty chamber was the equivalent of having an unloaded weapon.

Kincaid sat on his old bed and looked around the room. He was surprised that not much had changed since he had left fifteen years ago. His dresser still sat in the far corner. The large mirror whose wooden frame once held pictures of his friends, girls that he knew, and sports heroes he admired and tried to emulate, was gone. *Just one less thing Dad had to clean,* he thought.

He got up and walked over to the closet. It was full of clothes. He recognized some of his mom's old outfits. That surprised him. His mom obviously didn't want them, and his dad keeping them was a sign of what? That he still loved her? That he expected her to return? But she had been dead now for fifteen years. He tried to come up with a reasonable explanation, but couldn't. He shook his head and walked back to the bed.

He noticed the surfboard that used to hang from the ceiling was gone, as was the Nerf basketball rim and net that hung from the back of the bedroom door. He had once made thirty-five shots in a row from about right where he was sitting. None of his friends had even come close. He smiled at the thought.

McGuire yelling for him to quickly come down interrupted those thoughts. He grabbed the Sig and bounded down the stairs.

McGuire stood in the doorway of his father's den, holding an ice bucket full of ice and two glasses. He looked over at Kincaid. "You are not going to believe this."

12

When Rob was growing up, this office was his father's favorite room. Rob remembered it always smelled of lemon Pledge. And it did this night, too. Only now, it smelled of lemon Pledge and dust.

Every night after dinner, Rob remembered, he and his mom and dad would do the dishes together. Then he would be sent off to do his homework. His mom always went into the family room and watched television, while his dad retreated into his office.

He had made it into a working man's "man cave." Dominated by a large black walnut desk that always glowed as if newly polished. Even back then, if his father knew he was going to be out of town for a few days, he always took a polish rag to that desk. A large computer screen dominated the middle of the desk in front of a high-back leather chair. The telephone sat to the left of the screen. Behind the desk was a small table on which was a copier and fax machine.

But it was the two four-drawer filing cabinets in the corner that caught Kincaid's immediate attention. The top drawer on one was open and empty. The security locks for both had been drilled out, and a dusting of metal filings covered the floor like a fine mist.

"Better not disturb anything, Rob. Don't want to compromise what looks like a crime scene. Even though I'm not active duty anymore, let me call Robbery and get some techs over here pronto." He called on his cell phone. After a few minutes, he hung up. "Can't be over until morning. Eight-thirty. That gonna work for you?" Kincaid nodded. "Sure you don't want to come over and stay at my house?"

"Thanks, Uncle Mac. I'm staying here. I hope the fuckers come back. What the hell happened here, do you think? What were they after?"

"Well, if I had to guess, I'd say they were gang-bangers" McGuire replied. "These dirt bags wait for some kind of tragedy like an airplane crash. The paper publishes a list of the victims, and these assholes rob their homes while the next of kin are at the coroner's office, or, like in your case, flying in from somewhere. They're looking for money for their drugs. It's all about drugs nowadays."

"You sound a lot like my dad."

"Yeah ... well it's a fact. See it every day. Most burglaries ... hell, most murders are drug related."

"But does this look like that kind of robbery to you? Nothing else was disturbed. There are a lot of valuable things in this house. Or at least there used to be. Nothing hit but my dad's office? What would they have been looking for in here? Gold bars?"

"Yeah, maybe you're right. We'll let the robbery techs tell us what they think before jumping to conclusions."

They both just stared at the mess. Finally, Rob turned to McGuire and said, "I appreciate all you're doing for me. Why don't you go home and get some sleep. Will you be here tomorrow when the Robbery guys come?"

"You bet," McGuire said. "Maybe we could get a little breakfast? Ever think of visiting your dad's FBI friends?"

"I have, yeah. Thought I'd give them a call. I also have to contact Vinnie Delgado. Tell him I'm here. Have you met him yet, Uncle Mac?"

"No, but I want to."

"Good, I'll make that happen."

When McGuire left Kincaid's house that night, phase two of *Snow Plow* had been operational for twenty-four hours.

13

WEDNESDAY
MANZANILLO, MEXICO

As the de facto CEO of the fifty-first largest company in the world based on revenue, Victor "Angel" Lopez was, if nothing else, a shrewd businessman. As with so many other things in life, however, one person's "shrewd businessman" was another person's "sadistic butcher." Lopez fell most easily into the latter category.

Victor Lopez was the leader of the *Tormenta* Cartel, the most vicious of the seven Mexican cartels. *Tormenta* was the code name given to a special unit of the Mexican military who were trained by their American special op counterparts at the School of the Americas in Fort Benning in the nineteen nineties. The *Tormenta*'s mission was to return to Mexico and destroy the cartels. But upon their return, they found that money and power awaited them if they hired on as the armed wing of the Gulf Cartel, which at the time was the largest and most influential cartel in Mexico. When that relationship soured and came to a violent end, the remaining members of the *Tormenta* decided to form their own cartel.

Victor Lopez was a second generation *Tormenta*, the first leader not to have emerged from the Mexican army's elite *Tormenta* unit. Believing that inflicting fear into the heart of his enemy was the most efficient way of getting what he wanted, Lopez brought a new level of violence and brutality to the already violent drug wars. His sadistic reputation was sealed when he boiled alive three of his rivals in fifty gallon barrels of grease, and left their boiled remains, still in the drums, on the side of a major Mexican highway. His nickname was "*Ahn-hel*", the Spanish pronunciation for "Angel". In Mexico, Victor Lopez was known as the *Ahn-hel de la Muerta*, the "Angel of Death."

As befits one of the wealthiest men in the country, even a man with seven outstanding arrest warrants for charges ranging from torture to murder, he was that night hosting a lavish dinner party aboard his one hundred sixty-four-foot Delta Marine yacht he had named *M-40*, a play on the Mexican police radio code for "commander." The yacht was anchored at Lopez' beach estate, ten miles south of the Mexican resort city of Manzanillo. His guests that evening were Enrique Sanchez, the country's Minister of the Interior; Leon Cardenas, the chief of police of the Mexican state where Lopez' *Tormenta* Cartel was headquartered; and Alejandro Morales, the editor-in-chief of the largest newspaper in Mexico City. They were seated in the sixteen hundred square foot salon on the Delta Marine's second level, smoking expensive Cuban cigars and sipping Camus Cognac served to them by four scantily clad women. Except for the women and the twenty heavily armed guards strategically stationed on various levels of the yacht, the gathering could have been a high-level business meeting anywhere in the world.

And it was a business meeting.

"Sir," said Enrique Sanchez, "it is not possible for the coca plant to be grown on Mexican soil."

"That used to be true, Minister," Lopez replied. "But not any more. Tell him, El Papa." Alejandro Morales, the editor of Mexico City's *Gaceta Oficial*, was known as El Papa because he purportedly knew as many secrets about what was happening in Mexican government circles as the Pope supposedly knew about what was happening in the Vatican.

"Minister," Morales said. "Señor Lopez is right. The reason you are here smoking a Cohiba *BHK 52* with that lovely young señorita on your lap is because I know of someone who has developed a hybrid coca plant that will grow in Mexico. He has graciously allowed us to use it."

"How come I have not heard of that breakthrough yet?" Sanchez asked.

"Because you are not *El Papa*," replied a smiling Morales, blowing cigar smoke in the air.

"You need not know, Minister, who developed this plant," said Lopez. "All I want from you is to be given the ownership of the first five kilometers of hill country bordering Guatemala. And to be assured that no one from the government will harass me."

"How can I do that, Señor Lopez? I don't have that kind of power. I am but a lowly minister."

"Minister Sanchez," Lopez replied. "I know you will find a way. I won't even dishonor you with threats to your family. You will do the right thing, I know. Keep having fun with your playmate there. She is yours for as long as you want. Even all night if you are *that* much of a man. And when you leave, be sure to pick up that suitcase that Chief Cardenas has sitting next to him. It will handsomely finance the people you will need to ask to assist in our project."

A bodyguard appeared and whispered in Lopez' ear. He nodded and waved the gunman away. "You will have to excuse me gentlemen," he said. "I have to take a phone call. Ladies, show my friends a good time while I am gone." He went to his office and closed the door.

"My contacts just alerted me that someone of inter-est is coming from Washington, D.C. to nose around in our business," the voice said.

Lopez smiled. The voice was Rinaldo Palma, nick-named "*El Rhino*" not only as a play on his first name, but also because he was perpetually "horny." *El Rhino* was his boyhood friend, confidant and, if the truth were known, the second in command of the *Tormenta* cartel.

"Tell me, my friend."

"Robert Kincaid," Palma said.

"Ah, isn't that always the way?" Lopez said. "Family, the bane of our existence. Your contacts know us too well." He laughed.

"They knew we would be interested, *Ahn-hel*," Palma replied. "They, too, are concerned about cleaning up any potential problems occurring from us eliminating the senior Kincaid for them."

"And what do we know about the *el niño* Kincaid?" Lopez asked.

"He is a former Navy SEAL, *Ahn-hel*. So he could be a problem for us if we let him live."

"Then let's not let him live."

"That's what I thought you would say. Just making sure. I will make the arrangements."

Lopez hung up and tapped the top of the desk with his fingertips. He hadn't known the FBI agent had a family. But it wasn't a surprise to him that if he did, the son would come seeking revenge. They always did. That's why the *Ahn-hel de la Muerta* always made a point of killing the family of his enemies, and killing them in the most gruesome ways possible. It served as a warning. If you wanted your family to live, do not become his enemy. But if you did become his enemy, expect your family to pay the consequences.

He thought of the FBI's spy within his own cartel. The one they called *Munoz*. The man who told them about the bomb he had planted on the airplane. Not that they needed the warning, but still it made him angry. Munoz was a man Lopez had trusted. Not only did he execute him, but his wife and two children as well. Their mutilated bodies were dumped in an open sewer in Piedras Negras, on the Texas border. He smiled. The way he looked at it, he wasn't a bad man. He wasn't a *butcher*, as some people called him. He was simply a businessman discouraging competition.

But Robert Kincaid's military background presented a threat of a different kind. He wasn't worried, though. Rinaldo would handle it. He always did.

14

WEDNESDAY
LA JOLLA, CALIFORNIA

The man they nicknamed *El Rhino* was a practicing trial attorney in San Diego, California. He had known Victor Lopez since they were both in kindergarten together at Our Lady of Guadalupe in Tecalitan, a small town in the central Pacific coastal state of Jalisco.

If anyone ever had any doubts that opposites attract, their relationship would have erased those doubts. Victor Lopez was big for his age, and he exerted his physical superiority on everyone around him. Rinaldo Palma made up for his lack of physical strength with a mental superiority that bordered on genius. In fact, he was a genius. He had never beaten up anyone physically, but his mind had ground the strongest physical specimens into dust on many occasions.

It was Palma who saw the power in marrying his and Lopez' unique skills to become a powerful force in their surroundings. By the time they were twelve, they enlisted as mules in the La Familia cartel, delivering drugs throughout the states of Jalisco and Colima. Palma had figured out ways to skim and then resell what they had stolen without being caught. If some consumer made a fuss out of not getting the amount he paid for, Lopez would put a stop to his complaints by beating up his sister or mother. Their side business was making them a lot of money. Palma made sure they didn't spend any of it so as not to raise suspicions.

By the time they were sixteen, they had risen in the ranks of the Jalisco cartel. Now they were carrying guns and making a reputation for themselves in the shooting wars going on between rival cartels. It was in one such gun battle that their lives changed forever.

On a hot September night, a group of five armed men from a rival cartel arrived in Tecalitlan looking for Lopez and Palma. They found them in the main plaza where a Virgin of Guadalupe celebration was being held. They opened fire, killing eight people. Lopez and Palma escaped but knew their time living in Tecalitlan had come to an end. They took to the mountains and lived there for a month, deciding what they should do. It was during their discussions that a plan evolved. Over the last few years, they had saved over two hundred thousand dollars in their skimming operation. Palma would take fifty thousand of it and go to America. He had an aunt living in Tucson. He would complete his education there and then come back to rejoin Lopez.

Lopez in the meantime would take the remaining one hundred and fifty thousand and use it to bribe his way to influence in the Mexican government. With certain modifications along the way, the plan worked to perfection. Palma ended up staying in the States, receiving a college education and then going to law school.

Lopez, in the meantime, bribed his way to political influence at the same time he was making his bones in the *Tormenta* cartel.

It had taken twenty-five years, but Victor Lopez was now one of the wealthiest men on the planet, as well as one of the most wanted. He lived a protected and luxurious life on his yacht and in as many as fifteen haciendas he owned throughout Mexico. During that same time, Rinaldo Palma had moved permanently to the United States, become a citizen, obtained a law degree and ran one of the most lucrative trial attorney practices in California. His specialty was immigration law, which afforded him many trips to Mexico to obtain new clients.

It was common knowledge that Palma's practice entailed defending the cartels' interests in the US, but few suspected that he actually ran the US operation for Mexico's largest drug cartel.

The call from his contact in San Francisco had come at a very inconvenient time. But then, calls coming in any night after eleven would be an inconvenience. That's because Palma lived up to his *El Rhino* nickname virtually every night, and with a gusto that would have ordinary men swearing off their Viagra by the fourth month.

This particular evening he was entertaining a stripper from one of the many *Tormenta* cartel's *Gentlemen's Clubs* scattered around the San Diego area. The clubs were perfect for both money laundering and for keeping Palma supplied with an endless stream of young girls eager to please their boss. Tonight he was entertaining one of his favorite girls. Amber had been with Palma so many times that she was used to his "interruptions". It had become her habit never to let "interruptions" spoil the sexual mood. Unless told explicitly to stop, she just kept right on going. The original *Energizer* bunny. Because of her special talents, many nights Palma found himself conducting business on the phone in some very compromising positions.

This night was different. He told Amber to stop and bring him a Sapphire tonic from the bar. While she was gone, he dialed a number in San Jose, California. A woman answered.

"Lupe, forgive me for calling so late. I need you to get me a very competent shooter for a job I have for you in San Francisco. Can you do that?"

"Si, Patrón," she replied.

"Excellent. I will wire the money to your bank tomorrow with the name and address of the target. He arrived at the San Francisco airport earlier this evening. Have your person stake out his house for as long as he needs. Find out his patterns. Tell him his best bet may be to just ring the guy's doorbell, shoot him and leave. In any case, because of this man's background, I need you to hire the best you have. This man might prove to be a tougher kill than most."

15

WEDNESDAY
SAN FRANCISCO

Kincaid had been up three hours by the time the Robbery techs arrived at eight-thirty. After completing a two-hour, ten mile run through the streets of San Francisco, he showered and called Vinnie Delgado.

"Vinnie, it's Rob. I'm in town. Got in last night. I'm at the house. How fast can you make it over?"

"I'm in the East Bay, Rob. Depending on commute traffic, I can be there anywhere from an hour to an hour and a half."

"Perfect, I'll see you then."

He hung up and called the San Francisco office of the FBI, and asked for Special Agent Hartmann.

Kincaid introduced himself. After the usual *get-to-know-you* banter, he asked if it was possible to meet with Hartmann and his dad's old team sometime today. Hartmann said it would take him time to find out the schedules of his agents. Could he get back to him in two hours? Kincaid said he appreciated Hartmann doing this on such short notice and hung up. Ten minutes later, McGuire arrived. Five minutes after that, three

Robbery techs entered with a backpack full of little jars containing different kinds of chemicals, brushes, powders, baggies and enough cotton swabs to clean every ear in the city. It was going to be a busy day.

"How long will this take, Uncle Mac?" Rob asked.

"A couple of hours, at least," McGuire answered. "Just so you know, they are going to make a real mess here. But these guys are professional so will clean up after themselves. In fact, they spend almost as much time on clean-up as they do collecting evidence."

"Vinnie Delgado is coming over. I'm trying to get an appointment to see Hartmann and my dad's team. I want to get a lead on where Lopez might be. Care to join us?"

"I think I should stay here with these guys, Rob. The techs always do better when they have a fellow officer with them. Looking over their shoulder." He smiled. "I don't blame you on Lopez, but are you going to go in after him by yourself or will you have to get permission from the big boys in D.C. to carry out a mission like that?"

"The military is hoping the president will give us his blessing. But I'm going to get Lopez, blessing or not."

Hartmann called back forty minutes later. He had gathered his team together and would have them at their office in the Federal Courts Building in downtown San Francisco in an hour. Kincaid said he'd be there.

McGuire and Kincaid were having coffee in the kitchen when Delgado arrived.

"Vinnie, this is my Uncle Mac. He's going to be working with the Squadron. I know he is old," he said with a wink to McGuire, "but he was my dad's best friend and almost at retirement age so I felt sorry for him and agreed to hire him." Delgado looked confused, like he didn't know if Rob was kidding or not. "Come on, Vinnie. I'm just kidding," he said.

"Whew. Couldn't tell for a minute or two. Can I call you Mac?" McGuire nodded. "Mac," Delgado said, shaking McGuire's hand. "Nice to meet you."

"Likewise," McGuire replied.

"Uncle Mac has just retired ... on my recommendation and offer of a job he just couldn't refuse, by the way ... from a long and distinguished career as an SFPD Homicide Inspector."

"That's it," Delgado said, patting his forehead with his fingers. "I knew I had heard your name. Weren't you involved in the assassination of the governor a while back? I, for one, was glad you killed the son-of-a-bitch. He was a fucking traitor, no doubt."

"I didn't kill him. I tried to prevent it, actually."

Delgado gave him a disappointed look. "Well, he bought the farm in any case. Good riddance, if you ask me."

"I've got to tell him about you, too, Vinnie" Kincaid said. "Shall I give him the long version or the short version?"

"Short," Delgado said without hesitation.

"Okay." He turned to McGuire. "Vinnie was a SEAL with me and the other three Red Squadron guys you'll meet sometime soon. I don't want to embarrass him, but he was the toughest SOB I ever met or served with. Don't let his long hair and five foot two frame fool you."

"Five-five," Delgado corrected.

"Give or take," Kincaid said with a laugh. "Anyway ... he had, and still has, the record for the most bare-handed kills in the entire SEAL community. I don't know anybody who wants to mess with Vinnie. Why he's a former SEAL, you ask? That's the longer version of his story that I'll tell you sometime out of his earshot. He gets embarrassed when I tell people."

"If it's embarrassing, I don't have to know," McGuire said. "I've got enough embarrassing things in my closet that I wouldn't want anyone to know. It's none of their business and this is none of mine."

"Thanks, Mac," said Delgado. "I appreciate that."

"Vinnie, we have to go before this turns into a kumbaya moment and we all start holding hands and breaking out in song."

Delgado laughed. "Before we go ... do you know anyone who drives an older model blue Mercedes? A Mexican dude?"

"Not off the top of my head," Kincaid answered. "Why?"

"I was driving up here and noticed a car that slowed down out front of your house and drove past real slow. Looking up at it. Like casing the place. He went down the street, did a u-turn at the next intersection and pulled over and parked."

"Don't know why anyone would be interested in me," Kincaid said. "Hell, I just got in last night at about nine. Haven't had time to kick anyone's ass yet." He put his arm around Vinnie and laughed. "I'm going to be driving Mac's car to meet the FBI guys. If your antenna is up, why not let me go now, and you follow in your car. That way we can be sure if someone wants to see me." When he got to the door, he turned. "Mac, we'll be back in a few hours. Thanks for hanging out with the tech dudes."

16

Delgado pulled into the underground garage of the Federal Courts Building five minutes behind Kincaid.

"You've got a tail," Delgado said as they stepped into the elevator. "He followed you all the way. He kept going when you turned in here. Good thing you have some-body at your house now. This looks all the world to me like a burglary about to happen."

"Good luck. This guy is too late. Hope the pricks walk in on McGuire. Get a good look at him?" asked Kincaid.

"Not as good as I *will* get," he answered. "If I see him again, I'm going to take him. See what he is up to."

"Probably better if you coordinated that with McGuire," Kincaid said. "He's got law enforcement cre-dentials. You get in a scrape with this dude and all of a sudden we got lawyers involved. Or worse yet, what happened that night in National City."

Before Delgado could reply, the elevator doors opened on the twentieth floor. Standing there waiting to greet them was Special Agent in Charge, William Hartmann.

Bill Hartmann had crossed fifty several years before, but still looked as if his gym membership was current.

He had eyes the color of dark roasted coffee and a Prussian general's military bearing. He was immaculately tailored in a dark blue pinstriped suit, crisp white shirt with a navy and red club tie. Kincaid remembered his dad telling him that one of J. Edgar Hoover's first commands to new FBI recruits was n*ever embarrass the Bureau.* If nothing else, the way William Hartmann dressed would have made J. Edgar proud.

He grasped Kincaid's hand with a grip just slightly too strong for the occasion. "It's so good to finally meet you," he said with a practiced grin. "Your father bragged about you ... constantly." He laughed. Then the grin disappeared and was replaced by an equally practiced look of sorrow. "I'm really sorry about your father. He was a good man and a good friend."

Kincaid nodded. "Thank you for seeing me on such short notice, sir. My father always spoke well of you and the rest of his team." Kincaid didn't know that for a fact, since his dad had never mentioned Hartmann or any member of his team, for that matter, by name, but thought he'd do his best to meet insincerity with insincerity. "This is Vincent Delgado, by the way. A friend of mine. We work together."

Hartmann shook Delgado's hand, and then promptly forgot him. He took Kincaid by the elbow and guided him down a long corridor lined with windowed offices on the perimeter looking out on the city, and simple rectangular cubes down the middle.

At the end of the corridor was a steel security door with a small scanner attached. Hartmann gazed into the screen. The iris recognition software did its job, and

the steel door clicked open. Kincaid and Delgado were escorted into a small conference room with a round table surrounded by six executive-style office chairs. Three of the chairs were already occupied.

"Let me introduce your father's team," Hartmann said. "This is Agent Michael Gray."

Gray was of medium height and at least a decade younger than his three Task Force 64 teammates. He had chalky white skin and deep-set green eyes perched above a hawk-like nose. He shook Kincaid's hand. "I admired your father very much. We're sorry he's not with us."

"Thank you. I appreciate your words," said Kincaid with all the sincerity he could muster. Which wasn't much. He knew he wasn't going to like Gray. Maybe it was just the attitude. The way he had said *we're sorry he's not with us* instead of *I'm sorry he's not with us.*

"Agent Pete Garcia," Hartmann said, introducing the next man in line. Garcia leaned forward and shook Kincaid's hand. "Forgive the dress," he said looking down at his jeans and black Nike warm-up jacket. "This was supposed to be my day off. I was in the garage working when Bill called."

Hartmann waited politely for Garcia to sit, then said, "And last but not least, Brian Jackson." Agent Jackson was a thin black man of medium height with a painfully short buzz-cut and flat dark eyes. *Ex-military*, Kincaid thought. *Probably JAG, if I had to venture a guess.* The two shook hands.

Everyone sat. "Before we start to discuss business, I want to acknowledge Walt Kincaid's contributions to this project. He literally gave his life for it. Without him, our sitting here with *Snow Plow* hopefully about to go operational would not have been possible. Let's welcome his son, and Vincent Delgado, here with us today, and let's honor Walt's memory with a moment of silence."

The men in the room stood and placed their hands over their hearts. All except Mike Gray, who stood but didn't put his hand over his heart. Kincaid took notice.

17

"**O**kay, down to business. Rob Kincaid is with us today mostly to find out what happened to his father and why," said Hartmann. "Is that a fair assessment, Rob?"

"It is."

"Let me start from the beginning, but any of you, ..." he gestured to the agents at the table, "... who want to add something, please feel free to jump in.

"*Snow Plow* was a plan thought up primarily by your father to win America's war on drugs. Everyone who read it thought it was brilliant, including most of the president's cabinet. Unfortunately, the president himself remained resolutely opposed to some of its provisions, the biggest one being the sending of special operations forces into Mexico."

"And if I may be so bold," interjected Agent Jackson, "once we heard about your father's death, we were sure the president would change his mind. But he didn't. A real shame. We loved your father. Our leader, mentor and friend. We don't want his death to be in vain."

"If I may change the subject for a minute?" Rob asked. "How did you find out there was a bomb on board?"

"We had a man, code named Munoz, very high up in the *Tormenta* cartel. He found out about the bomb and tried to alert us. He sent his message last Saturday. Somehow, and we are still investigating why, it didn't arrive until Monday morning. Right before eight am. Your father's plane took off at eight-oh-two. God knows, Rob, I tried to get that damn plane turned around. It took me eleven minutes to contact the person in the FAA who could authorize the plane to abort its flight plan and turn back. We finally contacted the pilot and the plane was in the process of turning back when the bomb exploded. If I had gotten Munoz' message ten minutes earlier, or it hadn't taken so damn long to locate an FAA guy with the authority to get the plane turned around, we wouldn't be having this conversation right now.

"To add to the tragedy, Munoz somehow became compromised. He and his wife and two children suffered a horrible death at the hands of Victor Lopez and his friends."

"Wondering if I could ask something," Delgado said.

"Of course," replied Hartmann.

"I've been sitting here listenin' to everyone talking how they tried to get the plane back on the ground, how they knew there was a bomb on board, blah, blah, blah. For me, the most important question is how the cartels came to know that Walt was even going to San Diego that day, let alone the flight he was on. There had to be only a certain few people that had that information. Most of them in this room, I might add." He paused, then added, "Just sayin'."

A stunned silence gripped the room.

"I hope you are not accusing me or any of my men of leaking information to the cartels," Hartmann said, putting both hands on the table and half rising out of his seat.

"As my momma used to say back in the day," Delgado answered. *"If the shoe fits …"*

"Fuck you," said Agent Gray. Unlike Hartmann, he came all the way out of his chair. A direct, man-to-man challenge to Delgado.

Delgado just smiled at him.

Garcia put his hand out and pushed Gray back into his seat. "Let's not fight among ourselves, okay? Remember … we asked ourselves the same question. So why get our panties in a twist when someone else asks it. It's a legitimate question."

"We struggled with the same question, sir," Hartmann said to Delgado. "We went through our entire department. Who had access to Walt's files; what assistant may have inadvertently blurted out something at a coffee break or on the phone that could have gotten out? Kind of a *loose lips sink ships* kind of thing. We did a thorough internal investigation. The only answer we could come up with was the girl."

"The girl?" Kincaid asked. "Who the hell is the girl?"

"You want to fill him in, Pete?" Hartmann said. Garcia got out of his chair. "Hold on. Let me get her file. I'll be right back."

When he returned, he pulled a picture from a thin file he held in his hand. "It's not like we have a ton of stuff on her. Her name is Laura Simpson." He slid the picture to Kincaid. Delgado had moved his chair next to Kincaid's so he could see, too.

It was an eight-by-ten portrait, like a publicity still models and actresses use. The face was of a very pretty young woman with striking blue eyes and an intoxicatingly innocent, girl-next-door smile that on the one hand invited you to protect her from the big bad world, while on the other invited you to participate with her in delights yet unfathomed. She was absolutely stunning.

"Laura Simpson," Garcia said again. "Thirty-two years old. A stripper at a place called the Magic Kitty in San Diego."

Kincaid studied the photo. Auburn ringlets softly framed an oval face and slender neck.

"The Magic Kitty is one of four or five strip joints in San Diego owned and run by the *Tormenta* cartel. They used them primarily for money laundering. Your dad went down there to have a look around. Maybe recruit one of the women dancers. The FBI has been pretty successful over the years using dancers as informers. Probably because most of them had drug habits, and if the choice was becoming an informant or getting busted for drugs, they would almost always choose the former. Whatever the reason, they were worth their weight in gold because they always seemed to have a way of getting close to *people of interest,* so to speak. They were never purposely put in harm's way. Your dad met and cultivated Laura Simpson about two years ago. She in turn introduced him to the owner of the Magic Kitty. Your dad ended up recruiting him, too. A lot of useful shit came out of the connection with Laura Simpson."

"What's your gut tell you about this girl?" asked Kincaid. "Could she have sold him out?"

"No one knows." Garcia said. "No one in this room ever met her. Your father was pretty protective of Laura Simpson. Could she have sold him out? I guess it's possible. Anyone can be bought.

"But I'll tell you what. If she is clean, she had better be watching her back. The guys we are dealing with here would butcher her in a heartbeat if they found out she was sleeping with the enemy."

"Sleeping?"

"Just a figure of speech," Garcia said without a hint of embarrassment. "We actually don't know for sure one way or the other. Though we think she stayed at your house on occasion because we know she had a key. Walt told us that. Giving her the key to his house was a sign of how much he trusted her. It was highly unusual, trusting someone that much. But your father claimed theirs was an unusual and complicated relationship. And it was none of our business, anyway.

"So, yeah, there was talk among the guys. You know how that goes. It was mostly jealously, I'm sure. I mean, just look at her. Who wouldn't be jealous? But underneath it all, none of us really cared. All we knew is your father was getting a lot of useful information from her."

Kincaid looked at her picture again. "Can I keep this?"

Garcia looked over at Hartmann. He nodded. "Boss says it's okay, so I guess it's okay." Garcia said.

18

When Kincaid and Delgado got back to the house, the Robbery techs were gone. The blue Mercedes, however, was not gone.

"Whoever that guy is, he's got to be the dumbest fuck in creation," said Delgado as they walked in the front door. "Thinking he can sit in front of your house ... okay, a block down ... and not be made. Let me go get him, Rob."

"Let's talk to Mac first, Vin."

They found McGuire with a rag in hand wiping down the kitchen sink. "My boys didn't do a very good job of cleaning up, I'm afraid," he said.

"What did they find out?" Kincaid asked.

"They didn't find anything useful, Rob. Tons of prints, of course. Just what you'd expect in a lived-in house. Most of them smudged because the same surfaces were touched over and over by the same hands. Even in the office where we knew the computer and some files were missing, there were very few clear prints. They told me their guess was the ones in that room were either Walt's or yours. Unfortunately, whoever did this knew what they were doing."

"How did they get in?" Delgado asked.

"Good question," Mac answered, "The techs spoke to your neighbor, Mr. Popovich. He says he saw two men drive up in a van. Name of some house cleaning service on it. Popovich told them they went up the front steps and into the house. So they knew they didn't get in through a window or anything. Came through the front door, apparently."

"Wouldn't we have seen the doorknob broken off, or something?" Kincaid asked.

"Exactly. The techs said they expected the doorframe to be cracked. They said the burglars would have had to do that to get at the lock. But the doorframe was intact. So they looked for scratches around the lock itself. Looking for evidence that they used tools to pick the lock. But, nada! No scratches."

"So what are you telling me, Uncle Mac?" Kincaid asked.

"Rob ... the tech guys think they must have had a key."

Kincaid looked at Delgado. He nodded. They both were thinking the same thing. Laura Simpson.

19

Kincaid and Delgado filled McGuire in on the talk they had with Hartmann and Task Force 64, especially the part about the key to the house that Laura Simpson had.

"Maybe Vinnie and I should head down to San Diego tonight and have a chat with Ms. Simpson." He emphasized the word *chat*. "If she's dirty, it's time she paid the piper. Besides, we have a meeting with Admiral Thompson tomorrow at NSWC at 0900."

"How are you going to decide if she is or isn't dirty?" McGuire asked.

"If she still has the key to this house in her possession, I'm willing to give her a pass. What do you think, Vinnie?"

"Yeah, I think we should go tonight. As to our course of action with her? Let's just play that by ear," he replied. "In the meantime, we still have the blue Mercedes to deal with."

"I've had a guy on my tail since I arrived in the city," Kincaid explained to McGuire. "Vinnie spotted him out front when he came over this morning. The dude then followed me to the Federal Courts Building and back. He's down the block now. Vinnie's been itching to get at him, but I thought it would be better to wait for a real cop to make the collar."

"An ex-cop, but who's counting?" McGuire said. "But before we go charging over, let me see if there's a black and white in the neighborhood. I'm not carrying, so it's better to have a car here in case our perp decides to make a fight of it." He called dispatch. "Five minutes," he said.

"If they don't get here, we can even the scorecard. Wait here." Kincaid ran upstairs and got his Sig. "See?" he said, stuffing the gun in his waistband and pulling his shirt over it. "I'm like a boy scout. Always prepared."

They had just walked down the front steps when a police car pulled up behind the Mercedes with their flashers going. Both officers exited the vehicle with their weapons drawn. By the time Kincaid, Delgado and McGuire arrived, the officers had the driver spread-eagled on the hood. McGuire thanked the officers and asked them if he could ask the guy a few questions. In deference to his former rank, they said okay.

"Name?" McGuire asked, walking up behind the perp.

"You have no right to do this to me. I have broken no laws."

"Name?" asked McGuire again.

"Fuck you," the man snapped back.

"Wrong answer, asshole," McGuire said as he kicked the man's legs out further from the hood, making him fall to his knees. "Now, I'm going to ask you one more time, and if I don't get an answer, you and I are going to have a serious come to Jesus talk. You got that?" The man gave a short nod of his head. "Name?"

"Jorge Gallegos," he said through clenched teeth.

McGuire motioned for Kincaid and Delgado to come closer. "Look here," he said, pointing to the fingers of the man's left hand splayed out on the car's trunk. "See the tattoos there?" Kincaid and Delgado looked closely. The index finger had the number *4* tattooed on it; the middle finger had a *0*, and the ring finger had an *8*.

"*4-0-8*. That's the area code for San Jose," McGuire said. "Take a look at the tats on the right hand fingers. *W-S-M*. Stands for *West Side Mongrel*. The Mongrels are a badass motorcycle gang." He leaned closer to the Gallegos. "What were you doing following my friend around?"

Gallegos remained silent.

"Maybe we should just have a look inside the vehicle, then. See what I can charge your ass with."

"Hey, you have no right inside my car. Illegal search. Even if you find something, my attorney will have me out within an hour."

"We'll see," McGuire said as he put on the pair of plastic gloves he had borrowed from the officers. He climbed into the front seat. After a few minutes, he came back out with a big smile on his face. "Look what we have here, Jorge. A baggie full of what upon close inspection will probably prove to be cocaine. A whole baggie, Mr. Gallegos. It's gonna be large enough for at least one felony count."

"Planted," said Gallegos. "I'll just say you planted the drugs."

"You going to also claim I planted this?" McGuire held up a gun. "Glock 19. Nice piece. Gang-banger's favorite weapon. Gonna bet it has your prints all over it. And fully loaded, too. Now we *do* have a felony. Maybe more than one, actually. Especially if you're a felon, which I have no doubt you are." Gallegos said nothing. "That's what I thought."

McGuire turned to the two officers. "Can you guys take this creep to 850? Book him on the weapon and drug charges. See if they both stick."

As they stuffed Gallegos in the back of the black and white, McGuire leaned in and said, "Give my best to your attorney, asshole."

As the cops drove Gallegos away, McGuire turned to Kincaid and said, "Damn, Rob. I'm really gonna miss this shit."

20

WEDNESDAY
LA JOLLA

It was five minutes after nine that evening when Rinaldo Palma received the call from Lupe.

"I have failed you, Patrón. My gunman didn't kill Señor Kincaid. In fact, he got himself arrested in the attempt."

"Is your gunman in jail?" Palma asked.

Si, Patrón. Santa Rita."

"Kite him, Lupe, as a message that no one fails the *Tormentas*. That there are consequences."

"Si, Patrón."

Kiting was a method the gangs had of carrying out killings inside of prisons. A visitor carried the name of the person to be killed into the jail on a tiny scrap of paper. It was hardly readable and easily digestible. The message was passed around the jail yard until someone accepted the assignment. Accepting meant receiving some gift, maybe some extra dope, or some money for the prisoner's family. The person who accepted swallowed the *kite*.

"I'm sorry, Patrón."

"That is okay, Lupe. These things happen. But only once. Comprende?"

"Si, Patrón."

"Besides," Palma said, "We will plan something else for Kincaid the younger."

21

WEDNESDAY
SAN DIEGO, CALIFORNIA

An hour after Palma had put out a *kite* for Gallegos, Kincaid and Delgado were in San Diego driving their rental car up Highway 101 from the airport to the Magic Kitty.

"I'm gonna enjoy runnin' with you, Kincaid," Delgado said, looking up at the garish purple neon sign dominating the parking lot entrance to the strip mall where the Magic Kitty Adult Theater was located.

"Don't get too comfortable, my friend." Kincaid said, nodding his head towards two Hispanic looking dudes watching them from the doorway of the "open until three" Taco Plus restaurant located on the first floor directly below the Magic Kitty. "What do you make of those guys?"

"I've got them," said Delgado. "Convenient hours, huh? Nude theater closes around two, they close an hour later. Maybe serve eggs rancheros to patrons before they go home to mamma?" He paused. "Do those dudes look like chefs to you?" Smiling, he waved at the two. "How you guys doin' tonight? Business good?" They stared back at him through dead eyes.

"Cool it, Vinnie," Kincaid said. "We aren't here looking for trouble."

"Sorry, Rob. I'll be on my best behavior ... promise. It's just that those kinda guys ..." He shrugged, letting the thought die. "Tell you what, though. Them dudes ain't chefs."

"Shrewd deduction," Kincaid said with a smile. "Maybe they are here to keep away the riff-raff." They started up the wooden stairs leading to the second floor. "Speaking of riff-raff, Vinnie. Were you ever a customer of this place? I mean back in the day?"

"Nah. Made it a practice never to frequent strip joints located on the second floor of old, broken down strip malls. Especially ones advertising 'live nude girls'. You know ... like someone would come to see the alternative?" He laughed at his own joke. "And tell me, Kincaid. You're so smart ... what kind of genius puts his sex club on the second floor, for God's sake?"

"Maybe someone who wants plenty of lead time to clean up anything messy or inconvenient before the cops arrive. Maybe that's what our two friends downstairs are about. Cleaners."

"Yeah. Maybe." Delgado said, and then went off in a different direction. "Can you imagine the kind of poor fuck frequents a place like this? I'm guessing forty-five or older? Probably fat. Climbing these steps just to stare at pussy? Shit! Maybe those guys downstairs are doctors. Kinda like fucking ambulance chasing lawyers, but smarter cuz they are right at the source.

"And I'll bet the girls in this place are a piece of work, too. Nothing against the lady you are looking for, but I wouldn't let any of them get too close to an open wound or anything. Know what I mean? Never know what you might pick up."

"Geez, who wound you up all of a sudden?" Kincaid said. "But to tell you the truth, I don't plan on getting close to anyone." Kincaid ponied up two twenty-dollar bills to pay both of their twelve-dollar entrance fees. He was given change in one-dollar bills. "I'm just here to find a girl and collect my dad's key. That's it. Then we are outta here."

It took a few seconds for their eyes to adjust to the club's dark interior. Long and narrow, it obviously was the strip mall's only second floor tenant. There were two stages, one at either end of the oblong room. On the far wall, curtains hid a small booth area where the private dancing went on.

"I count thirty-two customers. Twenty-eight single guys and two couples," Kincaid said. "You?"

Delgado slowly looked around the room. "That's what I get."

"Anyone here look like trouble to you?"

Again Delgado's eyes trailed slowly over the room. "Nah. Even the two bouncers look like, forgive the pun, pussies."

They made their way to one of the tables on the outer fringe of the room. The ones used by guys who just want to look. Only trouble sitting there was you became marks for the girls roving around looking for lap-dance suckers. That's exactly who they got.

"What are you drinking," asked a young, raven-haired girl wearing a paisley g-string, matching pasties and sporting a large nose ring.

"Is there a cover?" Kincaid asked.

"Two drinks per hour minimum," answered nose ring distractedly. "Since the girls dance naked, we can't serve alcohol. Soft drinks, coffee and water."

"How much for the coffee?" asked Delgado.

"Eight dollars."

"And a Coke?"

"The same."

"Each?"

"Each."

"And we have to have two?" Delgado was having fun with her.

"Per hour. Come on, man. Don't give me hard time, okay. You guys know the drill, I'm sure. I don't set the prices. I just work here. I don't like the high prices, either. Cuts into the tips I get. And that's how I get paid. Tips. Have to work my ass off to make anything." She paused and looked seductively at both of them. "You guys want company?"

"What's your name, sweetheart?" Delgado asked as he put his arm around her waist and pulled her to him. She didn't resist.

"Tiffany," she answered.

"Well, Tiffany, I think we'll just order the Cokes for now. You're cute and all, but my partner here is spring-ing for all this, and he is notoriously cheap."

She smiled. "That's what all you big spenders say ... at first. I'll come back in an hour and you'll be begging me to sit with you. Or better yet, to dance privately for you." With that, she gave Delgado a bump with her hip and left to get the Cokes.

"Geez, Delgado. You are one smooth son-of-a-bitch."

"I know" he replied, shaking his head in bemusement. "That damn girl could be my granddaughter. Can you believe that? And she thinks I'm gonna take her up on that proposition?"

"Keep thinking that way," Kincaid said. "It will keep your dick in your pants. We'll all have a better chance of getting home early tonight. And in one piece."

"Hey ... I ain't lookin' to get laid. These girls are too damn young. Geez ... my granddaughter." He smiled and leaned closer. "And besides, what would Tiffany and I have to talk about in the morning?"

Some girl named Dawn was announced as the next dancer. The fact that Dawn was only about five-foot-two and more than pleasantly plump didn't detour the male groupies from placing dollar bills on the stage.

While Dawn was doing her thing, Kincaid leaned over to Delgado. "Go see if there is a back door to this place. Maybe some stairs to that taco dive downstairs. I'll buy the Cokes ... and even save them for you." He smiled.

"I'm gonna miss Dawn?" Delgado pouted. "Oh, well. Tell Tiffany I'll be back for her."

"I'm sure she'll be breathless."

A few minutes later, Dawn finished her set, picked up her clothes and money from the stage, blew her admirers a kiss and exited. The stage went dark.

A few moments later, the stage on Kincaid's right lit up. The announcer went through his routine. "And here she is, the one you have all been waiting for. The Magic Kitty's very own ... put your hands together and welcome to the stage ... Kimberly." The music pulsated, the curtain parted and, to polite applause, out stepped Laura Simpson.

22

Laura Simpson, who was now a blonde, had sparkling blue eyes and a smile that had "heartbreak" written all over it. Her stage persona was a combination of girl-next-door shyness and unbridled sexual energy. She had every guy in the place reaching for his wallet in the hope of bribing her for attention.

Kincaid watched her do her thing with more curiosity than lust. This was the girl his dad had recruited. He wondered if, at least on his dad's part, it was more than just a working relationship. It wouldn't have surprised him. She was everyman's fantasy female.

Kimberly was into her second number when Tiffany arrived with the Cokes.

"That will be thirty-two dollars, please," she said, flirting by rubbing her body on him. Kincaid smiled to himself and tipped her more than she was worth. "What happened to your friend? He didn't leave, did he? He was kinda cute."

"No, just had an errand to attend to. Told me to tell you he'd be right back." She smiled sweetly. "I have a favor to ask of you," Kincaid said, hoping the tip would be sufficient for her to do what I was about to ask. "I'd like to meet Kimberly."

That stopped her. She became decidedly less friendly, seeing her big scores going to another dancer. "You and every other guy in here, darling," she said. "But you don't have to go with her. You have me. Let's go in the back. I'll give you a lap dance you'll never forget. And maybe more if you are really generous." She cupped her breasts seductively and sat on his knee.

"Tiffany ... I like you. Really. But I have to talk to Laura," hoping the mention of her real name would give him some leverage. "It's personal. Friend of hers wanted me to look her up when I was in town."

She picked up her serving tray, already looking around the room for some other dumb bastard she could hustle.

"Yeah, I'll tell her" she said distractedly. "You a cop?"

"No, not a cop. Just a guy doing a favor for a friend."

"And what's the friend's name? In case she wants to know?" she asked.

"Walt. Tell her Walt asked me to give her a message."

Tiffany nodded and left.

23

Kincaid had just finished his first Coke and was sipping on the second when he felt a tap on his shoulder. He turned to his right and looked straight into the bare midriff of a girl who obviously knew her way around the gym.

"You asked for me?" came a soft voice with just a hint of the south. She laid her hand on his shoulder. "Do I know you?"

Kincaid looked up, almost getting lost in the deep blue of her eyes. "No."

"Then how did you know my name? I only give that out to very special people, of which, the last time I checked, you weren't one."

"I'm Rob Kincaid. Walt Kincaid was my father."

That heartbreak smile. She had not as yet picked up on the past tense. "Oh my god," she said, giggling girl-ishly. "I'm so glad to finally meet you. Walt has told me so much about you. Where is he? He was supposed to be here three days ago. Hope it's not something I said." She smiled again, and then turned serious. "Oh my god. I hope he's not sick or anything."

"He's dead," Kincaid said flatly.

She looked down at him, trying to gauge if he was playing with her. She couldn't tell. She took a step backward. "You're just teasing me, right?" Kincaid didn't respond. She turned to her left as if to leave, then swung back towards him. "You're not." This time she turned in a complete circle, not knowing what to do. Her hand flew to her mouth. "Oh my god," she cried. "What happened?" Her eyes filled with tears that sparkled in the fluorescent lights.

"I've got to talk to you," Kincaid said.

"No! This can't be right. You're lying to me."

Kincaid leaned in closer to her. "Probably not a good idea to make a scene," he said quietly. "Considering where we are and who could be listening."

She looked around, tears now lining her face. In a quieter voice, she asked, "What happened?"

"He was coming to see you. Did you read about the plane that went down in San Francisco on Monday?" She nodded dumbly. "He was on that plane."

"Oh my god, no!" She virtually collapsed into a chair at the table next to him, sobbing quietly. Kincaid was already beginning to think that Simpson had to be legit. Hard to fake this kind of reaction before a complete stranger.

Her distress had been noticed by one of the bouncers at the bar. He was already making his way through the tables, his right hand in his coat pocket. Kincaid quickly leaned over Simpson and whispered, "Can you get off early? I've got to talk to you about Walt."

Her head bobbed in the affirmative, her body still shivering with emotions. "Give me thirty minutes. I'll meet you in the parking lot out front."

Sobbing, she stood and walked toward the bouncer who, by this time, was just two tables removed. He put his arm around her paternally and whispered something in her ear. She shook her head and said something back. The bouncer looked back at Kincaid with a look that said "lucky you, asshole. You just got a reprieve on getting your ass kicked." Kincaid smiled at him.

Delgado was standing a few tables away, taking in the scene. As soon as everyone had settled back into their routine of watching naked girls dance, he came over and sat down.

"Shit. I can't leave you alone for ten minutes before you get yourself in trouble. Don't know what I'm going to do with you.

"By the way. I was just waiting for that bouncer to come over and start hassling you. I would have taken him out in less than a minute. I hate guys liked that. They bully you with their size. But inside? Inside they're as soft as little girls."

"That was Laura," Kincaid said.

"I figured. You told her about your dad, obviously."

"Yeah. She didn't take it well. She's either is the finest actress who ever graced a strip club stage, or she was genuinely torn up to hear about him."

Delgado nodded, sipping at his Coke. "Just remember though, Rob. These women? They are all actresses. That's how they make their money. Not sayin' she wasn't sincere. Just reminding you of the obvious."

"I hear you. I'm going to meet her in the parking lot in thirty minutes. She's taking the rest of the night off. I'm going with her to her house. To get my dad's key, if she has it. Shouldn't take too long. Want to meet me back here at, say, two? I'll cab it back."

"That will work for me," Delgado said with a smile. "I think I'll spend some quality time with Tiffany. She's starting to look real good to me about now."

"Yeah. Just remember, she's old enough to be your daughter."

"My granddaughter. And thanks again for the reminding me. Hey ... a question. What happens if Laura doesn't have the key?"

"Then get a room somewhere. I'll be later than two."

24

THURSDAY
SAN DIEGO

Kincaid looked at his watch as he saw Laura Simpson exit the far door of the Magic Kitty. One-fifteen. He was going to have to hoof it to get back here by two to meet Delgado. The tacoria was still open. No surprise there. Still no customers. No surprise there, either. The two Mexican dudes were still sitting at the front door. They watched him as he met up with Laura at the bottom of the stairs. She smiled wanly at him. Her puffy eyes indicators that this wasn't an act. She wore a short black leather skirt and a cream colored blouse under a knee-length black leather coat. He had just noticed how tall she was. The three-inch heels on her boots brought her at almost eye-level with him.

"You have a car?" he asked.

"No, I take a cab to and from work. Driving would be too dangerous. You never know what creep is going to find out where you live by tracing your license plate. I live about ten miles from here. Not far. I called for a cab. That's him there." She motioned to the far corner of the parking lot.

Kincaid looked back and saw the two Mexicans standing on the walkway looking at them.

"First of all," she said as they began walking toward the cab, "I want to apologize for breaking down in there. I was just thinking of myself. Selfish. I wasn't thinking of your loss. I'm sorry for you." She stopped and turned toward him, a single tear running down her left cheek. "And I want to thank you for coming all this way personally to tell me about Walt. I, ..." she reached into her jacket pocket for a tissue. "...I really liked your father." She let out a deep sob.

The cabbie was an older guy sporting a white turban and a matted black beard. "Where to," he uttered in a thick middle-eastern accent that Kincaid instantly recognized as Pakistani. Laura gave him the address and they both settled in the back seat.

"Are you in San Diego often?" she asked.

"Now and again."

"I asked because I was wondering why you never came in to the club with your father."

"Generally wasn't here when he was," Kincaid replied. "Besides, probably wouldn't have come with him to the Magic Kitty."

"Why?"

"Not my thing."

"What ... you don't like to see naked girls? You're different than most men, then," she said.

He settled back in the seat, looking out the side window into the darkness. "I've seen a lot of naked people in my life," he said. "Some because explosions had burned away their clothes along with half their bodies.

Some because their captors had stripped them naked before doing things to them you couldn't even imagine. I've seen naked bodies without arms. Some without legs. Some with their guts spilling out on the ground. Some without their heads. Naked bodies don't thrill me all that much. I wasn't there to see you dance. I'm only here to get the key my dad gave you to his house."

"His key? That's the only reason you are here? You actually lowered yourself to come to the Magic Kitty," her voice now dripping with sarcasm, "to get his damn key?"

Kincaid turned to her. "I'm sorry. I don't want to be harsh. Or diminish what you felt for my dad in any way. There are some things I have to do here in relation to his death and I don't have a lot of time. Under ordinary circumstances, I would have played this differently. Unfortunately, these aren't ordinary circumstances. How long a ride is this?"

"About twenty minutes." She paused. "You're nothing like your dad, you know?" she said looking over at him. "He was a very warm and caring person. You have no soul."

Kincaid didn't respond, thinking maybe she didn't know his dad all that well. On the other hand, maybe she was right. Maybe killing people destroyed your humanity. He was in no mood to think about that now. He closed his eyes and leaned back in the seat.

25

THURSDAY
LA JOLLA

Palma answered the phone. From the series of clicks that greeted him, he knew exactly who was calling.

"Sorry for the late call," the voice said. "I know I said no more business between us, but something just came up."

The voice told Palma that one of the dancers at the Magic Kitty, a girl named Laura Simpson, and Jairo Esteban, the manager of the club, were informers for Walt Kincaid.

"Esteban? An informer?" Palma barked into the phone. He was not in a good mood. He was being entertained by another special puta. She was lying in his bed, but instead of sharing her delights, he sat at his desk in a robe talking to the gringo from the north. "Why didn't you tell me? Do you think I am stupid?"

"Because we choose not to tell you everything," the voice answered. "You know that was our deal. You have the assets to eliminate people we can't, and in return we give you information that we think you should know.

Information that won't compromise us. This particular situation was a case we thought we could manage. And we did until Kincaid died. Now we have people snooping around. We have to clean things up around the edges. We have reason for not wanting the girl alive. If you can fix that, we owe you."

"I am more disturbed about Jairo Esteban," Palma said. "He was running four of our clubs in San Diego, and he was working for you behind our back? I gave him everything he ever wanted. I kept his whores in business in four different clubs, and look how he repays me. There is just no loyalty anymore. His family will pay dearly."

"Do with him what you want. But the stripper is who concerns us. She is more dangerous."

"He should never have done this to me," said Palma, not letting it go. "I will have him dealt with tonight."

"Good. Just don't forget the girl. We don't know what she knows. We think she was sleeping with Kincaid. No telling what he told her. We can't take any chances. And just so you know, it's Kincaid's son that is there talking to the stripper. You can take them both out together. As you have found out, he is not someone to be taken lightly."

Perfect, Palma thought. *Kincaid is coming to us.* "Don't worry. I will have my men take care of both of them tonight. I am glad you called."

Palma looked over at the girl squirming sensuously in his bed. He blew her a kiss and gestured he would be just one more minute.

He called the Magic Kitty. "I have a job for you, Ernesto," he said, recognizing the voice. "And Jesus. It needs to be done tonight. I will not accept failure."

"Si, Patrón."

"You have a puta there by the name of Kimberly?"

"Si, Patrón."

"I want her dead. Now!"

"She just left, Patrón. With a gringo."

"Perfect. Kill them both. Tonight. And Ernesto ... is Señor Esteban at the club tonight?"

"Si, Patrón."

"I want him dead, also. He has been talking to the American *federales*. I want you to make an example of him. Have Jesus get a soldier to go with him to kill the puta and the gringo. I want you to kill Esteban personally. Show the world what happens when our own betrays us."

As Palma hung up the phone, phase two of *Snow Plow* had been operational forty-eight hours.

26

THURSDAY
SAN DIEGO

Laura Simpson lived in a modest two-bedroom house in a modest suburb east of San Diego. Like all the homes in the development, it was defined by a patchy front lawn that ran twenty yards from the house to the street. Instead of fences, six-foot hedges separated the property lines. A cement walkway ran along the right hedge all the way to the front door. The stucco façade was chipped and faded. Metal wind chimes and colorful flowers held in small clay pots decorated the front porch.

"I have a dog," she said as she put the key in the lock. "He can be very protective, so don't follow me too closely until I can properly introduce you." She opened the door. Kincaid heard the growl first, and then saw him. Standing in the middle of the entrance hall, illuminated by nothing but the light from the street lamp, was a large beige and white pit bull, brow furrowed, teeth bared, and looking directly at him.

"Shush, Buck," Simpson commanded, taking hold of the dog's collar with one hand while the other stretched for the keypad to turn off her alarm system. Standing, she flipped on a light and motioned Kincaid to come toward them. "This is Buck," she said. "He is my protector. He'll get used to you in a few minutes, when he sees that you mean me no harm. In the meantime, just walk in slow motion." She knelt and hugged the animal who didn't quite know whether to be happy about seeing her or to do battle with this stranger. Laura whispered in Buck's ear, cooing to him that all was well. "He liked Walt," she said over her shoulder, "so I guess he should like you, don't you think? Come over slowly and offer your hand so he can smell you." Kincaid did as he was told, not wanting to have to kill the dog if he attacked. Which he would have.

Buck sniffed at him for a few seconds and then, apparently deciding he wasn't a threat, trotted back into the living room. "Come in and make yourself at home," Laura said.

The home was a small, box-like two bedroom, with all the rooms coming off a central hallway. Fully furnished, the interior was neat and clean. The kitchen was the first room off the hall on the right. Like a lot of homes built in that era, the kitchen looked over the front yard, while what served as the living room/dining room combo faced the rear of the house. A small bedroom that smelled of dog opened directly across the hall from the kitchen, while the door for the master bedroom opened into the hall across from the living room. Separating the two bedrooms was a yellow tiled bathroom with a small sink and an old fashioned tub.

She put her purse on the table in the hall and walked into the kitchen. "Can I offer you some coffee or maybe a drink of something? I think I have some beer in the fridge. I'm going to have a cup of tea, myself. Your dad always had coffee when he visited."

"Thanks. Just the key and I'll get outta here," Kincaid replied.

"Oh, for God's sake! Lighten up, will you? I won't bite, I promise." She paused. "I can tell you are wondering about me and your dad. It's written all over your face. You want to talk about that? I'll tell you everything. It's more complicated than you think."

Kincaid shook his head. "One cup. Then the key. Then I'm gone. Don't have to know about you and my dad."

She heated the water for her tea and his coffee in the microwave. When the bell rang, she gave him the cup and he followed her into the living room. It was medium sized and sparsely furnished. A large dried eucalyptus wreath hung on the wall over a small fireplace. The wall opposite the fireplace was entirely made of glass with a sliding door that led to an enclosed backyard featuring two producing fruit trees and a portable gas barbeque. Laura walked over and pulled the cord that closed the drapes. "Nosey neighbors," she said with a smile.

She offered him a seat on a white brocade sofa while she settled into a wing- backed blue chair that obviously had seen better days. She noticed him looking and said, "my parents' chair. From our house when I was a little girl. I inherited it when my mom and dad died within a month of each other. Kinda ratty looking, I know, but oh, so comfy." She smiled contentedly and curled her feet under her. Kincaid sipped his coffee in silence. "There was nothing going on between me and your dad, if that's what's bothering you," she said flatly. He didn't respond.

Buck stirred in the corner. Head up, ears cocked. A low growl escaped his throat. He leaped to his feet and sprinted into the hall towards the front door.

"Buck, what is it, boy?" Laura yelled after him.

"Quiet," Kincaid said, already up and following Buck to the front of the house. Just as he reached the hall, the dog burst past him and back into the living room, the cords of his neck knotted tightly. At the sliding glass, he stopped and bared his teeth, saliva glistening in the light of the lamp by Laura's chair. Kincaid heard what Buck heard. Footsteps on the patio.

"The light," he hissed to Simpson. "The light. Kill it."

She sat there dumbly, frightened by the commotion and not understanding what was going on. Kincaid didn't ask again. He grabbed her by the arm and yanked the light cord from the wall in one motion. The room did not go completely dark. "Shit," he said. The kitchen light was on and it softly illuminated part of the living room through the connecting door. He'd have to live with it. "The bedroom," he whispered, grabbing her by the arm. "Quickly! You have a gun?" She shook here head. "A knife?" Again, a shake of her head. He knew he could find one in the kitchen if he had the time. He didn't.

Kincaid pulled her roughly into the bedroom. "What's going on?" she said hoarsely, terror lining her face.

Kincaid tried to calm her. "It's going to be alright," he soothed. "No one is going to hurt us. Probably just a drunk neighbor. Besides, if someone tried to get in, he wouldn't get past Buck." He turned toward the door, listening. He heard the lock on the sliding door being jimmied. He could also hear Buck's growl. Lower now. More menacing. "Go lay down behind the bed. Don't get up until I tell you. It will be all right. Just do as I tell you, okay?" She nodded, but didn't move. He took her arm and pulled her around the bed. "Get down." Reluctantly she did.

Kincaid walked to her closet and unbent a wire hanger. SEAL training 101. When no weapon was near at hand, improvise. On soft tissue, a wire hanger was just as effective as a knife.

The lock on the patio door came free and the door slid open. He wondered why the guy wasn't too concerned about the noise he was making. Then it hit him. There were two bad guys. One was probably out front, he thought. Coming in from the back yard, this guy's job was to panic them into running out the front door, right into the sights of his buddy waiting in the front yard. They just made a fatal error!

After reminding Laura again that she was not to come out of the bedroom until he gave her the okay personally, he slipped out the bedroom door into the living room.

Just as Kincaid cleared the door, the intruder pushed the draperies aside and cautiously stepped into the dimly lit room. Out of the corner of his eye he caught sight of Kincaid coming at him. Pivoting sharply, he brought up the 9 mm he carried and leveled at Kincaid's chest. Before he could fire, Buck sprang and clamped his mouth on the exposed arm. Kincaid heard the bone snap under the power of the pit's jaw. The intruder screamed in agony.

Even with his arm broken, the bandit didn't lose his weapon. Still trying to transfer the gun to his good hand, Kincaid punched the coat hanger into his neck. Soft tissue. He pushed it clear through to the other side, puncturing the carotid artery on the way out. The intruder's eyes went wide with surprise, then clouded over in death as a stream of arterial blood turned Laura's comfy blue chair red.

27

Kincaid reached down and retrieved the intruder's gun. He checked to make sure the magazine was fully loaded and there was one in the chamber. Yes and yes.

He walked back and opened the bedroom door. "Laura?" he said quietly. Her head popped up from behind the bed.

"Everything okay out there?" she asked in a shaky voice.

"In the living room? Yes. I'm afraid I didn't treat our visitor very kindly. And I think he's got a partner out front. Stay right where you are. If bullets start flying, I don't want you to be a big target. You understand?" She nodded zombie-like. Still gripped by terror. "I'm going to close the door. Don't come out until I tell you."

Kincaid moved down the hallway, following Buck's bloody paw prints. The dog had stationed himself to the right of the front door. The low, menacing growl a warning that there was still someone out front.

Inching his way toward the kitchen, he reached through the doorway and hit the light switch, plunging the house into darkness. He deliberately slowed his breathing and focused.

He heard a soft scraping sound along the outside wall underneath the kitchen window. Someone was up tight against the house, sliding his way toward the front door. He brought the gun up and aimed it at the front wall, about where he thought the intruder might be by the sound he was making.

"Kincaid? Kincaid, it's Vinnie. I know that's you in there. Open up. I'm dragging the other sack of shit from the taco bar here with me. Don't shoot, okay?"

Opening the front door, Kincaid helped Delgado carry the unconscious gunman into the house. After securing his hands and feet with duct tape they found in a cabinet above the stove, Kincaid went and retrieved Laura from the master bedroom while Delgado found some instant coffee and started heating the water in the microwave. The three of them sat at the kitchen table and tried to make sense out of what had just happened.

"So I saw you and Laura leave in the cab," Delgado said. "Then I saw these two dumb fucks," Vinnie said, nodding toward the back of the house and then at the guy laying on the kitchen floor by the sink, "running over to get their car. The guy out back is the bouncer from the club, by the way. Remember him?" Kincaid nodded.

"Jesus Garza," said Simpson. "That was his name. The one here is Miguel Fox."

"Whatever," Delgado said. "Well, I didn't have to be Einstein to figure out where they were headed. Just to make sure no harm came to you and the lady here ..." he nodded his head toward Simpson and smiled, "I decided I should probably watch your back. Good thing I did."

"Nasty crack to the head," Kincaid said, looking down at the guy crumpled by the sink, the wound on the back of his head leaking blood on the kitchen floor. "Probably should clean that up before we leave." Buck was standing over Miguel, his knobby head just inches from his face. Even though unconscious, every time Miguel groaned, Buck would emit a low growl and his jowls would stretch back over his teeth. If the guy had awakened and been stupid enough to make a sudden move, Buck would have ripped half his face off.

"Yeah. He has a broken wrist, too," Vinnie said. "The broken wrist came first. Had to break it to get his gun. Then, when I got the gun, I whipped him upside the head with it. He went down like a stone in water. Anyway, that's where the nasty gash came from. He'll be hurting real bad when he wakes up."

"So ... what do you think we have here?" Kincaid asked, looking at Simpson. "These guys worked at the club, right? Why would they come out here to kill you?"

"I don't know why except somehow they may have found out I was working with your father. I got along okay with the owner. He wouldn't have any reason to want to harm me, though, because your father had recruited him, too. We were both supplying information to Walt. He knew and accepted that."

"What's his name?" asked Delgado. "The owner."

"Esteban. Jairo Esteban. A lot of the girls swore he was connected to the Mexican mafia in San Diego. That's because he ran four other clubs. You had to be connected to do that. At least that was the reasoning." She turned to Delgado. "Do you think you could get me some coffee, please? And there is some Bailey's in the cupboard. I could use a drink." She pushed errant strands of hair off her face.

Delgado got up. "Sure. You want anything Rob?"

"No thanks." He turned back to Simpson. "Tell me about Esteban and my dad."

"I don't know how much of any of this you know. Your dad came down here about two years ago. At least that's when I met him. He came into the club one night. And then another. And another. I noticed him because he was always at my stage when I danced. One night he asked me for a lap dance. When we got back into the private area, he said he only wanted to talk. That he'd pay me for my time. He started out telling me about my family. Where I grew up. He knew all about me. It was eerie. But he got my attention real quick. Knew who my favorite teachers were in high school. What beauty pageants I had been in, and which ones I had won. It was pretty flattering, to tell you the truth. Creepy, but flattering. He knew that drug use destroyed my family. Both my sister and my dad died from an overdose. He knew my mom killed herself because of it. He knew my first marriage broke up over it. Then he asked me out for breakfast. I ordinarily wouldn't have accepted, but he so enthralled me, I said okay."

"Did he tell you he was FBI? That he was running a special drug task force?"

"Later. The first morning he only told me he was FBI. That's how he knew so much about me and my family. It wasn't until he was satisfied, I guess, that I was just as much against drugs as he was that he started to level with me about why he came down here. Why he picked me out."

Delgado set the coffee in front of Simpson, and the Bailey's on the table. Simpson thanked him, opened the bottle of Bailey's and took a big gulp. She then poured some in her coffee. "Told you I needed a drink," she said, with a grin. "Thanks." Looking at Kincaid, she said, "Over time he told me what he was after. He knew about Esteban. Knew he was connected. Said he needed an introduction. I gave him one."

"Esteban is a drug dealer?" asked Delgado.

"No, strangely enough, just the opposite. He hated drugs, too. Said it was the scourge of my generation. Not because he was a saint or anything. Just pragmatic. Used to tell the dancers that if he ever caught any of us using drugs, he would fire us on the spot. It was bad for business, he would say. And that from a guy who would pimp his girls out. Go figure."

"How long ago was the introduction made?" Kincaid asked.

"About six months ago, I think."

"Somebody obviously got wind of your involvement," Delgado said. "And had to be recently, too. Otherwise they would have killed you long ago." He turned to Kincaid. "Your dad dying. This." His hand swept the kitchen. "It's all connected of course. And don't forget the guy in the blue Mercedes."

Kincaid nodded, picking at some of the flecks of blood that spotted his shirt. He looked at Simpson. "When exactly were you at my house in San Francisco?"

Her eyes hardened, and when she spoke there was an edge to her voice. "I was never at your house. I know what you are thinking, and it's the thing that bothers you the most, isn't it? Even more than his death, I think. Were Walt and I lovers! Well, first of all it's none of your damn business. Secondly, and I've tried to tell you this but you won't listen, so let me tell you straight out. No.... we weren't lovers. Not physically, at least."

"What the hell does that mean?" Kincaid asked.

"I loved your dad, okay? Is that what you wanted to hear?" Her voice was rising. "But I loved him like a father. Probably a lot like you did, if you are capable of loving anyone."

"But you had the key to the house."

"Yes, I did. Walt gave me one in case I ever wanted to R & R in San Francisco and he wasn't home. Said that I could stay at the house. Just like I told him he could do here. He had a key to my house as well. Did that mean we were sleeping together? No. He never stayed at my house, either. And I don't have the damn key to your house, by the way."

Kincaid and Delgado looked at each other. "Why? Where is it?" asked Kincaid.

"I looked before I came out here. As you two were pulling Miguel into the house. I knew you wanted it. The reason you came to the house tonight, remember?

"I kept it in my jewelry box on top of my dresser. Three weeks ago I had a break in. During the day. I was out walking Buck. I do it every day around three. I'm never gone very long so I don't set the alarm. Whoever broke in took my jewelry box, and not much else I could find, tell you the truth. Maybe I scared them away before they could get to the good stuff. Anyway, there was nothing in that box but junk jewelry. Nothing that looked even remotely valuable. I called the police about it and filled out a report. You can check with them if you don't believe me. I didn't mention the key, however. Since I never used it, I forgot it was even in there. That's the truth, and you can go to hell if you don't believe it." She stared into his eyes. Not blinking. Defiant.

Kincaid found himself returning her stare, not because of the challenge she threw down, but because he was captured by the beauty of those eyes. He broke contact, finally, knowing that Simpson would take that as a victory. That *he* had blinked first. She might have been right in the short-run, but in the long run he knew he had to report this killing to the police and that he had a date at 0900 with Admiral Thompson at NSWC. He looked at his watch. Only seven hours from now. They still had a lot to do.

28

The police arrived within ten minutes of Simpson's nine-one-one call. They went over their stories one more time. She knew Kincaid's dad. Kincaid had just happened to be here visiting. A home invasion had occurred. Being a former Navy SEAL, he knew how to protect himself as evidenced by the corpse in the living room. For her part, yes, she did know the guy and, no, she had no idea why he wanted to break in. Could be that he didn't know she was home, and just wanted to rob her. Could be he saw her leave with Kincaid and was jealous. Could be that he was there to rape her. She just had no idea.

Delgado had already left in Simpson's car with Buck and Miguel. It was just easier that way. One guy breaking in, the cops would believe. Two guys? Cops would start asking questions. And Miguel could answer those questions in ways that could be uncomfortable for them. Delgado was to dump Miguel somewhere in the hills, and sit tight until Kincaid and Simpson were released by the police. Because someone was actively trying to kill Simpson, it was Kincaid who came up with the idea that Delgado and Simpson should drive to San Francisco and stay at his house. Kincaid figured he would be back in San

Francisco by ten tonight. None of the three missed the irony of Kincaid passing Simpson the key to his house.

Once the cops heard Kincaid had been a SEAL, they breathed a sigh of relief. It gave them cover not to spend a lot of time investigating what they considered another unfortunate home invasion perpetrated by some Mexican gang-banger who had a rap sheet going back twenty years. That he was a fatality? Good riddance as far as they were concerned. They weren't going to spend much time on him. The police took both their statements, asked where they would be staying for the next week or so, waited for the coroner to finish up his work, and let them leave. Simpson packed a suitcase full of clothes and toiletries, and she and Kincaid drove away to meet with Delgado. He looked at his watch. Only five hours before he had to be at NSWC.

Just as Kincaid turned into the Coronado Hotel to get breakfast before showing up at NSWC, his cell rang. It was Delgado.

"Hope I'm not bothering you, Rob. I'm out front of the Magic Kitty. Since Laura won't be coming back to work, she wanted to grab the clothes and outfits she left, and also to leave her key. You should see this place. Lotta shit going on here."

"Like?"

"Police running all over the place. Parking lot lit up like Christmas. Yellow crime-scene tape strung across both entrances. I had to park a block away. Not sure what went down, but after what happened to us, I'm thinking it's a good chance they're related."

"Where's Laura now?" Kincaid asked.

"Told her to see if she could sweet talk some young officer into letting her get to her locker. Her flirting worked. He's escorting her inside personally as we talk." Delgado laughed. "And you'll never guess who else is here." He didn't wait for Kincaid to answer. "Tiffany." He laughed again as he heard Kincaid groan. "Don't worry, partner. I'm cool." He was silent for a few moments, then said, "Hold on a second, Rob. Laura's coming back. I'll find out what happened. Want me to call you back?"

"Nah, I'll hold."

Kincaid could hear muffled talking between Delgado and Simpson. "Okay, here's the skinny, Rob," said Delgado, coming back on line. "The owner of the club was found murdered."

"At the club?"

"Yeah. That Esteban guy. They told Laura he was tortured and then executed. Gotta tell ya, Rob. First Laura, and then this guy? Seems like the cartels are trying to sweep the area clean."

"Get her up to my house safely, Vinnie," Kincaid said. "I'm counting on you."

29

THURSDAY
NAVAL SPECIAL
WARFARE COMMAND
CORONADO, CALIFORNIA

At 0900 hours, Kincaid walked into Admiral Thompson's temporary office quarters at the NSWC base in Coronado. Chris Fuller, JJ Johnson and the Rosen were already seated around the table with Thompson. They had arrived last evening and spent the night on the base.

"Look what the cat drug in," Fuller said as Kincaid joined them at the table. "You look like shit, Rob. Rough night?"

"You'd never believe me," Kincaid replied. "Long story. I'll fill you in later."

"Glad you are all here," Admiral Thompson said. "I've got another meeting at 1100 regarding some concerns about what is happening up your way, Rob. In San Francisco."

"Like what, sir, if I may ask."

"Like the ten mysterious deaths reported to the Center for Disease Control in Atlanta. Caused by anthrax."

"Anthrax?" said Fuller. "There's a blast from the past. Deliberate?"

"That's what we're trying to find out now," Thompson said. "I'll find out more details at this meeting coming up. So, because we don't have a lot of time, let's get down to business.

"Remember I told you on the phone when you were still in J-bad that Red Squadron had been brought up in my conversation with the president? Specifically as it related to *Snow Plow*? The fact is the president, unless something absolutely draconian happens, is never going to authorize Special Operation troops into Mexico. Just too politically risky.

"But, as long as we can provide him with plausible deniability, he assured me that he would turn a blind eye to black-ops in Mexico. Let's see. Black-ops ... Red Squadron." Thompson said, using his hands as if he were weighing both phrases. "Synonymous as far as I'm concerned.

"That's why you are here today. JSOC is going to sponsor you. As *consultants*. We don't need any special budget approval to hire consultants. That will be our public cover if this arrangement ever sees the light of day. Which, hopefully, it won't. It will be an open-ended contract. I'll have my E-6 work out the monetary details with you. Questions?"

"Are we essentially on stand-by now?" asked Rosen.

"Something like that. I am assuming your first target will be Victor Lopez? That would be our preference, and I'm guessing yours, as well."

"You've got that right, Admiral," Kincaid said.

"Good. That will give the president the additional cover he wanted in case your operation in Mexico was discovered. That you and your buddies were there to kill Lopez for what he did to your dad." He paused, accessing Kincaid's reaction. Satisfied, he said, "Then I am going to give you everything we have on Lopez and his operation. I'll send his file electronically to your secure server. Your server is secure, is it not?"

"It is, sir," Kincaid replied.

"Where will you be headquartered, by the way?" Thompson asked.

"Right now," said Kincaid, "we'll be working out of my house in San Francisco. It's a big place. We'll be living there, too."

That was a surprise to the three Red Squadron members. Their voiced responses ranged from "No shit?" to "Aw, shit."

———

Earlier that morning, the phone awoke Palma from a deep sleep. He had sent the whore on her way just thirty minutes before. He was exhausted and gave a thought about letting the call go to voice mail, but knew that messages coming in on this line had important business implications. He hadn't gotten this far by letting those calls go unanswered.

"This is Ernesto Calderon, Patrón. Pardon the early call. I wanted you to know I took care of Señor Esteban. The police are just wrapping up their investigation. By the mutilated condition of his body, they will undoubtedly conclude it was a drug deal gone bad."

"Excellent, Ernesto. I knew I could count on you. A bonus is in order."

"Thank you, Patrón. But I do have bad news, too. The girl and the gringo escaped death. In fact, both the gringos escaped death."

"Both gringos. What do you mean?"

"There were two of them. Came into the club together. Only one went with her to her house. The other must have followed Jesus and Miguel. The police found Miguel in a dumpster. He is at a local hospital. They knew that he worked here, so they called us. He is in very bad condition. Jesus is dead."

"That's too bad, Ernesto, but we can always find replacements," Palma said, his voice not betraying his anger. "Do you know where the girl and the gringos are now?"

"The girl is at the club now, Patrón. Picking up her clothes. Only one of the gringos is with her. Sitting in a car about a block from the club. I don't know where the other one went."

"What's he look like? The gringo with the girl?"

"Short. The other one was taller. This one has long hair. Tied back. Do you want me to kill them both?"

Palma thought for a moment. Kincaid had to be the other one. "No, Ernesto. It's the other gringo I want. Follow this one and the girl. They will lead you to him. Once you find the tall one, kill him. You can also kill the girl and the short gringo, too."

"Si, Patrón."

30

Thompson let them use his office while he was gone. "Let's make a list of what we think we might need," Kincaid said. "Mostly just basic weaponry since we don't have specific targets, yet. Wolfman, can you keep track of this?" He nodded and retrieved a pen from his shirt pocket and a pad of paper from the desk.

"First thing I would vote for would be Molle chest rigs," Fuller said "The one with the ballistic plates. If we had a quick deployment, too quick to get down here, for example, those puppies stop high caliber rifle bullets. Life savers."

"I wholeheartedly agree," Rosen said.

"Speaking of higher caliber rifles," Johnson said, "you all know I just love my HK 417. It will be good for at least one of us to carry the heavier caliber. I'll volunteer." He laughed. "And while I'm at it, let's not forget the EOTech Thermal sights."

In the Teams, EOTech Night Vision Thermal sights were known as *the sight for all seasons* because of their high-resolution thermal imagery. The EOTech could penetrate fog, rain, light snow, and darkness.

"Any objections?"

"None at all," Kincaid said. "I'm thinking we all should carry it. I know it's a little bulky for the MP7s, but, like the Molle rig, it's one of those things that tends to be a life saver."

"Cateyes?" said Fuller.

"Definitely," said Kincaid. "Don't leave home without them." Cateyes were essentially night vision contact lenses. They had replaced the helmet-mounted, night vision tubes. Not only were they less bulky, they allowed the operator complete peripheral vision, which the helmet-mounted tubes didn't.

"You sure they have them here?" Rosen asked.

"Hey, this is the most complete fun-store armory on the planet. They have everything here," said Fuller. "When I was stationed here, I used to just wander through to see all the new toys. It's the reason I became a SEAL. They got first access to all the hottest gear."

"Okay, what else?" Kincaid asked. "Grenades?"

"Flash bangs, for sure," Johnson said. "Two each." Everyone nodded in agreement.

"ChemLights?"

"I think we should carry them. What the hell, they don't take up a lot of room and they are always helpful. Especially if we have to clear rooms."

"Breaching tubes?"

"I don't see the use for them," said Fuller.

"I agree with Chris," said Rosen. "No use for them as far as I can see. Hope not, anyway."

"Scratch breaching tubes," Kincaid said with a laugh. "Last but not least, rifles. We all comfortable with the MP7?" They all nodded in the affirmative. "With three mags and a thousand rounds each?"

"Might be overkill," Johnson said, laughing "but what the hell. We might be facing a small army someday."

About the time Red Squadron was boarding a plane in San Diego, Ernesto Calderon called Rinaldo Palma and told him that he had followed the puta and gringo to a house in San Francisco. The tall gringo was not there. Palma had told him that he would no doubt be joining them soon, and to call as soon as he arrived

Kincaid and his team flew into Oakland International, rented a black Chevy Suburban and drove to the airport's north field to await the arrival of their gear. Forty minutes later they saw an older model C-23 Sherpa on approach.

"Thompson must have pulled in some favors," Kincaid said as the plane taxied over to where they were parked. The Sherpa was a small, prop-driven military transport that had been decommissioned for regular military use years before and now was used almost exclusively by the Army National Guard. The Guard pilots helped unload a heavy wooden crate into the Suburban and took off.

As they were driving out of the airport, Kincaid called Delgado and told him where he was and that the house was about to get crowded.

An hour and ten minutes later, the Chevy Suburban pulled into Kincaid's driveway, and the four men exited carrying three large pizza boxes and three six-packs of Stella's they had picked up from a local store.

While Kincaid and his group were devouring the pizza and beer, Ernesto Calderon called Palma back.

"The gringo just arrived at the house, Patrón. He came with three other men. Friends, by the looks of them. What do you want me to do?"

"Screw it. Come on back. We'll deal with him later."

31

THURSDAY
LA JOLLA

Palma called Victor Lopez and told him about having to kill Jairo Esteban but not being able to kill Kincaid. That he was back in San Francisco.

"Rinaldo, how long have we been together?" Lopez asked with a venomous voice. Palma had heard the tone before so knew what was coming.

"Many profitable years, *Ahn-hel*. And many more on the horizon," he answered, attempting to deflect the coming, predictable onslaught. Lopez got in these moods often. Violent and ugly. The fact was they were occurring more frequently, which worried Palma. But he couldn't do anything about it, and he knew they didn't last long. Just as quickly as the mood came, it would fade away.

"So why is this happening? Why do we have defectors like Esteban? When we pay them so handsomely? Why no loyalty?" he asked, his voice rising in intensity. "And this prick, Kincaid? Why are we having such trouble eliminating him? That doesn't happen *here*. I keep control of *my* people. If they fuck me, I cut off their balls in front of their wives. And then decapitate their children and place their heads on poles alongside the highways. They soon learn."

Lopez was like a hot air balloon. Once the burner was turned down and the hot air cooled, the balloon drifted back to earth. Lucky for Palma, it was at that moment the burner turned down, and Lopez came down to earth.

In a very calm voice, he said, "I want to come to visit you, my old friend. I love America. So peaceful. I'm having bad dreams lately. Maybe we can get together, eh? I'll tell you about the dreams."

Oh-oh, thought Palma. He wasn't up for dispensing psychological advice to the boss. Especially a boss so volatile. Lopez once had a therapist whose tongue he had cut out because he didn't like the advice she gave him. Palma cherished his tongue.

"What about the casa in Borrego?" Lopez asked.

"When would you like to come, *Ahn-hel*?"

"Tomorrow. Can you arrange it?"

"I can. You will fly, of course?"

"Of course. Mid-morning. Is that okay?"

"Perfect, *Ahn-hel*. I will prepare the casa."

32

THURSDAY
SAN FRANCISCO

At eleven that night, after everyone had retired to the beds they had been assigned, Rob sat alone in his father's office pouring over some of the electronic correspondence Thompson's E-6 had sent regarding Victor Lopez. He heard a noise and looked up to see Laura Simpson peeking in the door.

"Sorry to disturb you," she said. "I was just going to the kitchen to see if you had some milk."

"No problem," he replied. "I'm sure there is some. Help yourself."

A few minutes later, she walked back into the office holding a glass of milk. She was barefoot and wearing a man's long-sleeved, blue-striped shirt that barely covered her thighs. Her hair was pulled back into a ponytail, and she wore no makeup. Kincaid's eyes couldn't help but take in the whole package. "Mind if I join you for a few minutes?"

Kincaid minimized the computer screen and leaned back into his dad's leather chair. "Of course not," he said. "Have a seat."

"I'm such a creature of habit. I always have to have a glass of milk every night before I go to bed. It puts me right to sleep."

Sensing his stare, she turned to him and smiled, the top of the shirt gaping just enough to show the swell of her breast. "Your father's shirt. A little long for me. Only thing I could find. Hope you don't mind."

Kincaid suddenly felt distracted by her presence. It hadn't happened to him often, so he was surprised by its power. She was a very pretty woman, no doubt. But this was something more than just looks. She had an aura about her that was unmistakably female, and unmistakably inviting.

"This was your dad's study?" she asked.

"Yes. His most favorite room in the entire house. I remember as a kid what a treat it was to be invited into his *office*. That's what he called it ... his *office*. It was the original *man cave*, before *man caves* were invented. He'd be ashamed of it now." Kincaid half twirled the leather chair around so he was facing the violated filing cabinets and the hole in the wall where the safe had been. "After he died, a couple of scumbags broke in here and stole things from this room."

"Is that the reason my 'key' became important? How they got into the house?"

"Precisely. Sorry about the way I came on to you. There were, and are, a lot of loose ends surrounding the circumstances of his death. The way they got in here is one of them."

"Well, I'm glad the key was an issue. If it hadn't been, I probably would have not heard about Walt's death, and certainly wouldn't have met you."

Kincaid looked at her, wondering if she was teasing him. Her smile told him she wasn't. *Damn,* he thought. *This girl is flirting with me. And doing a damn good job of it, too.* "I hope you didn't think I was being rude by putting you in my father's room," he said, changing the subject. Trying to pretend he hadn't noticed. "Only reason I did was because it had its own private bathroom."

"You're thoughtful," she replied, again flashing that heartbreak smile. "I appreciate it. Haven't ever lived in a place with five guys and me being the only girl. A nice, *protective* feeling."

"Nothing will happen to you, that I can guarantee." He leaned back in the chair, appraising her. "How long have you been in California?" he asked.

"I came out when I was twenty-two. Six years ago. My family was pretty screwed up, as I told you at my house. In spite of all that, though, I was a pretty good student in high school. Got good grades. Played sports."

"Oh? Which ones?"

"I ran track and played baseball. Well, softball. Girls play softball." She sighed. "I was pretty good, too. Enough to get some college scholarship offers. I was even recruited by Northwestern."

"Impressive," Kincaid said. "You must have been really good."

She laughed. "I love telling that story. People are always so impressed. Like you. But I was offered by Northwestern *College*, not Northwestern *University*. It's a Christian school in Orange City, Iowa. Division three. But at seventeen, I was just glad *someone* had noticed. I was a happy girl."

"And well you should have been. Not many people get scholarship offers to college. No matter what division."

"Your dad told me you played baseball."

"A little," he replied.

"More than a little. He said you were drafted by the Cubs out of high school. Beats the hell out of my Northwestern story." She laughed again.

My, my, my said the spider to the fly, Kincaid thought. She was drawing him into her web. He could feel it. And he wasn't resisting. "You want a glass of wine or something?"

"Sure. Do you have white?"

"I'm sure we have a bottle in the fridge. My dad always kept one on ice. Hold on." He came back with two glasses and an open bottle of Sauvignon Blanc he found on the refrigerator's second shelf. "Probably not the best, but it's cold," he said, putting the glass in front of her and filling it. They sat there in silence for a minute or two sipping their drinks.

"How'd you go from high school baseball star to the stripping business?" Kincaid asked.

"Dancing," she said with a smile. "We're *dancers*. Being a stripper sounds so sluttish." She looked over at him. "You've probably heard my story a dozen times if you ever watched Oprah, or Jerry Springer, or Ellen."

"I'm *not* sorry to say that I've never watched any one of those shows."

"I don't blame you," she said. "They are generally not guy kinda shows. But, if you had watched them, one of their recurring story lines was interviewing young women who have fallen on hard times. The cliché is of a young girl, almost always from the Midwest, who came from a dysfunctional family. So far that's me. To escape from that family, this cliché girl runs away from home and marries her bad-boy high school sweetheart. Ditto me. Also in the cliché story, the "bad-boy" part always beats out the "sweetheart" part, and in three years the husband has gone off with someone else and left her in some shack with a baby.

"It's here where my story deviates a little from the cliché. There was no shack, and no baby. But if you're watching this on Jerry Springer, his cliché girl can't go back home, so she and her baby hop a bus for the West Coast where she turns to prostitution to support herself. The prostitution leads to dope, dope leads to stealing, stealing leads to jail, followed by a pretty shitty life for her and the baby that ends, many times, in violent death.

"Fortunately, my story took a different path. I did take that bus ride to Los Angeles. But I had an aunt there who turned out to be a wonderful, caring lady. And by this time, I'm twenty-two years old. Not really a kid, anymore. And it didn't hurt that I'm okay-looking and pretty smart, so it didn't take long finding a job. My aunt invited me to live with her, and a week after I moved in, I found a job at a savings and loan company in Tarzana.

"A year went by, and I met a guy. We dated for a while and then I moved in with him. It turned out he knew a guy, who knew a guy, who ran some *Gentlemen's clubs* in San Diego and was looking for dancers. Mostly to impress me, as I think back on it now, he asked if I would audition for that job. I've never been a real prude about my body, and since the pay was, like, triple what I was making at the savings and loan company, I said I would. This guy who ran the club, by the way, was Jairo Esteban, the manager of the Magic Kitty and three other clubs in and around San Diego. I liked Jairo. He was a very nice man and very respectful. He liked my audition and offered me a job. I took it. It didn't take long for my boyfriend, however, to become almost insanely jealous of me taking off my clothes for other men. After many arguments, some of which became violent, I insisted he leave.

"That was four years ago. In a relatively short time, I was raking in scads of money, but I wasn't happy. As a little girl, I had dreamed of making a difference in the world. To do something really good or really important. It didn't have to be inventing a cure for cancer, but it sure as hell had to be more important than sending men home to beat off while thinking of me.

"But then your dad entered my life. I told you, he was like the father I never had: talking to me for hours about life, and happiness, and religion, and stuff like that. He talked about his passion to rid America of the scourge of drugs. Of what that would have meant to families like mine. And what that *could* mean to families in the future, especially families in the inner cities who are simply being torn apart by the amount of drugs in their communities. He said I could help him accomplish that goal. He said I could make a difference in the world." She wiped away a tear from her eye. "Can you see now why I loved your dad?"

Kincaid nodded. "It's funny," he said. "I never got that close to him. I left home after high school, like you did, but I never got a chance to see him much after I left. I wish to hell I had."

She looked at her watch as she stifled a yawn. "It's getting late," she said. "I should be getting to bed." She put her glass down. "Anything new happening on the anthrax front?"

She was referring to a call Kincaid had received from Admiral Thompson right after they had finished dinner that night telling him that the anthrax deaths had passed twenty and were causing great concern in the highest circles of the government. The concern was caused by the fact that the deaths weren't contained to just San Francisco. If they had been, one logical explanation could have been that some local lab had inadvertently released spores into the air. But the reported deaths were now coming from different parts of the Bay Area and beyond: from Sacramento to San Jose, to as far north as Chico. When Thompson told him that Homeland Security was involved, Kincaid knew that this wasn't going to go away soon.

"Nothing since he called earlier," Kincaid replied. "I'm hoping there will be some simple explanation, but my gut feeling is this is a lot bigger than anyone thinks."

By the time Kincaid and Laura Simpson had gone to bed that night, phase two of *Snow Plow* had been operational seventy-two hours.

33

FRIDAY
SAN FRANCISCO

"**S**orry to wake you at this ungodly hour, Rob. Homeland Security has just elevated their Security Advisory threat level to "Imminent.""

"*Imminent*? That's the highest possible level, General. Forgive my language, but what the fuck is going on?"

"The San Francisco Bay Area, and beyond, is under biological attack by an as-yet unknown terrorist group using anthrax as the preferred weapon of mass destruction. They have fifty-five confirmed deaths so far. That's thirty more than there were at ten last night. And the hospitals are filling up quickly. A very serious situation."

"I guess. Where do we fit in, General?"

"There was a *sit rep* meeting at the White House this morning. Since I was here and not there, I can only tell you what was told me. It was the unanimous opinion of everyone present, and the heads of every major government agency up to, and including, the Joint Chiefs *was present*, that JSOC and the FBI be given joint operational control over the attack until further notice."

"Why JSOC, sir? This sounds like domestic terror-ism to me, and domestic terrorism isn't in the military's charter, is it? I always understood that domestic terror-ism was a law enforcement issue."

"You're correct, Rob. But I was told that the feeling at the meeting was that since anthrax is classified as a WMD, this attack could very well be state-sponsored, and might, therefore, need a military response. That's where Red Squadron is perfectly positioned to be our liaison to the FBI. Hell, Bill Hartmann has been named the officer in charge."

"Why him, sir? Do you know?"

"Their director told the White House this morning that he appointed Hartmann because he was the only person locally who knew anything about anthrax. He had been stationed on the East Coast in November of oh-one, and had assumed operational control over the first anthrax attack that occurred right after 9/11."

"Has the press gotten on this yet?"

"I'm afraid they have. They all get Homeland Security's Threat Assessment report. As soon as the threat went Imminent, everybody knew. It will be all over television by now. Check it out."

"I will." Kincaid turned on CNN, and there was a somber faced newscaster with the DHS logo filling the screen behind him, anxiously gesticulating as the screen changed to the number of deaths attributed to the attack. Kincaid flipped through a few channels. All were carrying the same feed. He turned the TV off.

"If I'm not mistaken," Thompson continued, "your agency now offers a law enforcement component."

"That it does, Admiral. But you already knew that. A fellow named Tom McGuire. Former SFPD homicide inspector. Highly respected. Knows everyone in law enforcement. I'll call him immediately. He will have to get used to getting early morning phone calls if he is going to work with us."

"Amen to that, Rob. Give Hartmann a call, too. Offer your services. I don't know if he knows you work for us, but you can tell him if you think appropriate."

"Thank you, sir. I'll get right on it. But no matter how this emergency turns out, I want you to know, Lopez is still mine."

Rob looked at the clock next to the phone. Four thirty-five. He dialed McGuire's number. *McGuire better start getting used to these hours,* he thought. *If he objects, he doesn't belong with us.*

McGuire didn't object. In fact, he was highly energized. "You mean I get in on the ground floor of what will become the biggest manhunt in history" he said, "and in addition I pull a pay check? Michele will be thrilled. Me out of the house, and she with money to spend. She'll think she died and went to heaven."

"You might as well get dressed, Uncle Mac. I'm going to call Hartmann now and see if we can come over. I'll be back to you in a few minutes."

McGuire had showered and dressed before Kincaid called back. "Hartmann is up to his ass in alligators. He would like us to come over ASAP to help him sift through the data before the shit hits the fan media-wise. I'll pick you up at five-thirty."

34

It was early still, but the word of the anthrax attack was out. The first National Guard units had arrived and were starting to deploy. Barriers had already been erected at major intersections to keep the growing crowd of demonstrators from causing problems. McGuire made a left on Van Ness. Big mistake. There were fifty or sixty demonstrators milling around. The Guard had cordoned off the sidewalks on both sides of the street so the opposing sides wouldn't start killing each other. On one side of the street were about sixty left wing crazies, chanting and carrying signs and placards that read things like "Bush's Revenge," conveniently forgetting that Bush had been out of office for eight years, to "G-8 Sucks," to "Bring Down Corporate America".

"Where are the *Free Huey* banners?" Kincaid asked. McGuire chuckled and shook his head.

On the other side of the street were the right wing nuts. Not as many of them, but, given the political profile of San Francisco, that's exactly what you'd expect. They were chanting and carrying signs, too. Their shtick was how the attack was obviously a sign of God's displeasure and anger at San Francisco. "The Wrath of God," as one sign said. There were signs proclaiming that God was so pissed off about gay marriage, abortion, Obama's presidency, and governmental taxation that He was letting the terrorists attack the Bay Area as payback.

"What the hell time is it?" McGuire asked, looking at his watch. "Six-fucking-thirty. And you got all these creeps on the street protesting already? Welcome to San Francisco." He shook his head in humorous disbelief.

"Yeah. I had forgotten what a nut case city this can be," said Kincaid.

The press also happened to be out in force. Kincaid counted almost as many news people as demonstrators. Because of all the people milling about, the Guard could only allow a few cars through at a time.

By the time they arrived at the Federal Courts building, the National Guard was setting up their command post. About two hundred troopers milled about, all wearing masks.

Kincaid looked at the troopers. "How's this anthrax shit spread, anyway? Any idea?"

"I think mostly by breathing it in," McGuire said. "Not exactly sure if that's the only way it can be transmitted, but I'll bet we're going to find out real soon."

"Since we didn't get the word to wear masks, I guess you and I could be breathing in the shit right now and never know it. At least for however long the incubation period is."

"Comforting," McGuire said.

Coming off the elevator on the twentieth floor, McGuire saw his old partner, Bill Murray. He called him over and introduced him to Kincaid.

"I've heard a lot about you," Murray said with a friendly smile. "Welcome to San Francisco, home to Fisherman's Wharf, Cable Cars and terrorist attacks."

"If this is any kind of sample, I can't wait for you to introduce me to all your San Francisco treats," Kincaid said with a smile as they shook hands.

"Sorry about your father," he said. "Terrible tragedy."

"Thanks," replied Kincaid. "I appreciate it.

National Guardsmen in full battle dress were escorting people down the corridors to their destination.

"Who are you seeing here?" McGuire asked Murray.

"There is supposed to be some kind of theater on this floor where I was asked to show up," he answered. "Kearney and O'Brien were asked to attend, too."

"Just like old times, huh?" McGuire said with a smile.

"The FBI wants us to learn about how anthrax is spread and then use our undercover contacts to find out who the perps are."

As they waited for their escorts, McGuire pointed to the windows that lined the floor.

"I find it rather ironic," he said to Kincaid. "All this security here? National Guard called out to escort us to wherever. Everyone worrying about biological terrorists. Look at this building. Twenty stories high and virtually all glass. One well-placed explosive and the glass shards from those windows would simply cut all of us here in half." He looked around. "I wouldn't be at all surprised if this anthrax shit was nothing more than a grand pretext by some disgruntled voter to get the city's brass up here in one spot and blow them all to hell at one time."

"Ah, but don't forget the barriers," Murray replied with a cynical smile.

"Yeah. Right! The barriers! I forgot about them." McGuire laughed. "After wrangling back and forth for years, the city and the federal government finally came to an agreement on whose responsibility it was to make the building secure from terrorists. Together, they got as far as splitting the cost for placing cement barriers on the street out front so that cars had to park at least one hundred yards away. About the same distance McVeigh parked his truck full of fertilizer that blew the shit out of the Federal Building in Oklahoma City."

"Thanks for sharing," Kincaid said. "I feel so much better now."

"Oh, speaking of sharing," Murray said to McGuire, "did you hear about that Mexican kid you arrested in front of Rob's house?"

"Gallegos?" McGuire asked.

"That's him," Murray said. "He's dead."

"Dead?" McGuire said. "What ... the anthrax get him?"

"No, he was kited."

"No shit?"

"Why would anyone want Gallegos dead?" asked Kincaid.

"I'm guessing it has something to do with you. Maybe somebody put out a contract on you and this Gallegos guy didn't fulfill it," Murray said. "Tell you what, Mr. Kincaid. You got some powerful enemies for someone so new in town."

35

FRIDAY
BORREGO SPRINGS,
CALIFORNIA

Just as the National Guard was coming to escort Kincaid and McGuire to the private offices of Task Force 64, Victor Lopez was settling into his Casa at Borrego Springs.

Borrego Springs is part of what, in the United States, is called the Anza-Borrego desert, but topographically is the westernmost section of the Sonoran Desert of Mexico. It was from Sonora that Juan Bautista de Anza came north seeking an overland route to Monterey, California. He made camp at Borrego in seventeen seventy-four because he found a natural spring that bubbled up from the desert floor.

Lopez didn't know where the name *Borrego* came from, and he didn't care. Its remoteness and the general inhospitable nature of the weather made it the perfect spot for him to come to conduct business on the American side of the border.

In the late nineties he had Rinaldo Palma purchase a ten-acre parcel of land there. They registered it to a shell corporation run by Palma's aunt. In order not to draw attention to the site, Palma had taken a number of years to construct what turned out to be an eight thousand square foot, ten bedroom, ten bath hacienda, complete with a twenty bed dormitory for Lopez' body-guards, all surrounded by a seven foot wall of sand colored plaster over a reinforced steel core.

Lopez had christened the site Casa Moraga, in honor of Gabriel Moraga, who not only was a member of Juan Bautista de Anza's two expeditions to consolidate Spanish, and later Mexican, claims to the entire south-western part of United States, but also happened to be born in the same Sonoran town as Lopez' father.

To solidify the anonymity Lopez needed, Palma made an offer to the owner of the small airport on the north side of town that, in return for allowing Lopez to fly in and out of his airport without having to file flight plans, he would give him a yearly stipend of twenty thousand dollars ... and a promise to let him live. It was an offer the owner couldn't refuse.

Lopez and Palma were sitting together in the study. Lopez had leaned back in his chair and was silently looking out at the Laguna Mountain range that pro-tected Borrego Springs from the marine influence of the Pacific Ocean seventy miles to the west. He was in a foul mood again.

"It is your job, Rinaldo," Lopez began, "to recruit local talent. Obviously, you haven't been training them well. They are proving unreliable. Look at what hap-pened in San Francisco when you tried to get someone to kill Kincaid, and now in San Diego. Failure after failure."

Palma was getting tired of taking the brunt of the blame, but he just nodded his head and agreed with everything Lopez was saying.

"My organization has been made to look foolish," he continued. "The people on this side of the border will need a reminder of who we are and the dangers to them of crossing us." He took a sip of his drink, then looked over at Palma. "Do you have any suggestions as to how we can recover?"

"First of all, Victor, let me say I am sorry if I have let you down. It was not intentional. You know that. You are my oldest and best friend. We have been through many good times, as well as a few bad times, together. This is one of those bad times. Actually, more annoying than bad. Nothing here that can't be fixed rather quickly and easily."

"I hope so, for all our sakes."

"Have you heard the latest news from up here?"

"You mean like *news* news? I have been too absorbed in business to pay much attention these last few days. Something happening I should know about?"

"There has been what they are calling a terrorist attack in Northern California. Primarily in the San Francisco Bay Area."

"Terrorist? What kind of attack?"

"Biological. Anthrax. Many people have died."

"¡Mierda!" Lopez cursed. "Who would do such a thing? More importantly, who could do such a thing without telling us?"

"They are saying Al Qaeda, but no one has yet taken responsibility."

"How come we weren't informed? Hezbollah certainly would have known." Lopez' voice was rising in anger. "We let them use our courier systems into the US, and this is how they repay us? This world is going to shit. Heads will roll. They don't respect us anymore."

"I've taken it upon myself to speak to Sheikh Obedani. He denies knowing anything about it."

"Impossible, Rinaldo. They had to know. Something is going on here that is not good for us."

36

FRIDAY
SAN FRANCISCO

The Guard escorted Kincaid and McGuire to the private offices of Task Force 64.

Agent Hartmann met them. "Thanks for coming," he said. "Have a seat. Let me fill you in on where we are to date.

"As you can imagine, ever since the DHS raised the security threat level, my office has been deluged by phone calls from everyone: from the federal and state government to every news outlet on the planet. So, if I have to interrupt our conversation periodically, you'll understand why.

"At three this morning, the governor activated the State's emergency preparedness media center so that citizens statewide could get the latest news and information on how to protect themselves from anthrax, and who to contact if they started to feel sick. Implicit in his activation was the admonition that if anyone knew who was behind this atrocity, it was their duty to let his office know. He has instructed all citizens in San Francisco, at that time the epicenter of the attack, or so we thought, to shelter in place if possible. This city's police and sheriff's departments, along with the Guard, will try to keep everyone off the streets as much as possible until they can determine how the anthrax is being distributed. Since we know that anthrax has to get into the body somehow, every off-duty paramedic will be taking air samples at fifteen minute intervals in assigned sections of the city." Hartman held up his hand as the phone rang. He hung up three minutes later.

"That was Homeland Security. Four hundred and fifty-five deaths, so far, and rising. Death reports are now coming in from Nevada, Arizona and even Oregon and Washington State. Bad shit."

"Has any group claimed responsibility?" Kincaid asked.

"In my view, this has to be Al Qaeda. No one else could conduct an operation this big, with these many causalities. But to answer your question, no one as of yet. I'm sure we'll be getting a communiqué from the bastards soon enough."

"Anthrax! That is really surprising," Kincaid said. "As a SEAL, we were trained what to do if attacked by chemicals like Sarin, or Tabun, or Phosgene. Those were the ones we thought the pricks would use if they came after us chemically. The thinking was that a biological attack was too complicated and unpredictable. That's why we never did too much with anthrax."

"I know," Hartmann said. "Anthrax was thought to be too old-school for sophisticated players like Al Qaeda. Boy, were we wrong.

"But let's talk about where we are now. We've set up a command center in the next room over. The data streaming in is current within a five-minute interval. I'd like you two to give me a fresh pair of eyes. Tell me what you see. Maybe together we can come up with a pattern of distribution, and then stop the bastards."

"I'm not sure I'll be able to help, Agent Hartmann," McGuire said. "I don't know enough about anthrax to offer any opinions."

'Glad you said that," Hartmann responded. "Oh, by the way ...the name is Bill." McGuire acknowledged the courtesy with a nod of his head. "Next door we are sponsoring an *everything-you-ever-wanted-to-know-about-anthrax* seminar for the local police, sheriff and firefighters. Probably something you should attend. You've already missed some of it, but it will be repeated continually for the whole day, so everyone will have a chance to hear it."

"I'll go, too," Kincaid said. "I could use a refresher."

37

They went to the conference room next door and found a seat. Dr. Leslie Coombs, head of the Infectious Disease Department at the University of California San Francisco medical center, had just been introduced and was at the podium.

Dr. Coombs was a tall, angular woman of about fifty whose gray hair was pulled back and kept in place with a blue, dolphin-shaped barrette. Behind the half-glasses that perched precariously on her nose, her eyes told the story of sleepless nights and harried days.

"I'll try to make this short and sweet," she began. "I've been up all night looking at this data. To put things in perspective, anthrax derives its name from *anthraces,* the Greek word for "coal". It is so-named because of its ability to cause black, coal-like cutaneous lesions in the lungs. The bacillus anthraces organism is usually only deadly if inhaled or gets into your bloodstream in heavy doses.

"Historically, human anthrax in its various forms has been a disease of those with close contact to animals or animal products contaminated with Bacillus anthracis spores. In the mid-1800's, inhalational anthrax contracted by those in the textile industry became known, in England, as woolsorters' disease while in Germany it was known as ragpickers' disease because of the frequency of infection in mill workers exposed to imported animal fibers contaminated with the anthrax spores. In the early 1900's, human cases of inhalational anthrax occurred in the United States in conjunction with the textile and tanning industries. In the latter part of the 20th century, with improved industrial hygiene practices and restrictions on imported animal products, the number of cases of reported anthrax fell dramatically

"It was almost wiped out worldwide by the early nineteen thirties. In fact, before the 9/11 attacks, the last reported case of human inhalational anthrax in this country was in nineteen seventy-six. So when it showed up again in November of two thousand one, everyone knew it had to be a biological attack."

"Is it usually this deadly?" someone in the audience asked. "I think I read somewhere that if you caught anthrax early enough, and treated it with massive doses of antibiotics, it wasn't all that lethal."

"Antibiotic treatment," Coombs replied patiently, "especially at the early stages, certainly increases the chance of survival. But not lethal? I can tell you that anthrax is *very* lethal. Even with antibiotics, approximately forty percent die. Two out of every five. That's deadly. And fifty years ago? Fifty years ago if you got anthrax in your lungs? You died! Period! So, I guess the direct answer to your question is ... it's not as deadly as it was fifty years ago, but it's still deadly enough."

"Dr. Coombs," McGuire said. "I just got here, so someone else may have already asked this. What is the incubation period between the time anthrax got into those peoples' system and when they got sick and died?"

"That is a good question and I was just about to get into that," replied Coombs. "The period between contracting anthrax and the symptoms showing up is usually just a few days. Maybe a day before you start getting cold-like symptoms, and another day before the symptoms start to get violent. You get severe breathing problems, and then within a day or two after that you go into shock. Death follows rapidly. So, the answer to your question is, in general, three to five days. Very quick."

"So, for the people dying now," continued McGuire, "they had to be infected anywhere from last Monday onward. Is that approximately right?"

"Approximately, yes," she answered.

Another question came from the back of the room. "Since there aren't a lot of sheep in this city, do you have any idea on how it is being spread?"

There were a few chuckles in the room that a stare from Dr. Coombs soon quashed. "We don't have the answer to that yet," said Coombs. "I understand that is partly why you are all here today. To answer that mystery.

"In the meantime, I think we can definitely rule some things out. It's not in the water supply, for example. I'm not sure if that is even possible, but if it were, we'd all have contracted it by now. And it would be the intestinal kind of anthrax, not the inhalational type."

"But what about human contact?" continued the questioner. "I mean, by coughing, for example, can spores being expelled from someone's lungs and be ingested by another person's lungs. Or by kissing? Stuff like that."

Coombs took a sip of water and replied. "No. At least we are pretty sure. If I thought there was any danger of it spreading human-to-human, I would have insisted that we make it a law that everyone in the city wear a mask until we find the people responsible for this. But there has been no study that has shown it to be contagious human-to-human.

"Now ... the spores can be on someone's clothes and be spread that way, if you happen to touch the spores and either bring them to your mouth and ingest them or get them on an open wound or cut or something. That's why when we are first treating these patients, we are in the Gumby suits which we then thoroughly disinfect before we re-emerge in civilian clothes."

"Well, if not human contact, how 'bout aerosol?" McGuire chimed in. "You think they are spraying it, like, from a spray can?" Again there were a few chuckles in the room. "Could somebody be walking around the city with an aerosol can, like, spray paint, spraying people he passes?" There were chuckles around the room.

"No, I don't think that is what's happening," said Coombs with a tired grin. "Besides having no reports of a mad aerosoler out there ... if the guy was actually using that method of dispersal, he'd be at risk of contracting it himself."

"Unless he was vaccinated," Agent Hartmann interjected from the side of the room.

"Yes! That is correct. Unless he was vaccinated," replied Coombs. "And that's a good point, too. As part of the effort to catch those responsible for the anthrax attacks in the fall of two thousand one, and Agent Hartmann here can vouch for this since he was in charge of that investigation, they formed a task force to look into people who had been vaccinated, and then they cross-referenced them with scientists or anybody else who worked at labs that produced anthrax. The list of vaccinated people included every one who was in the army during the Desert Storm years. That's a lot of folks. They didn't even come close to finishing that list. And couple that list with the soldiers from the Iraq and Afghanistan wars, and that list is even larger.

"But back to your aerosol thing. Silly as it sounds, we haven't entirely dismissed your deodorant can theory. And for one very good reason. In nineteen seventy-nine, an accidental release of aerosolized anthrax spores occurred in a military biological facility in the former Soviet Union. Seventy-nine people contracted inhala-tional anthrax. Sixty-eight died!

"So, we know it can be done. Whether or not it *has* been done is another story. But, again, for at least thirty years, bio-weapon groups on both sides of the divide have been trying to aerosolize anthrax as a method of delivery. Maybe somebody succeeded."

38

The seminar went another fifteen minutes before going to a break. Kincaid and McGuire walked back to the command center with Hartmann, who passed them off to Agent Jackson, saying he had to brief some presidential aide in D.C. because the president was going to have a news conference in twenty minutes and needed facts and figures. Jackson nodded acknowledgement to Kincaid, introduced himself to McGuire and shook his hand. He showed them to an open computer terminal and went through the same speech they had heard from Hartmann an hour ago. How they needed a fresh set of eyes to look over the data that was streaming in. Jackson booted up the computer while Kincaid and McGuire found some chairs. A few minutes later the screen came alive.

"Just so you get an idea of how fast this is moving," Jackson said as he played with the mouse. "I wanted to show you the data as of five thirty this morning."

Anthrax Poisonings
CONFIDENTIAL
First Case Diagnosed: Thursday, 1:30 am.
Reported Cases as of Friday, 5:30 am: 548
Reported Deaths as of Friday, 5:30 am: 263

Geographical Distribution of Reported Deaths as of Friday, 5:30 am

San Francisco: 77
SF Peninsula: 24
San Jose: 41
Sacramento: 28
Marin County: 18
Stockton: 17
Calif. Penal System: 58
Total Deaths: 263
Number of Hospitals Reporting: 19

"Now take a look at this," Jackson said, bringing up the next chart. "This is the newest data as of a few minutes ago."

Anthrax Poisonings
CONFIDENTIAL
First Case Diagnosed: Thursday, 1:30 am.
Reported Cases as of Friday, 8:40 am: 1824
Reported Deaths as of Friday, 8:40 am: 760
Geographical Distribution of Reported Deaths as of Friday, 8:40 am
Mendocino to the Oregon Border: 53
Sonoma County: 26
Marin County: 24
San Francisco: 135
SF Peninsula: 43
San Jose: 89
Sacramento: 52
Stockton: 15

Bakersfield: 27
San Luis Obispo: 19
San Fernando Valley: 41
Nevada: 48
Arizona: 25
Oregon: 18
Washington State: 10
Calif. Penal System: 135
Total Deaths: 760
  Number of Hospitals Reporting: 67

"What do you think?" Jackson asked.

"Holy Mother of God," said McGuire.

"Not sure I'd use that exact phrasing," Jackson said. "But it is curious that, besides the enormous jump in reported cases and deaths in just the last few hours, we are now getting reports from all over the West."

"Not sure *curious* is the exact phrasing I'd use," McGuire said, pushing back a little on Jackson. "More like, how the hell can these assholes be covering such a wide area? Doesn't make sense."

Jackson acknowledged McGuire's *dis* with a nod of the head, then said, "And notice that Los Angeles' stats aren't even included. They had some computer glitch down there and went off-line about thirty minutes ago"

"Uncle Mac is right, though," Kincaid said. "The big mystery is the width and breadth of the geographic distribution. How in the hell can an Al Qaeda cell, two or three guys max, or even ten cells, do this much damage over such a wide area? Even in Afghanistan, where they had a ton more bad guys and a sympathetic population, they couldn't have pulled this off."

"Hold on," Jackson said, putting his left hand out to quiet the conversation while using his right hand to push in his earpiece so he could hear better. He shook his head twice in rapid succession and then said, "We can carry on this conversation after we hear what the president has to say."

They followed Jackson to Hartmann's office where Hartmann and the other TF 64 members were seated around a big-screen television. None acknowledged their presence.

The news conference took all of ten minutes. An emotional president assured the nation that the terrorists spreading the anthrax would be caught and brought to justice. He mentioned that all the evidence pointed to an Al Qaeda operation centered on the West Coast. He gave essentially the same data report that Jackson had just shown to Kincaid and McGuire. The president also said that if their investigation concluded this attack was State sponsored, he would authorize a military strike against the offending nation. That was greeted with applause and fist pumps from the assembled TF 64 group.

It took a minute for Agent Jackson to disengage himself from talking to his excited team members. "Where were we?" he asked as they reassembled around the computer.

"Rob was wondering how an Al Qaeda cell could do so much damage," McGuire said. "That's the first thing that jumps right out at you. I mean Arizona and

Nevada? And San Luis Obispo, for God's sake? Why there? Come on. If anthrax is really *inhalational,* then the only way they could have done this amount of damage is by airplane. Maybe these guys had rigged up a number of planes with nozzles, like crop dusters use, and flew them over the nine western states. I know that sounds ridiculous, but maybe we should be looking into airfields."

"Not so ridiculous," said Jackson. "We thought of that, too. An airplane or airplanes could explain what we see here. But when we started calculating the number of airplanes you'd need, and the number of pilots, and the number of airports you'd be flying out of ... well, we just didn't think it was plausible that *someone* wouldn't have noticed and notified us, or at least their local law enforcement people." He paused, looking down at the computer screen. "Let's not forget that anthrax poisoning is not only inhalational, you also get poisoned if it gets into your blood stream. Like if you eat something with the spores on it, and the spores get into your blood stream, then you also have a chance of dying. It's another avenue to explore."

"There is another puzzle here, too," McGuire said. "Even if they had airplanes, when I look at these charts, something jumps right off the page at me. It's the second biggest mystery. What's with the number of deaths in the State prison system? Now *that* just doesn't make any sense. The cop in me doesn't buy it. Unless it's in the food supply, something is wrong here."

"Agreed," Jackson said. "Maybe it's something you could look into. We don't have the access to the prison system like you do, and you probably know half the population." He laughed at his little joke.

"I'll take a crack at that," McGuire said. "And I do know a few dudes in the system. Not many of them are very friendly to me, but what the hell. I'll find out what I can. Do you have a list of the prisons affected?"

"All of them," said Jackson. "Pick one."

"Ok. I'll pick one where I know a few of the guards. No use going now. By the time we reach any of them, it will be lunchtime. Rob and I'll go home, get cleaned up, have a bite to eat, and get on the road."

39

Kincaid and McGuire didn't have as much weirdness getting out of the city as they had getting into it that morning.

"Why not pick up Laura and come over our house for lunch," McGuire said. "I'd love to meet her, and I'm sure Michele would, also. Hell, Michele's going to love meeting you, too. She loved your dad."

Kincaid demurred. "I've got four guys staying at my house, Uncle Mac. Teammates of mine. And now yours, too. And you want me to leave them there, and take Laura with me? I'd never hear the end of it."

McGuire laughed. "That's because if that girl looks like I think she looks, any one of them would leave your sorry ass at the altar for a chance to be with her. Don't be so sensitive. I know you want to bring her."

Kincaid smiled and put up his hands in surrender. "I give up. You persuaded me."

He called the house and asked Laura if she would like to come to McGuire's for lunch. She accepted immediately. He told her he would be there in ten minutes but to take her time, as he needed to brief the guys on what was happening with the anthrax attack.

While Simpson was upstairs dressing, Kincaid and McGuire filled in Red Squadron on what they had learned. The group had the same questions Rob and McGuire did - how's the anthrax being distributed, and why in such a haphazard manner? McGuire had printed out the data from the command center and laid it out on the dining room table for everyone to see.

"And this thing is spreading so fast, what you see here is probably old news by now." Kincaid said, pointing at the pages.

"How long does it take anthrax to incubate in the body before it becomes lethal?" asked Johnson.

"Three to four days, depending on the body it invades," McGuire replied.

"Which means," he continued, "most of the people who have already died, or will die tomorrow, were most likely infected on Monday or Tuesday. Maybe the reason you're not seeing how it *is* being distributed is because they're not distributing it any longer. It's possible they did whatever they did, and however they did it, on Monday or Tuesday, and are now just sitting back watching the fruits of their labors. The pricks."

"Shit," said Kincaid. "I didn't think of that. This is making my head hurt."

"What we did see," said McGuire, "and I'm sure you saw it too, was the number of people in jail up and down the State who have contracted the disease."

"And dying from it," said Fuller, looking at the stat sheet.

"And dying from it," said McGuire in agreement. "I know some people over at San Quentin. Guards and people I personally put there. Rob and I will go over there after lunch and talk to inmates and guards alike. See if they saw anything that could help us."

"Speaking of lunch," the voice of Laura Simpson said from behind them. All heads turned toward her. They didn't want to be obvious and stare, but they couldn't help themselves. She was wearing a simple white sundress clingy enough to highlight every curve, and with what would be called in fashion magazines a *flirty* hemline. That hemline hit her mid-thigh and gave the deliberate impression that a slight breeze would lift it just ... enough. It was accompanied by gold strappy sandals and a large gold wrist bracelet.

"I hope this is okay," she said. "I didn't know what to wear. If this isn't appropriate ..."

"Don't be silly," Kincaid said. "You look fine. Don't let the reaction of these troglodytes bother you. The only problem may be it is a little chilly out there today."

"Nonsense," roared McGuire. "Don't let these flatlanders get to you. Where I'm going to take you it *is* sunny ... and warm."

"Enough of this," said Kincaid. "We have to go. Eat your hearts out, men."

McGuire wasn't kidding about his house being in the sun. He lived on one of the city's larger hills, just a few short miles from Kincaid's house. About halfway up that hill, Kincaid's van broke through the cloud cover, the sensation much like that of being on an airplane right after take-off. Looking out the side window of the van, they saw what looked liked an ashen carpet that covered most of the city.

They pulled into the garage of a three bedroom, two-bath house at the very top of the hill. "This was Michele's house before we were married," McGuire explained. "A modest house, by anyone's standards." He laughed. "Before home prices tanked in this city about five or six years ago, this 'modest' little house would have sold for over a million and a half. Do you believe that? The market's coming back, but if we sold it today, probably only get a little over a million. But am I complaining? Hell, no. Let's see ... I marry Michele and inherit a home valued at a million and some change. She marries me and inherits a big-screen television, a Tivo and the bed we sleep in. Hey ... I'd say we are even, right?"

They were all laughing when Michele opened the door.

40

Kincaid remembered his dad telling him what a stunner McGuire's wife was. He was right. About twenty years Mac's junior, Kincaid now understood why McGuire had stayed in such good shape.

She was wearing a fuzzy purple turtleneck over jeans. Her auburn hair was swept back from her face and held in place by one of those clippie things women wore. Not much makeup, at least that you could notice. McGuire had met her on a murder case where she was one of the witnesses. He didn't let her go afterward. *Good move on his part*, Kincaid thought.

Michele took Kincaid's hand. "I'm very happy to meet you after all this time. I'm really sorry about your dad. We went to many a Giant game together." She smiled at the thought. "I liked him a lot." She turned to Laura and took her hand, too. "I'm very happy to meet you. Are you from here?"

"No. San Diego. I came up here yesterday."

"First time in San Francisco?"

"It is. And I'm enjoying it very much." She looked at Rob and took a step closer to him.

"Well, welcome. What say we have lunch? Are sandwiches okay?"

They ate ham and cheese sandwiches with chips at the kitchen table. The women had a beer. The men, thinking it would be better not to show up at San Quentin with liquor on their breath, had Cokes.

"How'd you two meet?" Laura asked.

Mac told the story of the murder case he was investigating. Michele happened to be living across the street from where the crime took place, and had seen the perp.

"I walked across the street to interview her. I came under her spell right away."

"The bathrobe I wore with nothing on underneath probably had something to do with that, I'm sure," she said with a chuckle.

"That it did," he replied. "It kept gaping open just enough to entice me to ask her out in the hope I could see the rest of it sometime."

"As I remember, you got lucky shortly thereafter," she said, winking at Laura.

"Because I took you out on good dates."

"Yeah ... a Giant game. No surprise there, huh Rob?"

"Not at all," he replied.

"I wasn't a big fan at the time," Michele continued, "but I soon became one. Rob's dad came with us a lot. He was as big a fan as we were. Now we have season tickets."

"I knew Walt from my time in San Diego" Laura said. "Don't know if you knew that. He told me all about going to games with you guys. I've heard so much about you, it's like I've known you for years."

"We'll have to give you our tickets sometime. Are you a baseball fan?"

"A fan? Hell, she used to play baseball," Rob interjected. "Had scholarships to play in college. Northwestern even recruited her."

"Oh, stop," Laura said, reaching over and squeezing his hand. "Not *that* Northwestern."

"She's just too modest," Kincaid said, squeezing back.

"I'm impressed," McGuire said. "And Michele's right. We'll give you tickets anytime. Maybe this'll be the start of a great romance." Kincaid felt Laura's hand flinch ever so slightly.

"They are a lot like us, don't you think Mac? I mean, you only married me cause I'm a lot younger and hot." She looked over at Rob and Laura. "She's younger and hot, too."

"Time to go, Uncle Mac," Kincaid said, a smile creasing his face. "It's either San Quentin this afternoon or me getting married." He stood and looked down at Laura, still holding her hand. "I'd at least like to take you to a Giant game first."

41

San Quentin was the oldest prison in the state. The inmates called it the "Death House" because it featured the state's only "death row" for male inmates. In the hierarchy of criminal notoriety, if you hadn't spent time at San Quentin, you were a nobody. Charles Manson and Sirhan Sirhan, the assassin of Robert Kennedy, each spent time on "Death Row", as did serial killers Juan Corona and the "Night Stalker", Richard Ramirez. On the other hand, the prison had equally famous people who, it turned out, were just passing through: like Merle Haggard who was busted for grand theft auto before he found an easier path to fame and fortune. Same went for Neal Cassidy, the author and poet who became an icon of the Beat Generation in the fifties. He was truly a man ahead of his time as he was incarcerated at San Quentin in nineteen fifty-eight for smoking pot.

For McGuire, however, none of the rich criminal folklore of San Quentin mattered. For him, his job had been to send bad guys to jail, and a number of those bad guys ended up in San Quentin. It was to visit one of those bad guys that he and Kincaid had driven to the prison that afternoon.

J.D. Prichard was one of life's losers. McGuire had first arrested him for attempted murder back in the late eighties. Prichard had beaten that rap because of a hung jury. McGuire had chalked that up to inept prosecutors. That failed prosecution, unfortunately, cost the life of a young woman three years later when Prichard struck and killed her while driving under the influence. He served nine years of a fifteen-year sentence at Soledad, being released as an *exemplary* prisoner in one of California's periodic prisoner release programs to lesson prison overcrowding. He had stayed relatively clean for a while, or at least under the police radar, until his name surfaced in a SFPD drug and prostitution sting that McGuire had been part of in the early part of the century. J.D. was convicted and sentenced to live the next fifteen years of his life at San Quentin. This time he didn't get released in any of the state's prisoner release programs.

Today was an anniversary of sorts for Prichard, as it marked the first day of his thirteenth year in confinement. Only two more years left. He was feeling pretty good as he was ushered into the visitors' room and seated at a table with McGuire and Kincaid.

Prichard looked like a biker. It was a common prison persona. Made him loom large in the general prison population. Big and thick. Six foot three. Pushing two hundred and fifty pounds. Arms like ham hocks. Cops called them prison arms. When you have nothing to do all day but pump iron, your arms get ripped. Doin' curls for the girls, was the mantra. But McGuire knew that once Prichard was out of prison, the pumping would stop. Always did. Then the biceps went soft, surrounding themselves with a layer or two of fat. They still were big, but no longer defined. Even at that, most normal people stayed away from guys as big as Prichard.

"Nice seeing you again, J.D.," McGuire said. "How's life treating you?"

"Can't complain," he replied, looking around the room. "Well, I can complain, I guess, but who the hell would listen, or care? What brings you to these parts, Inspector? It's been a while."

"First of all, let me introduce my friend, Rob Kincaid." Both men acknowledged one another but didn't shake hands. "The word may not have reached you yet, but I'm no longer at SFPD. I'm actually working for this guy." He motioned to Kincaid.

"No, I hadn't heard. Doing what?"

"Rob runs a kind of quasi-government security agency. Hired me as his token cop."

"Hey," said Prichard, turning to Kincaid. "I've only got two more years in this hole." He stopped and gestured toward McGuire. "Unless, of course, *Inspector* McGuire here can work his magic and get me time off because I'm about to be so helpful to him. Anyway, when I get out, if you need *real* security, especially in terms of muscle, I'm your man. I'll be honest with you. I'm getting too old for *this* shit." His arm swept the room.

Kincaid smiled. "Could be. We'll see," he said.

"Reason I'm here," continued McGuire, "is because of this anthrax attack. You've heard of it, right?"

"Of course I've heard of it. What? You think we live under a rock at this place?" Kincaid and McGuire chuckled politely at his play on words. Prichard glanced at Kincaid. "Your security agency involved?"

"On the periphery," Kincaid replied.

"First thing is," McGuire said, bringing Prichard back to the issue, "have you heard any scuttlebutt regarding who is behind it?"

"Tell you the truth, Inspector ...Wait! What do I call you now?"

"Mac is good enough."

"Good. Well, to tell you the truth, *Mac*, I thought you'd ask about those two bitches I knew who actually died of that shit."

"Tell me about them, J. D. We have all afternoon."

"When you arrested me back in the day, I was running these girls. Guilty. You got me on drugs and pimping. The pimping was a bogus charge. I never pimped them, swear to God. I was their bodyguard, so to speak. You remember, Inspector ... oops, Mac. You remember, they were strippers." McGuire nodded. "I got them their gigs. They paid me to protect them from the hustlers, pimps, thieves ... you know who I mean. Believe me, that was the truth."

"Makes no difference whether I believe you or not, J.D. A jury of your peers didn't believe you. Have this conversation with them. With me ... tell me about the girls."

"Susan and Sandy. Met 'em in Fresno. We maintained our connection even with me up here. They visited often. Like once a month. Regularly. To tell you the truth, they kept me supplied. You know what I mean? But then about four years ago, this place had a *come to Jesus moment* about drugs. Now, none of that shit gets through. Believe it or not, this is now a completely drug free establishment."

"I knew that, of course," McGuire said.

"And to tell you the truth, it's really a better place now. Betcha don't hear that too often, huh? Drugs tend to fuck you up, man, 'cept marijuana, of course. And it's legal. I got my card and everything."

"So now you can get stoned legally."

"It gets even better. This is *medical* marijuana. I've got this prescription now. And since it is a prescription, and the state pays for all prescribed drugs, the taxpayers are keeping me high. And I thank you all." He sat back in his chair and laughed until his eyes watered.

"The girls, J.D.?"

"Oh, yeah, the girls. Well, they visit on Wednesdays. Once a month. This past Wednesday was their day. They didn't show, and no phone call, which I thought was strange. But it had happened a few times before. You know, they get busy or are traveling or something. But when they didn't come Thursday, I got worried. Used one of my allotted phone calls. A guy answered their phone and told me that both had been taken to the hospital on Wednesday night, and had died about three in the afternoon yesterday. From that anthrax shit."

"You've heard that there are guys in prison who are dying from anthrax poisoning. We want to know why. It doesn't make sense to us."

"Isn't everyone dying from anthrax?" J.D. said. "That Al Qaeda outfit spreading all this shit around. We shoulda finished those guys off when we had the chance."

"Well, that didn't happen and won't happen now, J.D.," McGuire said.

"We're trying to make sense out of how it is being distributed," Kincaid interrupted. "And we look at the prison population getting hit and wonder how it's getting inside the walls."

"Can't help you with that," J.D. replied. "I guess we're just lucky here. I think we've had three infections total, and no one died. At least so far. Maybe the doctors are better here. Maybe they care more. Maybe at those other prisons the officials are just letting the prisoners die. Ever thought of that? Maybe all this is nothing more than the new state program to solve the prison overpopulation problem."

"I'm thinking that was a complete waste of time," said Kincaid as they got in the car to drive back to the city.

"Maybe not," McGuire replied. "While we're driving, I'll call and get the latest updates from the command center. We should maybe pay attention to what Prichard said. About the prison system. I know it sounds far-fetched, but it *is* an answer as to why the prison population is getting hit so hard."

"But it doesn't answer why the prison system *and* the general population are both getting hit. There's got to be a reason that encompasses both populations."

"Maybe," said McGuire. "But with the politics in the state being what they are, and having one group clamoring for releasing prisoners and another clamoring that building more prisons is the answer, maybe someone came up with a solution that will make both sides happy."

42

While Kincaid was driving, McGuire called Agent Jackson at the command center asking for the latest casualty figures. Over the next fifteen minutes, McGuire wrote furiously on a tablet pulled from his jacket pocket.

"Are you ready for this?" he asked, leafing through his notebook. "The death toll so far? When we left this morning, I think it was, what, seven hundred and some? Care to take a guess?"

"From the way you were writing and cursing, I'm gonna guess a lot. I don't know, I'll say two thousand."

"Close. Twenty-seven hundred."

"Son-of-a-bitch."

"You bet. But that's not all. Death reports are now coming in from the entire West Coast. Hell, even Montana and Utah. And we still have that anomaly with the prison systems. Now every state is reporting their penal systems, even in the small towns, are experiencing a huge number of cases with their corresponding death rates. Way out of line with the general public as a percentage of the population."

"So it kind of shoots down our idea of a political conspiracy centered on lowering California's prison population numbers," Kincaid said.

"Would seem so, unless the states are in collusion. Which would never happen." McGuire looked at his notes. "As of now, only the people at the command center are privy to this. But when it goes public, Katie bar the door." He sat looking out the window, thinking. "According to Jackson, what's got everyone scared out of their jocks is how big the conspiracy has to be for the scope of damage they are seeing. This is national emergency kind of stuff. This is call-out-the-damn-Army kind of stuff."

"We're missing something," Kincaid said. "I feel it in my bones. To pull something off like this? Jackson's right. The terrorists would have to have some kind of world-class distribution system, which I seriously doubt, because nobody could put something like this together without *someone* leaking *something*. And there are so many people becoming infected. How are they doing that? They ruled out just about everything, right? Crop duster-type airplanes? No. Aerosol spray cans? No. What else? Water supply? Could the water supply be contaminated? Something everyone uses? God damn it, Uncle Mac, it has to be *something* people have in common to account for just the raw numbers."

"Can't be the water, Rob. Someone asked that Dr. Coombs lady, remember? She ruled out using water. I think food, too, but I forget."

"There were two things that bothered me this morning about the data the command center was getting. Well, three things, actually, if you count the prison population anomaly. But that jumps out at everybody. What wasn't so apparent was the distribution of sickness in the population centers. The numbers are out of whack. There are the usual places you'd expect, for sure. High-density places like Los Angeles and Sacramento and San Jose. But some of the other places ... like San Luis Obispo. What's up with that? And Bakersfield. It's in the middle of nowhere, for god sake. And Chico. Your son lives there, right? Is he okay, by the way?"

"Yeah. I called him before we left for San Quentin."

"I'm glad to hear that. But what I was getting at was, Chico is nothing but a freakin' college town. I'm telling you, terrorists don't give a shit about small towns. That's what I mean about the numbers. There shouldn't be so many small towns, so many college towns. San Luis Obispo? Give me a break. Something is wrong. That distribution pattern doesn't make sense. And I'll tell you another pattern that doesn't make sense. Read me the geographic distribution again."

McGuire read off a state-by-state death toll from his notes.

"Let's take a state," Kincaid said. "Take Nevada, for example. How many people reportedly died in Reno? Forget the prison system for now. Whatever their numbers are, they won't make any difference to where I am going with this."

"Two hundred and seven," McGuire answered. "Four hundred and sixteen in Vegas. Winnemucca ... fifty-two total. Bunch more in some of the smaller towns. Carson City, for example, just nineteen. The list goes on and on, Rob."

"Yeah, I know. Let's just stay there. Walk those numbers through with me."

"I think I can see where you are going," McGuire said. "How many people did they say died in Reno? A couple hundred something?"

"Yeah."

"The question you're asking is why *only* two hundred something, right? Why not *two thousand* something? Or *two hundred thousand* something? And Vegas? Four hundred and some? Why not *four hundred thousand* and some? Or why not the whole damn city?"

"Exactly. What the hell is going on? What causes only four hundred and sixteen deaths in a city of more than two million people? From something that's supposed to be in the air, for God's sake? Something you breathe in? Here in San Francisco, we've got all those paramedics going around testing for air quality, and not one anthrax spore has come up on their radar. Not one. We're looking at this wrong. We're not interpreting the data right. I'm convinced of that. It's got to be telling us something we haven't figured out yet."

"You said it before," McGuire interrupted. "The victims have to have something in common. That's the only way any of this makes sense. There has to be something that explains why a whole city comes under attack, but only a certain few get infected. Genetic?"

"Like race?" Kincaid asked.

"Something *like* that, yeah. I'm not saying it *is* race. But it has to be something the victims have in common."

"Well, let's just go through the possibilities," Kincaid said. "Male-female? No commonality there. It wouldn't answer why only two hundred and seven in Reno and not the entire *male* or the entire *female* population in the city. Water system? That's been ruled out. What else? Maybe food? Like only those who eat sushi? Or only meat eaters? Or veggie eaters?"

They sat quietly for a few minutes, McGuire staring out the side windows at the Marin hills. "Holy shit," he blurted out, looking over at Kincaid. "They had to have something in common, right? I think we've got a big fucking problem on our hands." He pulled out his cell and opened the address book.

"Mind filling me in on what you're thinking?"

McGuire found the number he was looking for and hit the call button. He held up his hand. "Hold on." They both waited for the connection to go through. "Fly? Inspector Tom McGuire. I need to meet you. Tonight." McGuire shook his head. "No, Fly, you don't understand. I don't care what you had planned. I'm meeting you tonight at nine o'clock. You'll have your worthless ass out of bed by that time, I know. Cassies. If you're not there, I'll tell you what. I'll roll up your whole goddamn network. Got that?" McGuire listened to the reply, a small grin framing his lips. "I knew you'd see it my way. Cassie's at nine."

McGuire disconnected and punched in another number, again holding up his hand to silence Kincaid's questions. "Agent Jackson, please." McGuire waited for a few moments for them to make the connection. "Brian? Tom McGuire. A favor. Can you email me the locations of all the hospitals where people have died? Forget about the prisons. That will only confuse matters. I need the whole state. I'm going to need to sort the data by counties. Your system allow me to do that? Great. Thanks."

"Okay, I give up. What is your great breakthrough?"

"Just a hunch. I was chewing around the edges on this thing like you were. The infected people have to have something in common. We both agree on that. What if the commonality was not where they lived, or what they ate or drank, or the air they breathed? What if the commonality was a lifestyle choice?"

"I'm not getting this." Kincaid said. "You mean whether they are health nuts? Run marathons? Or choose to be child-free? Drinking gin as opposed to bourbon? Lifestyle choices like that?"

"I was thinking of something a little less healthy. I was thinking of drugs. What if the people who were infected were all dopers?"

43

By the time Kincaid and McGuire got back to the house, Michele had prepared what she called her "international" dinner - Omaha steaks, Idaho potatoes, French cut beans, Greek salad, and Spanish wine.

"That was a great dinner, Michele. Thanks. Let me help you clear the plates. I'm sure Mac can entertain Laura for a few minutes."

"Indeed I can," Mac said. "You just come with me, lass. I'll show you delights unfathomable." They all laughed.

After they had cleared the table, Michele said, "Mac told me how you guys met. I wouldn't let that bother you. She seems like a really nice girl, and it's clear she really likes you."

"She's nice," said Kincaid. "But I haven't been in the dating scene for a long time. First of all, I never had the time for it. And SEALs aren't prime husband material, or so I've been told by my buddies."

"You're not a SEAL anymore," she replied.

"True enough, but still busy."

Michele good-naturedly commented about how lucky a girl would be to capture a guy like him. A guy who knew his way around the kitchen like he did.

"Yeah, right," Kincaid said. "I used to have a stock line for that kind of talk. I'd say I'd much rather be breaking down and cleaning a M-4 than cooking dinner for anyone. That always put a quick end to any romance issues."

"I can see why," she answered, taking his hand and walking back into the living room where McGuire was entertaining Laura with cop stories.

"Did I hear the name Dirty Harry?" Michele asked as she sat on the couch next to McGuire. "Laura's not old enough to even know who Dirty Harry was. In fact ..." she patted Mac's knee. "... no one in the room but you is old enough to remember him."

"Spoil sport," he responded, slumping down in the cushion.

Michele turned to Laura and said, "I hope you don't mind, but this is the first time I've met Rob. I've heard so much about him from his dad, I'd like to ask him a few questions."

"Ask away," Laura said. "His dad told me a lot about him, too, but I'm still curious."

"You're a celebrity with the girls, boy-o," Mac said.

"Swell," Kincaid replied.

"I was always curious why you went in the Navy," Michele said, "after having what looked to be a possible career in baseball."

"Not pursuing baseball was a personal decision, not worth going into here," he replied. "But my choosing the Navy had a lot to do with Uncle Mac's influence, being a war hero and all."

"Where'd you do basic?" asked McGuire.

"After I graduated from Annapolis, they sent me to Orlando," Kincaid replied. "Tell you the truth, I thought it was too easy. I was in pretty good shape and hardly broke a sweat. I started asking my instructors for something tougher. They all thought I was crazy, but if I was such a tough guy, they said, I should try SAR, Search and Rescue. I applied right after Basic and was accepted. I'd been a good swimmer in high school, so I thought this would be a snap. It wasn't exactly a snap, but I was still looking for more."

"I trained with SAR, too," said McGuire. "If you wanted to become a pilot, you had to. So I know what you went through."

"Probably a lot tougher during the Vietnam era," Kincaid said. "I found it challenging, but wanted to be in an elite unit. The SEALS offered that."

"I'll bet," McGuire said, laughing.

"Yeah," Kincaid replied. "I found out quickly they took their motto 'the only easy day was yesterday' seriously. BUD/S was tough. But I learned a lot. Coming from Annapolis, I entered BUD/S as an officer. That meant exactly squat. In fact, most officers washed out. I was determined not to let that happen. I learned that physically you could endure just about anything. It was all about your mind. The mind simply had to overcome the pain. Hell, with what you went through as a POW in Hanoi during Vietnam, Uncle Mac, you must have learned the very same thing." Mac merely nodded. "Anyway," Kincaid said, "I got through it. A proud member of BUD/S Class 221. Graduated three weeks before 9/11. Been busy ever since."

"And what about this girl, here," Mac teased. "When are you going to marry her?"

Kincaid sat there not knowing what to say. Not thinking kindly of McGuire for blindsiding him like this.

"Don't I have a voice in this?" said Laura, rescuing him from his discomfort. "I haven't even kissed the guy yet." With that, she got out of her chair, walked over to Kincaid, leaned down, looked into his eyes, and kissed him. She stood back up, turned to Mac, smiled broadly and said, "Yeah. If he ever asks, I think I'd give him a shot."

44

They got back to Mac's office a little after eight. "We're going to have to hurry if we are going to meet Fly at nine," he said.

"Right. You wanted the locations of the hospitals where people have died?"

McGuire booted the computer. "Yes. Let's start with a radius of a hundred and fifty miles from San Francisco. I'm going to query for the hospitals that reported the most anthrax patients in each area. Does that seem right?"

"I would have queried for deaths, but that's just me. I'm content with your way," Kincaid said.

McGuire entered his search parameters. "I asked for the patient count for all major metropolitan counties, then asked for the two top reporting hospitals within those counties. So, for example, we'll get the count and two top hospitals for San Francisco because it is its own county. But most of the data for the San Francisco peninsula will be reported in San Mateo County; the South Bay will be reported in Santa Clara County; the East Bay will be reported in Alameda, Contra Costa and Solano Counties, and so on. Doing it this way will isolate the more rural population areas. I don't know about you, Rob, but it's those counties I'm most concerned with."

"God, this is slow," Kincaid said. "What time are we supposed to be meeting with your man Fly?"

"Nine. Plenty of time still. Don't be impatient. We get really shitty internet service up here," he said. "Sometimes takes forever to retrieve files. Especially big ones like these."

It didn't take forever, but to the two men waiting if sure seemed like it. But finally the screen popped back to life and they moved their chairs closer to the small screen.

"Okay, in the immediate Bay Area, San Francisco pops up, of course. The East Bay from Vallejo through Berkeley, especially Berkeley, had high incidents of infections. Hayward more than Oakland. Anyone looking at that figure would be surprised, but it fits my theory. Look at San Jose. Huge patient load. Again, consistent with my theory. Let's see, here's an interesting one. The Monterey Peninsula ... including Santa Cruz. Going east, Stockton has a fair number, Sacramento, of course. Going north from Sacramento ... not much until you get to Redding and Eureka. Have to throw in Chico."

"I want you to know I'll keep your boy in my thoughts."

"Thanks, I appreciate it," McGuire said.

"Care to tell me what theory you are testing out?"

"I don't want to be secretive here, honest. What I'm thinking is so radical that I'm embarrassed to say it out loud. You'll think I'm crazy."

"No I won't. Promise."

"Let me plow through these reports first, ok? If my theory is validated by the data, I'll tell you. Fair enough?"

"I love watching a real detective at work," Kincaid said. "And, yeah, fair enough. Anything in the North Bay?"

"Coming south from Eureka. Let's see, the next major concentration is around the Santa Rosa area. Then not so much until San Rafael. A small spike there. And then really nothing until we are back in San Francisco."

"You wanna test that theory of yours in the southern part of the state?" Kincaid asked. "Might be a good thing to do. If you end up taking your theory to Hartmann, you'd better have all the lose ends tied up."

"Agreed," McGuire said. "Let's take a look." He put in the same search terms for the Southern California area.

"In Los Angeles, it shows South Central has been hit really hard," McGuire said. "That could be because there are only three hospitals in the entire area, so all three were overwhelmed."

"That's where USC is, isn't it?"

"Correct," McGuire replied. "There's also a big concentration in Orange County, especially in Fullerton. That hospital was also overwhelmed. The San Fernando Valley got hit hard, too; specifically Northridge, Pomona, Riverside and San Bernardino. That corridor along Interstates Ten and Sixty." He minimized the computer screen. "That about does it, I think."

"And that shows what, exactly?"

"You were the one who put me on to this when you were talking about the population distribution of those infected. You kept referring to college towns. It was one of the triggers that started me thinking about the drug connection. For the young, at least according to my boys, going to college really *is* all about *sex, drugs and rock and roll.*" Kincaid laughed. "But your insight about what the data showed was right on." McGuire scrolled down the distribution chart on the screen. "Some of the biggest clusters of infected people are around where colleges are located. That could just be by chance, because there are colleges everywhere. But look here. Berkeley hospitals have a high infection rate. UC Berkeley. And Hayward, for goodness sake. Nothing special about Hayward except California State University has a thirty thousand-student campus there. It's the same with all of these high-density infected areas.

"You were the one who said early on that terrorists weren't concerned about small towns. When you look at the small towns that have the highest infection rate per number of people living there are those with college campuses. San Luis Obispo has Cal Poly. Chico has Chico State. And so on. For me, that's the only explanation. What is the one thing that all these college towns have in common? Drugs. We can test this out tonight with Fly. If I'm right, he'll know."

45

Kincaid and McGuire pulled into the parking lot at Cassie's at exactly four minutes to nine.

Cassie's was an old Bernal Heights establishment that became famous during the sixties as a place where lots of cute hippie chicks hung out and where drugs were plentiful and cheap. When the hippie movement started to move from free love into violence, Cassie's became less relevant and fell on hard times. In the past few years, though, it had reincarnated itself as a homage to those glory days of the sixties when, if you were not coming to San Francisco with a flower in your hair, you were like "nowhere, man." More a bar now than a restaurant, its bartenders all wore red bell-bottomed jump suits, and the walls were festooned with pictures and posters from the glory days of the hippie movement. The wall behind the bar was devoted to photographs of "flower children," mostly young girls with flowers in their hair. And mostly topless. It seemed tourists never got their fill of looking at topless teenage girls with flowers in their hair.

On another wall was a picture of Abbie Hofmann raising hell in Chicago at the Democratic Convention in nineteen sixty-eight. Smaller photos of Kent State and Woodstock also made the cut. On the side wall was a montage of the famous rock stars of that era that had the good sense to visit Cassie's in its prime: Janis Joplin was pictured; Dylan; Glen Frey and Jackson Browne pre-Eagles; the original Jefferson Airplane before Grace Slick; a poster of Buffalo Springfield and the Doors jamming together at the Whisky-a-Go-Go in L.A.

Along the back wall, under a huge poster of Jimi Hendrix at Woodstock, sat Kenneth "Fly" Neuson, sipping a rum and Coke and conversing with some Mission District gang-bangers. Neuson was a legendary street hustler and drug dealer in the Bay Area. McGuire had known him for a long time and was one of the few police officers that Neuson would actually talk with.

"God," said Kincaid as he and McGuire ordered a drink while Neuson held court in his booth. "Look at the dudes your friend is hangin' with. Not the most savory looking characters. You sure you picked the right guy?"

Kenny Neuson was born in an affluent area in the hills of Oakland. Coming out of high school, he supposedly had scholarships to one or two of the Ivy's. Neuson's teachers had told any number of police officers intent on finding out what made Neuson tick that he was one of the brightest students they ever had. Most were convinced he could have ended up as CEO of one of the Fortune 500 companies.

The way Neuson told the story of how he went from being known as *Kenny* to "Fly" was due to a research paper he was assigned to do in high school. He had to write a paper on someone who had made a big impact on the African-American community in this country. While most of Fly's classmates chose to write about

Martin Luther King, Jr., or Malcolm X, Fly chose to write about Freeway Ricky Ross, the man responsible for the rise of rock cocaine in the black community in the seventies and early eighties.

Starting in South Central Los Angeles, Freeway Rick built one of the biggest cocaine distribution networks the country had ever seen. As a consequence of his success in peddling crack cocaine, a huge swath of black urban America was engulfed by violence from which it was still recovering. At his height, Freeway Ricky was reputed to have been pulling down one-to-two million dollars a day.

As Neuson told it, by the time he finished writing his paper, he knew where and how he was going to make *his* millions. But he wasn't going to emulate Ricky Ross from A to Z. Ross had made mistakes. Those mistakes had sent him to prison for a long time. Kenneth Neuson was going to be smarter. What his research paper had shown him was that Freeway Rick's downfall came because he didn't treat the white establishment with enough respect, and they finally brought him down. Fly wasn't going to make *that* mistake. First thing he did out of high school was join the Marines. It wasn't necessarily a patriotic move. He knew he had to get physically tougher, and being a Marine certainly would do that for him. But more than anything, being a Marine held a certain cache in the white establishment. But that was just the beginning. Over the years, Fly learned how to cultivate the white establishment. Especially the cops.

After 9/11, this country's major metropolitan police departments underwent a dramatic shift in classifying the hierarchy of crime. Before the Jihadists crashed those airplanes into the Twin Towers, solving or preventing a murder was the crime around which you could make a solid career. Murder was now relegated to second place. The number one crime that had to be stopped at all cost became terrorism. If a cop wanted to make his bones, all he had to do was help capture a would-be terrorist. Or prevent a terrorist attack. Do one of those, and a long law-enforcement career would be assured. A distant third was arresting drug dealers.

Fly learned early-on how to play *that* trifecta. He understood clearly that a cop having a choice between arresting a drug dealer or stopping a terrorist threat would be a no-brainer.

In recognition of the psychological pressures on most policemen, Fly formed a special unit in his drug syndicate whose sole responsibility was to steal dynamite and other explosives from local construction sites and then either sell them to naive San Francisco anarchists or hide them in rented public storage lockers around the Bay Area. Since very few people had stolen dynamite in their possession except would-be terrorists, Fly had discovered his get-out-of-jail-free card. Every time a cop wanting to make a name for himself by arresting Fly, or someone in his syndicate, Fly would trade the name of one of the anarchists or the address of one of his storage lockers for his freedom. Cops always went for the explosives because they could brag that they had foiled another terrorist plot, and Fly always went free.

His high school teachers had been right. Fly had a gift. And so far, his business model was working.

46

McGuire caught Neuson's eye as he and Kincaid walked over to his booth. He had dismissed his posse and was sitting back, appraising them both over the edge of his half-filled glass.

"Fly knows you," he said, gesturing with his glass at McGuire.

Neuson always talked about himself in the third person. He said he picked it up from his boyhood idol, Ricky Henderson of the Oakland A's. Henderson always gave media interviews in the third person.

Q. "Hey, Ricky. How'd you steal that base in the fourth?"

A. "When Ricky saw in the pitcher's eyes that he was intent on throwin' home, Ricky took off. Ricky stole that base without even a throw."

"But don't know you," he said, looking straight at Kincaid.

"Even if you had, you probably wouldn't have remembered," said McGuire. "You could have been in a drug- induced stupor. He's my new partner, Rob Kincaid."

Neuson nodded at Kincaid, then turned back to McGuire and said, "Come on, man. You know Fly don't touch no drugs."

"That's true. I forgot. You just sell 'em." McGuire said. Neuson glanced sideways at McGuire, a thin smile creasing his lips. "In any case, you should get along with Rob. He's a former Navy SEAL. You piss him off and he'll reach across this table and turn you inside out. Turn your black ass white. Make you a reverse Oreo."

Kincaid tensed, but then saw Neuson's smile get a little bigger. Obviously normal patter between Fly and McGuire. Trash talking. A sign of respect. At least Kincaid hoped so. He didn't relish having to explain to Admiral Thompson why the head of his newly con-tracted "Security" agency had to fight his way out of a retro bar in San Francisco

"A SEAL, huh?" Neuson looked over at him with a new respect. "Fly served, too. First Marine Division. Desert Storm. Best time Fly ever had. Whole war over in six damn days. First Marines captured Kuwait City. Hardly fired a shot. Fly had tougher days in the hood, man. Biggest challenge was what to do with all those mothers we captured. Had to be twenty thousand or more."

"Mothers? Mothers?" said McGuire. "You cleaning up your act, Fly? In front of my partner here? I've never known you to say only half a word."

Neuson laughed out loud at that one and raised his glass as if to say *good one*.

"You must be on hard times, Fly," McGuire contin-ued. "You never associated openly with trash like that before." He nodded toward the gang-bangers still hang-ing around at the end of the bar. "What ... you slowin' down?"

"You know … Fly don't need no honky jive-ass cop telling him who to hang with. Besides, you know, tomorrow they gonna be askin' *me* the same questions about *you*. You know what I'm sayin'?"

He took a sip of his drink and motioned to someone at the bar to bring him another. "You know … the only reason Fly is even talking to your white asses is because you makin' it impossible for Fly to make a livin'. You know what I mean? You and your candy-ass white friends. Not doin' their jobs. You know what I'm talkin' 'bout? Makin' Fly hang with low-life motherfuckers like that." He pointed with his glass to the group now huddled around one of the pool tables.

"Come on, Fly. I'm not for certain, but I always thought you could read. Was I wrong?" Fly leaned back and looked at him through hooded eyes. "The city happens to be under a major threat from terrorists. I'll bet you ask your gang-banger friends there, they probably tell you they at least *heard* about it. In the old days, Fly would know all about what's happenin' in the city. Guys like me would come to Fly *for* information. You never even alerted me about the terrorists, Fly. There was a time when the Fly I knew had game. You would have known who these terrorists were even *before* it all went down. Shit, you better catch the worm, dog. You *are* losing it." Neuson smiled again, obviously getting a kick out of McGuire trying to speak ghetto. "You are right about one thing, though. We've been busy. Way too busy even to bring your sorry black ass down to *850* … where it belongs."

"Busy? What you been busy doin'? Fly tell you what you *ain't* been busy doin'. Fly puts out a strong product.

Someone is lacing Fly's grade A product with anthrax powder. Trying to murder all Fly's customers. I know you *ain't* been all that busy tryin' to find out who tryin' to put Fly out of business. I know *that* for a fact."

"Fly … up until now I always admired the quality of your info," said McGuire. "But this is straight-up bullshit. You've just wasted a good bar-hopping night for us. We're outta here." He started to slide out of the booth. Neuson stopped him with a hand to his shoulder.

"Why you think those dudes was in here talking to Fly? Because every one of them dead people Fly been readin' about in the paper are *their* customers. And, therefore, Fly's customers. And guess what? Fly's starting to have fewer and fewer customers cause everyone is afraid someone is tryin' to poison 'em with that anthrax shit."

McGuire looked over at Kincaid. "You got one minute, Fly. You better not be gaming me."

"Somethin' funny going on, Inspector," said Neuson. Getting serious now. No more trash talk. This was business. A whole different relationship. Except for the language, Fly could have been the CEO of Gap talking about return on investment. "Someone is fuckin' with my supply. Either my suppliers are fuckin' with my product, or someone is fuckin' with my suppliers' product. Maybe it's them Mexicans. They be tired of killing their *own* people, now they be killin' *my* people. You go home and look up the victims of this so-called terrorist attack. They most all be consumers, man. *My* consumers. First victims were cocaine users. Now heroin users are dying, man. Tomorrow, probably crank. I knows who's dyin', man. This is my business. Go home and do *your* business so I can do *mine*."

"Tell me about losing customers, Fly. Entertain me."

"Total business is down twenty-three percent, man. First time that's ever happened. Usually just keeps goin' up. That's what I be talkin' about to those dudes tonight. We all bein' squeezed. Them dudes thinkin' someone is out to get Fly, so they blamin' me. Thinkin' that their business is down 'cause I lost leverage with *my* suppliers. They be talkin' about leavin' me for a safer supplier. But I spent the afternoon talking to business associates up and down the state. It's not just my supply. You heard the news tonight. Terror has spread beyond the state, man. You may or may not know, but the terror has spread to Colorado and New Mexico and Arizona. And north, man. To Oregon and Washington. All in my network. Know what I'm sayin'? It ain't hit the news yet. I know, 'cause my people callin' *me* up. Wantin' to know what's goin' on and why. Know what I'm sayin'? All my bros' businesses are down 'cause our clientele be scared.

"You know, man, that I don't deal in crack. Not like Freeway Ricky, man. Him and his shit messed up my neighborhood real bad. Never again." He smiled. "Thought I'd mess up y'all's neighborhoods instead.

"No little white rock for me. You know what I'm talking about? My cocaine is so smooth, put you right in the middle of heaven. Sold that heaven to the white neighborhoods for years, man. It's been a good business for me. Lots of powder parties goin' on in them white hoods. And in them colleges, too, man. Big customer base in colleges. But let me tell you, that customer base is down almost forty-eight percent. Mostly white kids cause my bros don't get to college too much. Know what I'm sayin'?

"I keep track of who's buyin'. Call it recreational. Call it anything you want. I call it profit. But my profit is hurtin', man, cause the white hood is scared. Whitey ... hey, he see what's goin' down. And he don't want to die while partyin'. So whitey stops buyin'. Accounts for about sixty percent of my net profit. So I be hurtin', man. But we all be hurtin'. Cocaine use be down forty-five percent in just the Bay Area alone, man. People who only use it sometimes? They have just stopped buyin' all together 'cause the word is out. Believe me, my users know. They see what's happenin'. They be no dummies. They don't wanna die choking to death on their own spit. The word be out, man. The word be *out*!"

McGuire looked at Kincaid. "Let's go. We've got some people to talk to." They said their goodbyes to Fly and slid out of the booth. By the time they were at the door, Neuson was again surrounded by the gang-bangers.

"Gotta hand it to you," Kincaid said. "You had this nailed. Glad you're going to be on my team. What do we do now?"

"We go wake up Hartmann and the boys and tell them they have a different kind of terrorist at work here."

47

"The brainchild of the cartels?" Kincaid said. "How the hell did you come to that conclusion?"

"Doesn't make sense any other way," explained Hartmann. "They are the only group that would have been able to contaminate so much product to kill so many people. Thirty-six hundred so far, by the way."

=

After meeting with *Fly* Neuson, McGuire put in a call to Hartmann. He told him that he and Kincaid had been made privy to some anecdotal evidence that may make all of them rethink and retest their assumptions. Hartmann agreed to assemble Task Force 64 and look over whatever new evidence they brought to the table.

After carefully digesting the evidence McGuire and Kincaid had, Hartmann said, "I agree, this theory *can* explain the data we've been getting. I'm not saying it *does* explain it, only that it deserves to be looked at very carefully. Any objections?" His question was aimed at the TF 64 members sitting around the table. They remained silent. "At the very least, I think it's compelling enough to make us go back to the Center for Disease Control in Atlanta and ask them to collect toxicology scans of every anthrax victim from the reporting hospitals." He turned to McGuire and Kincaid. "This may take some time. If you guys want to go home and get some sleep, we can fill you in tomorrow."

"I think we'll stay. Okay with you, Rob?" McGuire said.

Kincaid nodded his head in agreement. "For me, curiosity is insomnia-inducing."

Two hours later, the reports from the CDC started arriving. They were prefaced by an apology that only ninety-two percent of the hospitals replied to their request. However, every one of those reports showed that the victims, not only those who had died, but the whole of the infected *set*, had illegal drugs in their systems. While cocaine and heroine were, by far, the most prevalent, meth had showed up a solid third.

"I guess that pretty much explains how the poison was being distributed," Agent Mike Gray said as they all finished reading the report. "Someone has laced the drug supply in this country, at least the 'powdered' supply, with anthrax."

"We've got to alert the president immediately," Hartmann said. "This is a big change from an Al Qaeda terrorist attack. This attack was obviously cartel inspired. I have no doubt it is their brainchild."

=

"You're saying the cartels contaminated the drug supply?" Kincaid asked. "For what purpose? To kill their own customers? That makes no sense at all."

"There could be any number of reasons," said Hartmann.

"And they are all valid," Gray interrupted, slapping the table with an open hand for emphasis.

"It could have been one of the junior cartels," Hartmann continued, shooting a *don't interrupt me again* look Gray's way. "Maybe a cartel who sees the drug business has reached its zenith, and there are better, easier and safer ways to make money. Like the human trafficking business, for example. Do you know how much money the smaller cartels make by escorting those Central American kids up through Mexico to our border? Hundred of millions per run."

"That's a real stretch, Bill, if you ask me."

"Or political extortion? A growing business down there."

"You haven't convinced me."

"Fortunately, I don't have to convince you, Rob. I only have to convince the president."

48

Kincaid dropped McGuire off, and he and Laura drove back to the house. They sat in the silence of their own thoughts most of the way, until Laura said, "Did I make you uncomfortable earlier tonight? Kissing you like that? If I did, I apologize. I could see you were uncomfortable with Mac's question. I thought I should help you out."

"Well, first of all ... yeah, it was a little uncomfortable. But I definitely didn't mind the kiss." He looked over at her and smiled. "And thanks for being so thoughtful."

Once they got home, Laura went to her room and Kincaid sent an email to Thompson giving him a heads-up on what had transpired with the anthrax investigation, that Hartmann was dead-set on blaming the cartels, and the president had probably already been informed.

Thompson wrote back immediately, making Kincaid wonder if the guy ever slept. His return message was cryptic. Have Red Squadron report to NSWC at noon tomorrow. *If president wants us to move, we need to be ready.*

Kincaid had packed and was lying on top of his bed when images of Laura floated through his consciousness unannounced. Even though he tried to shut her out, he was not successful. He wondered if she was still awake.

Was she thinking of him like he was of her? He shook his head and turned on his side, knowing if he kept this up, he was lost. The next thing would be him asking her out to a movie, or something like that. Those damn baby steps. Wrong road, he told himself. Wrong road. Don't go down it. But he knew he had already started down that road. And he was pretty sure he would stay on it until he found out where it led.

He fell into a deep sleep. He had a dream that Laura had come into his room. That she knelt by his bed for a long time, just looking at him. When he awakened with her lips on his, he knew it wasn't a dream. He smelled her hair, and his arm went around her back to bring her close. But her arms wrapped around him and pulled him to the floor in a tangle of blankets. He had a brief thought of the guys in the next room being able to hear, but soon dismissed the thought, not caring. When two people were determined to be lovers, the sound they made was the last thing on their mind.

49

SATURDAY
SAN FRANCISCO

Red Squadron was up early that Saturday morning. Turning on the television, they were told that the president had scheduled a news conference for nine a.m. Pacific to give an update on the anthrax attack occurring out west. They decided to book their flight to San Diego at ten so they could listen to the president's news conference before boarding.

They left the house at seven-thirty, returned the rented Chevy Suburban, and were in the terminal by eight-forty. At eight-fifty, Kincaid's cell phone rang. It was Admiral Thompson. "There's a flight leaving at nine-fifteen. It's boarding now. I booked you and your team on it."

"Sir," replied Kincaid, "we already had a flight booked at ten."

"I know. I cancelled it. I need you down here immediately."

"That means we're going to miss the president's press conference."

"If you don't get your ass down here on that nine-fifteen flight, you're going to miss Victor Lopez. He's in Borrego Springs."

"Son-of-a-bitch," Kincaid replied with a rush of adrenaline rarely felt outside of combat. He looked around for a departure monitor. The flight Thompson booked was taking off from the next terminal over. "Stay on the phone, sir. Talk to me while we to hoof-it to the gate." He quickly told his team about the change in plans. They all started to sprint.

"I'll make this quick," Thompson said. "I asked Hartmann to come, too, but he can't because of the president's speech. He's got to handle the press questions afterward. We needed a federal law enforcement-type present when we take Lopez down, so he's sending Agent Garcia. Garcia gets into San Diego about a half hour after you do. I'll have a van waiting for your team curbside. Don't wait for him. He'll have to make it over on his own."

Red Squadron arrived at their new gate before the boarding process had begun, so Kincaid sat down and called McGuire. Michele answered.

"I wanted to thank you for last night. I hope it wasn't a bother."

"No bother at all. You sound out of breath."

"I am. Had to run to catch an airplane. I have a favor to ask of you. Could you take care of Laura while I am gone? I feel sorry for her in that big house all alone with no transportation."

"Of course we can. I'll go get her myself."

"Thanks. Could I have a quick word with Mac?"

"What's happening?" McGuire asked. "We were just about to catch the president's talk. Curious about what Hartmann fed him." He laughed. "Michele said you were running for a plane. You gonna miss his talk?"

"Gladly. Thompson has word that Lopez is on this side of the border. In Borrego Springs. We're going down to take him out, once and for all."

"Shit. That's great. You get a chance, put one into him for me, too."

"Count on it."

50

SATURDAY
BORREGO SPRINGS

The call came at nine-ten on one of the twenty burner phones Palma had stocked at the Casa Moraga. *One and done,* he thought as he walked toward them. *Worth their weight in gold.*

"They know you are there," the voice said. "You've got to get Mr. Lopez out of there in the next hour, or he won't be leaving. Ever!"

"How do they know?"

"They are monitoring your phone calls. From now on, be very careful who you talk to."

"I will sue the United States government," Palma spat. "They have no right. I am a citizen. I am an attorney. I am afforded attorney-client privacy."

"Yeah, right," the voice said. "They'll have a drone over your place in thirty minutes. Get out now. Not by airplane. By car. They already have the air corridors covered."

"I can arrange that."

"Now, you have to do something for us. We've asked this before, and you've failed. You can't fail this time. Understood?"

Palma thought of his recent talk with Lopez, hoping he wasn't jinxed. "I will make sure that whatever you ask of me gets done."

"We want you to take out Robert Kincaid once and for all. He is not trustworthy and can cause us a lot of embarrassment. We have the plan. All you have to do is follow it step-by-step. No deviations. We will have our people nearby to make sure you carry this out exactly as we tell you. You understand?" Palma said he understood perfectly. "Good. Now, get Lopez out of there. I'll call back in twenty minutes to tell you our plan. By the way, have you ever met Robert Kincaid?"

"No," said Palma.

"You're about to."

51

SATURDAY
NAVAL SPECIAL
WARFARE COMMAND
CORONADO

I t was after eleven when Kincaid and his men walked into Thompson's office. They couldn't help but notice the four MP7s and the one HK 417 leaning against the wall in back of his desk. "I hope you don't mind. I took the liberty of obtaining weapons for you," Thompson said, acknowledging their looks.

"Before we begin, I want to tell you about the president's news conference. He mentioned how many people have died so far. I forget the exact number. Somewhere close to four thousand. He said the evidence now shows that the attack was perpetrated by the Mexican drug cartels. Normally an attack of this nature would engender an military response, he said, but because of the historic closeness of the two countries, he has requested, and received, a meeting with the president of Mexico to see if the two countries can work together on an appropriate response to this cowardly attack."

"Where does that leave us, Admiral?" Kincaid asked.

"Where we've always been, Rob. The president is hedging his bets publicly because he knows he has *us* to respond in a way that will count. Undercover, but with the end game being the same." He raised his palms upward, the gesture asking if there was any more anyone wanted to know. When no one pushed him, he said, "Then let's get to why you are here."

He played with his computer for a minute and brought up a picture of a Mexican-style hacienda on the fifty-inch flat panel screen hanging on the side wall. "The Casa Moraga," he said.

"Shit," Rosen exclaimed. "A casa? Looks more like a friggin' army base."

"Could be," Thompson said. "The locals we've contacted tell us there's been a lot of activity there over the past ten years or so. Big parties. Expensive cars coming and going. Lots of armed men patrolling the perimeter. But right now that's not the case. As far as we know, there are only two people in there. We've had a drone over it for the past twenty-five minutes. No sign of anyone. We're getting two heat signatures from inside the house. Hopefully one of those belongs to Lopez. The other, probably a fellow named Rinaldo Palma."

"How'd you find out Lopez was in Borrego?" Delgado asked.

"When we first heard that Rob's father had been murdered by this guy Victor Lopez, and that JSOC might be involved in surgical strikes against his operation, I reached out to an old friend of mine in SIGINT, Signal Intelligence, and asked if he could keep an electronic eye on Victor Lopez. He found the guy had some very sophisticated counter-measures, so he switched to known business associates of Lopez, hoping they would be less guarded when talking to friends and associates.

"One of Lopez' business associates lives right up the street. In La Jolla, for god's sake. An attorney named Rinaldo Palma. Took them a few days to set up the surveillance, but it produced dividends immediately. Just today they deciphered a call Palma received on Thursday from our good friend Lopez. They made plans to meet in Borrego. He's here, and so are we."

Thirty minutes later, Pete Garcia arrived. The formulation of their plan of attack could now be finalized. They decided to helo in on an *AH6 Little Bird* and land right in the middle of the courtyard. From there, Red Squadron would follow normal SEAL training to effect a take-down in a hostile environment.

"Are we there to capture or eliminate?" asked Kincaid.

"You are there to do whatever is necessary to maintain your safety," responded Thompson, purposely not answering the question. "Anything else?" The room was silent. "Then let's go visiting."

52

SATURDAY
CALEXICO, CALIFORNIA

The *Little Bird* was just taking off from NSWC when Victor Lopez and his bodyguard entered the house on Andrade Avenue in Calexico, California. The car ride from Borrego to Calexico had taken a little over three hours.

Lopez owed his long career as a *narcotraficante* to being unusually imaginative in figuring out more cost effective and safer ways to conduct business. Safer meant not getting caught, and so far it had proved successful. In the early days of his career, he built a grocery store in the middle of Guadalajara as a front to launder his money. But in a short amount of time, he had more money than the store could launder, so he commissioned a local architect to design a secret place under the store to hide his growing stash. But soon that place grew too small, so he began buying houses all over Mexico under which he built his secret money vaults.

Over time, it came to him that if he could build a hideout for money under a house that happened to be close to the United States border, why not just keep digging until he came out on the other side?

The cross-border tunnel from the house in Calexico to the one in Mexicali was just one of a hundred and ten such tunnels Lopez had built over his long career. This particular one was air conditioned, had a modern drainage system, and featured tracks so that large quantities of drugs could move more efficiently into the US.

On the way from the Casa Moraga, he had listened to the president's speech on the car radio. He couldn't believe what he was hearing. Who in their right mind could believe that the cartels would mount an anthrax attack against the United States using their own customers as victims? He was starting to feel squeezed. That damn dream. It was driving him loco. He didn't get a chance to tell Palma about it.

Lopez and his bodyguard opened the passageway and walked through the tunnel to Mexicali. Once there, he was picked up in an Escalade for the two-hour drive south to San Felipe. From San Felipe, he would board a small plane to Culiacan and safety.

=

Lopez had already crossed into Mexican territory by the time the *Little Bird* flared and dropped into the courtyard of the Casa Moraga. Red Squadron fanned out, setting up a defensive perimeter. Into that perimeter walked Rinaldo Palma.

"What is the meaning of this?" he demanded. "Who are you? How dare you attack my home like this."

Kincaid made a hand gesture for his men to scour the premises looking for Lopez, then turned and said, "My name is Robert Kincaid."

"I know who you are, Mr. Kincaid. My name is Rinaldo Palma."

"And I know who you are, Mr. Palma. You're the man whose friend murdered my father."

"Ah, that. Regrettable, Mr. Kincaid. But don't feel so privileged. Victor Lopez has killed many fathers. If I were you, I'd be worried more about your own life, not your father's. You can do nothing for him now except join him. My advice to you is to forget about Señor Lopez."

"Dry hole," Kincaid reported to Thompson from the courtyard of the Casa Moraga. "Palma swears he was never here. He's making noises about suing us for profiling him because he is Mexican."

"Throw enough shit against the wall ..." Thompson chuckled. "Have him talk to Agent Garcia. Fellow Mexican to fellow Mexican. That should quiet his ass down."

"It hasn't. He's with Garcia now, and I can still hear him threatening to take us all to court for violating the attorney-client confidentiality laws. That we spied on him while he was talking to one of his clients ... Victor Lopez."

"The guy has balls, I'll give him that. Anyway, wrap it up soon, okay? Nothing for us there, and Admiral Vaughn is here and wants to meet you guys in the Blockhouse. He was the reason I wanted your team down here in the first place."

53

SATURDAY
NAVAL SPECIAL
WARFARE COMMAND
CORONADO

In ordinary business parlance, the Blockhouse might have been referred to as a conference center. It was, after all, a place where meetings were held in classroom style rooms under one roof. While the Blockhouse had meeting rooms, no one at NSWC called it a conference center. It was a steel-encased, four thousand square-foot structure built three stories underground.

Kincaid and his Red Squadron team were met at the entrance by three armed guards that checked each ID and relieved them of all electronic gear, including their watches. The group was then escorted through a foot-thick, soundproof steel door to an elevator that deposited them outside the conference rooms on third level. They were then turned over to another set of armed guards who escorted them to Room One, where Admiral Thompson and Rear Admiral Roger Vaughn sat waiting.

The group took their seats around a thirty-foot square steel table. Open laptops sat on the table top like place settings in a restaurant. Four giant flat-panel television screens lined the walls. In the far right corner was a large printer.

"Where the big boys hang out, huh L-T?" Johnson whispered to Kincaid as they sat.

"I guess we should be honored," Kincaid whispered back with a smile.

Admiral Thompson called the meeting to order, and introduced Admiral Vaughn.

Roger Vaughn was a short man, built much like a bowling ball - big arms, big legs, big chest and big hips. He had a ruddy complexion and whitish hair. He was a SEAL, so he had everyone's trust. Within the SEAL community, he was known as a no-nonsense commander, a stand-up guy who, it just so happened, was also well respected by D.C. politicians.

Vaughn was commander of Advanced Force Operations for JSOC. AFO had the responsibility for the targeting of all clandestine operations undertaken by Special Op troops, and for those *special* Special Operators who worked off book.

"Please sit," he said. "I am Rear Admiral Roger Vaughn. I am honored to know everyone in this room, and more honored to have served with many of you. That was when you were tender young pups, though, and I was thirty pounds lighter." He paused. "And six inches taller." The men gave the requisite polite chuckle.

"The president, as you know, *has not* signed off on a ground operation inside Mexico to be conducted by Special Operation units of the United States military. He has given us permission to degrade the cartel leadership as we see fit, as long as it's carried out by private groups that can't be traced back to the White House. Red Squadron has been chosen to lead the mission to find, fix, and neutralize, by whatever means necessary, Victor Lopez, head of the largest drug cartel in Mexico. The *Tormentas*.

"This is, as you can imagine, an extraordinarily sensitive operation. You were picked because you are not strangers to these kinds of missions. Just be aware that this is even more sensitive than the operation that netted us Osama bin Laden. If our operators had encountered trouble when taking down bin Laden in Pakistan, three fully loaded troop helicopters on the Pakistani border were ready to come to the rescue. That will not be an option here. We, that is JSOC, will give you all the assistance we can. Just be aware there will be limits. Understood?" All heads nodded.

He opened a small carton he had in front of him, retrieved some file folders, and passed them around.

"Each file here is the same, and each has summaries of reports we received over the past year about the whereabouts and habits of Victor Lopez. Of particular value will be the one on top." They all opened their files and took out the top dossier. The identifying label said *La Voz*. "We had a woman close to Lopez whom we code-named, as you can see, *La Voz* ... The Voice.

"The code name was given her because she acted for a time as the *voice* of Victor Lopez." Blank stares looked back at him. "Sorry," he said. "I forget you are not narco cops. So let me tell you about Lopez. I've studied the man for a long time. I think you will find this helpful when you go after him.

"The first thing to realize is Lopez is paranoid about his safety. That makes sense. He's got to watch out not only for the people the government sends after him, but also rival cartel factions out to grab his territory. He's better now than when he first went into the business, but he is still very, very careful. He actually employs over one hundred former military personnel, ex-Mexican Special Forces. In his early years, when he was growing his drug business, he stayed pretty much to himself near his home in the Sierra Madres. But as his fame, fortune and power grew, he found bribes and killings worked wonders for his security. Those two things alone allowed him enough peace that he could live at least a few weeks a month aboard his yacht in Manzanillo. That was a plus for us.

"But his paranoia for his own safety never left him. We know he has secure hideouts all over Mexico, but he keeps their whereabouts highly compartmentalized. Except for his yacht, he is constantly on the move. He rarely stays anywhere two nights in a row."

"What about communication?" Thompson asked. "Our friends in SIGINT never heard a peep."

"His M.O. is to use cut-outs," Vaughn answered. "That's where La Voz comes in. She was one of his cut-outs."

"And you recruited her?" Delgado asked.

"Actually, she was recruited by Walt Kincaid." He paused to take a sip of coffee. "But when dealing with a paranoia as deep as Lopez', being a cut-out is not an ideal career path. If you know what I mean."

"How'd he use her?" Kincaid asked.

"Lopez uses a system that makes it virtually impossible to compromise his whereabouts. It combines a sophisticated encryption system with a software program initially designed by the US Navy to protect secret military data transfers.

"It's too complicated to go over here in detail, but briefly ... instead of taking a direct route from source to destination, the Navy system used random pathways, or cut-outs, that covered their tracks so that no one observer at any single point could tell where the data came from or where it was going.

"Of course, thanks to Walt converting La Voz to our side, *we* knew where at least some of it was going. For more than six months, we read every message Lopez was receiving through La Voz. Remember, he may have had six other people just like La Voz, but at least we had her. Unfortunately, Lopez didn't use La Voz as a cut-out on any of the preparations regarding Walt and the bomb. Instead, the FBI in San Francisco got that message from one of *their* plants. A fellow we code-named *Munoz*. It came in via other means, and it got caught up in the damn system with, as you all know, disastrous consequences."

"Where is La Voz now?" Delgado asked.

"In a small town in Chihuahua called Batopilas. She's actually there hiding from Lopez," said Vaughn. He turned to Thompson. "We want to mount a mission to get her out of there, and back here, alive. The why and how I'll leave to Admiral Thompson."

Thompson nodded. "The why we need to extract her is easy. First, she knows more about Lopez that anyone on the planet, except maybe his mom. She will be invaluable in our search for him. Second, she is in danger. Lopez has tentacles in every corner of Mexico. If he doesn't know where she is by now, he will in a very short time. Then she will be tortured and killed. He has already killed part of her family. For what she has sacrificed, we owe her." He then switched gears. "Best I show you where you will be going to extract her. Please look at the computers in front of you." All eyes looked down as the computers came to life. "Batopilas is a village more than a town. Population of about a thousand. In the mountains about three hundred miles northeast of Culiacan, where we think Lopez has a base of operation." He used the mouse to point out where both were.

I think this mission is best accomplished with two operators, and I think Rob should be one since La Voz knew his father. In these kinds of scenarios, as you know, trust can be a critical component of success."

Kincaid looked around the room for volunteers. "If it has to do with rescuing a female, Rob knows I'm the best," Delgado said.

"I can't complain," Kincaid said with a smile. "Look what he brought home to me last time we hooked up. When do we leave?"

"I can have a private jet at North Island at 0800 tomorrow, if that would fit your schedule."

"Good by me," Kincaid replied. "Vinnie?"

"Let's do it," he said.

"The jet will take you to a city called Parral, about two hundred miles east of Batopilas. Because both locales are in the mountains and the road between them is not a super highway, you're looking at a six-hour car ride from Parral to Batopilas. With the flight and time zone change, you'll be arriving in Batopilas sometime around 1800 hours.

"Since you don't know the terrain, nor speak the language, I've spoken to officers I know at the Mexican Marine base in Hermosillo to get a driver for you. They are sending a young Marine named Emilio Hernandez to pick you up in Parral. He'll drive you to Batopilas, and then get you back. He knows exactly where to pick up our lady."

"We can stay here tonight, sir?" asked Kincaid.

"Of course. And if you need use of the armory, please, be my guest."

54

SUNDAY
BATOPILAS, MEXICO

Kincaid and Delgado had made the connection with Emilio Hernandez as soon as they landed. It was 1130 hours, and they were already an hour into their drive from Parral to Batopilas. They were slightly ahead of schedule thanks to both a favorable tailwind and having the Commandant of the Marine base at Hermosillo arrange for them to get free passage through Customs. Even though it had saved them time and probably a lot of hassle, they knew it meant their arrival would be noticed. They took it as a mixed blessing. On the one hand, it meant that Lopez would certainly be alerted about the two Americans who had come into his territory with enough juice to bypass Customs. On the other hand, that juice meant they didn't have to declare their weapons, which for Kincaid meant his Sig p226, and Delgado his Glock 21, each with its own three fully loaded magazines.

As an added benefit, however, it gave them reason to be extra sensitive to their surroundings. The drive from Parral to Batopilas only heightened that sensitivity. The road was narrow and windy as it traversed through the mountain passes of the Sierra Madre from Parral's fifty-three hundred foot elevation to Batopilas' fifteen hundred feet. Even Hernandez was wary, and it showed in his attitude.

"This is very dangerous," he said. "Even for me. We usually wear ski masks to hide our faces when dealing with the cartels. These people come after your families."

"You're doing a good thing, Emilio," Kincaid said. "Good people have to stand up if the world is going to rid itself of this cartel curse."

"I am a soldier, Señor. And a good one. But like my comrades, I have to be careful. My family is always vulnerable." He let that thought sit a moment, then said, "Lillianna Martinez ... they killed her family. Now they are after her. That is why she is here."

"And who is Lillianna Martinez?" asked Kincaid.

"La Voz," Hernandez replied. "I thought you knew."

"No. We didn't know her name. Tell us about her."

"At one time she was Victor Lopez' girl friend. She had a fight with him and decided to give him up. She had met one of your agents."

"That would be Walt Kincaid?"

"Si. Lopez found out she was working for the gringos. He had her house raided one night when he knew she wasn't home. He wanted her to know he was the *Ahn-hel de la Muerta*. That he would be coming for her, too. But that night? That night, he was after her family. His men butchered her grandmother, her father and her cousin."

"Jesus," muttered Delgado. "How safe is she here?"

"No one is safe in Mexico, Señor," Hernandez answered. "No matter where you are. Too many people are indebted to these, how you say ... assholes?"

"That's as good a word as any," said Delgado.

"A man like Lopez? He is Santa Claus. Everyone loves Santa Claus. If you are poor, he helps you financially. If you get sick, he'll provide you with a plane to get you to a hospital and pay your doctor bills. Your child gets baptized? He sends a gift. Need a well in your village? He sends money and workers. He is a hero to many people. They even write songs about him. *Narcocorridos*. Ballads praising him and sung in local coffee houses. What they don't mention in those ballads is, if you cross him, he will kill you ... and your family."

55

Darkness came early in the mountains of the Sierra Madre. It was twilight when they reached Batopilas, a stuck-in-time village straggling virtually un-noticed along the bottom of the Barranca de Batopilas. The temperature gauge in the car said it was still over one hundred degrees outside.

"Does it ever cool down here?" asked Delgado, his shirt stuck to him even though the air conditioning was going full blast.

"Maybe to ninety," Hernandez answered with a smile.

"Do you know where we are supposed to meet Señorita Martinez?" Delgado asked. "The quicker we can talk to her, the quicker we can leave. Safer for everyone concerned that way."

"Roger that, Vinnie," Kincaid said. "Though we probably should wait until it's completely dark before we make the rendezvous. If Emilio is right about Lopez' reach, even this tiny village has too many eyes."

"I am right about Lopez, Señor. You are smart to be wary. Señorita Martinez is on the other side of town. I am going to continue driving. There is a small chapel about a mile from here. At the bottom of the Barranca, near the river. There is a place I can pull off the road and hide the car in the brush. We can hike back to where she is staying."

"How far off the road?" Kincaid asked.

"About half a mile. There is a path leading to it. She has taken up residence in an old pulqueria."

"Are we supposed to know what that is?"

"A tavern, Señor," Hernandez responded. "These little towns were famous for making *pulque*. It's an alcoholic beverage made from the maguey plant. The maguey is plentiful in these mountains, and each village had its own pulqueria. Some had two or three. But the government cracked down on the beverage sometime in the nineteen fifties. You could make it, but it was illegal to be sold in anything but a government-approved tavern. All of which they owned, of course. But in these mountain villages? I'll bet everyone in this town still makes their own *pulque*."

"Has the Señorita taken up residence in one of those? A government sponsored tavern?" Kincaid asked, the needle on his *wary* meter flirting with the red zone.

"No, Señor. This tavern has been closed for, maybe, sixty years."

It was completely dark by the time Hernandez drove the car into a copse of trees and brush behind a weathered hut that he swore was, at one time, a thriving church.

"Are many people aware of this particular pulqueria?" asked Delgado.

"People who live in the area would know of its existence," Hernandez answered. "But the chances of anyone finding her there would be remote. She's only been here a week, at the most. And Batopilas is at the far end of the earth."

"Feeling uneasy about this, Vinnie?" asked Kincaid.

"Just being careful," Delgado answered. "Being remote can be a good thing, or it can be a death trap. I think we should at least spread out walking down this path."

"Probably a good idea to put our *Cateyes* in now," said Kincaid. "We have a pair for you Emilio. They are night vision contact lenses." He gave a set to Hernandez.

"Gracias, Señor, but I could never wear them. I can't stand to put anything in my eyes." He did put on a ski mask, however. "You can't be too careful," he grinned.

"That's okay," Kincaid said. "Just walk between us. Vinnie will lead the way. I'll take the rear." After putting in the *Cateyes*, they drew their automatics, and walked slowly forward.

Twenty minutes later the pulqueria came into view. There was no light spilling out from inside. *A good sign, or a coffin*, thought Kincaid, as the three men moved off the path and into the bordering brush.

"You speak the language," Kincaid whispered to Hernandez. "You go to the door. Put your hands out in front of you so she can see you are unarmed. Be sure you tell her who you are. You don't want her shooting you." Hernandez nodded but remained silent. "Vinnie will stay in the brush line and circle to your left. I'll do the same on your right. Once she opens the door and we can see it's safe, we'll come forward."

They moved out. Hernandez was almost to the old pulqueria' steps when Delgado looked over and saw a red laser dot flitting over his back. "Emilio ..." was all he could yell before a shot rang out. Hernandez was blown forward, crumpling on the building's front stairs. The echo had not died before they heard a woman scream from inside.

They both knew Delgado's warning to Hernandez had given away his position, and within seconds bullets started to pepper the brush surrounding him. Two shooters. The one who took out Hernandez was off to Kincaid's right. He was the closest. He'd be the first to die. While Kincaid was circling right, Delgado had quietly crawled deeper into the brush and sat, listening. There was no sound. They'd be coming for him shortly. They thought he was the only opposition left. A fatal mistake.

As Kincaid slowly circled to his right to find the shooter that had taken out Hernandez, he wondered how many new tactics the SEALs had adopted for close quarter battles since Vinnie had left active duty. None, as far as he remembered. That was a bonus. In this CQB, he and Vinnie needed to be on the same page tactically.

As Delgado lay quietly in the brush, all those years of training came rushing back to him. In situations where one member of the team had been compromised, the compromised member was supposed to cause just enough commotion to keep the bad guys focused on him while the other team members, in this case Kincaid, found and eliminated them. And that's exactly what he did. Each time he caused a slight rustle in the bushes or a twig to crack, shots rang out. None very close, but he knew it was just a matter of time before they would fix him and one of those shots hit him. He prayed Kincaid would do his work quickly.

It took Kincaid the better part of six minutes to find the shooter who was sitting cross-legged on a small rise about forty yards from the pulqueria, sweeping the area to his left through his scope trying to pinpoint Delgado. Kincaid was above him now and about ready to break cover, when a shot rang out from the area where Delgado was. A rifle. The second shooter was zeroing in on Vinnie. His shot was immediately answered by four quick shots from Delgado's Glock. Kincaid didn't like where this was going. If a real gunfight broke out, Delgado would lose.

The shots distracted the shooter in front of him just enough for Kincaid to come up silently behind him. He put one hand on the guy's head while the other grabbed his chin. With one violent jerk, Kincaid snapped the neck sideways, breaking the shooter's spinal cord. He waited to make sure there was no sign of life, and then placed the body silently on the ground. He picked up the shooter's weapon. A FN SCAR. *A nice piece*, he thought. *These guys know what they're doing.* Having a rifle in his possession evened the playing field.

Hoping he could get to Delgado in time, Kincaid moved obliquely to his left. Passing the pulqueria's mid-line, he came to a small clearing. The second shooter lay prone at its far edge. Kincaid knew there was at least one bad guy in the pulqueria, so for deceptive purposes, he shot the shooter in front of him with his Sig. Three rounds in rapid fire. Then he fired two bursts from the SCAR he had taken off the guy he killed. He wanted the shooter in the building to think that since the last shots fired were from rifles, his guys were winning the battle.

Kincaid crouched behind a bush and aimed the crosshairs of the SCAR's night scope a foot and a half above the front doorknob. If the bandit inside became curious enough about what was happening outside, he just might open the door a crack to take a quick peek. If he did, he would be a dead man. He did, and he died.

"Three down," Kincaid yelled to Delgado and took off sprinting toward the open door. Stepping over the corpse by the door, he found La Voz in one of the back rooms, tied to a chair. Her face was bloodied and her left eye swollen shut. But she was alive. That's all that mattered. Kincaid cut her free and was getting her a damp towel to clean her facial wounds when Delgado walked in.

"Clear out front," he told Kincaid as he walked over and helped the woman wipe the blood from her face.

56

"**W**e have to find a way out of here, Vinnie," Kincaid said, looking at his watch. It was 2340 hours. An hour had passed helping Lillianna Martinez attend to her injuries. "Nothing serious," Delgado had told her, thinking of the plastic surgery she would need to soften the facial scars that would surely accompany the healing process. But none of that would make any difference if they couldn't get out of Mexico alive.

Kincaid kicked himself for not bringing a satellite phone along, but it never dawned on him that this would be anything more than a routine operation. He had a cell phone, but there was no reception in these mountains. They could take Hernandez' car to Parral, but that was a six hour trip, and by that time Lopez would have concluded that they had escaped his ambush in Batopilas and sent his men after them. He calculated they had no more than two hours before the three of them became the subject of an intense manhunt.

"The only way we are going to make it is if we can get in touch with people who can help us before Lopez' people come looking for us. Do you know anyone in Batopilas?"

"I do not," Martinez replied.

"Are there landline telephones here?"

"Si. The people who own the grocery store certainly must have one. Others, too. If there is one phone in a town like this, there will be many."

"Let's take Emilio and put him in his car. We'll come back for him later. Right now, let's go find a phone."

Martinez asked them whom they were thinking of calling. When Kincaid told her a very senior officer of the United States Navy in San Diego, she said to let her make that call for them. Having worked for Lopez for two years, she knew what to say to any inquisitive exchange operator. And there would be questions. She also told them they should walk to town, as the noise of a car that early in the morning would draw unwanted attention. Both Kincaid and Delgado were properly impressed.

The walk gave them the chance check out what houses had telephone lines coming from them. They counted eight.

"A wealthy community," Martinez said.

"Which house should we choose?" Delgado asked.

Martinez looked around. "The second one we passed," she said pointing to a house a quarter mile behind them. "It's the most remote. Fewer people will hear their cries if they are unwilling to help."

"Here's how we'll do it," Kincaid said. "We'll look first in all the windows. If there are children, we'll go to another house. Children are a pain in the ass to keep quiet. Can you handle a gun?" She smiled and nodded. "Good. Here's a pistol we took off one of Lopez' men." Kincaid released the safety and handed it too her. "We don't want to shoot anybody. Too noisy. Too messy. But we have to make them think we will. Got that?" She nodded again, instinctively checking the slide to see if a round was chambered, then put the safety back on.

"I can see you're not a stranger to firearms," he said with a smile.

The first two houses they checked had small children, so they passed over them. The third house had only two rooms, the living area and a bedroom where a male and female were asleep in a double bed. No children. Delgado was prepared to break in, but the front door was unlocked. "We'll go straight into the bedroom and wake them," Kincaid whispered to Martinez. "You do the talking. Tell them we work for Lopez. That you are his girlfriend. If they don't cooperate, tell them they will become his enemy, and they know what Lopez does to his enemies. Ready?"

They walked silently into the house and directly to the bedroom. The couple was frightened, but did exactly as they were told. Martinez placed the call. It wasn't easy to connect to the States, but every time she encountered resistance, she had no hesitation in dropping Lopez' name. Twelve minutes after she dialed the number, Martinez handed the phone to Kincaid. Admiral Thompson answered on the third ring.

"Admiral, it's Rob Kincaid. We're in trouble."

57

MONDAY
BATOPILAS, MEXICO

Kincaid had to stay on the line while Thompson handled all the details. It took over an hour. Every now and then, Martinez had to get on the line and evoke the name of Lopez to keep the connection open.

Thompson again contacted his counterpart in the Special Forces unit of the Mexican Marines. Between them, they agreed to extract Kincaid, Delgado and Martinez plus Hernandez' body.

Their extraction would take place at the clearing on the grounds of the abandoned chapel in Batopilas at 0230 hours, and they would be taken back to the Mexican Marine base outside of Hermosillo. As they ended the call, Kincaid promised Thompson an update on Lopez as soon as he had a chance to talk to La Voz.

They took the couple back to the pulqueria, telling them if they left before the helicopter arrived, they would be shot and killed. They walked back to Hernandez' car, unloaded the body, carried it to the clearing near the chapel, and sat. They had a two-hour wait.

"This tells you how times have changed here," said Martinez. "A two hour wait for a helicopter used to be a death sentence."

"How so?" Kincaid asked.

"The military was so corrupt, it would sell this kind of information to the cartels. The military wouldn't even have to send the helicopter because they knew the parties they were supposed to meet would already be dead."

"Tell us about Lopez," Kincaid said.

Martinez spat on the ground. "Are you going after him? Your military?" she asked.

"I am going after him," Kincaid replied. "With my team. He killed my father. He will pay for that act with his life." He leaned back against a tree stump. "That's why we came to get you."

"I lived with him for two years," she said. "I know him well. What he is like. His habits. But even at that, he is still a very secretive man." She gave a contemptuous laugh, but didn't go any further.

"That is something I can't understand," said Delgado. "Why does a man who has made, maybe, hundreds of millions in the drug trade still act as if he is afraid of his own shadow? Except for his yacht, I hear from people on our side of the border that he lives like a pauper."

"That part of him is changing, my friend," said Martinez. "The young ones in the trade are now saying it is better to live one good year than ten bad ones. And Victor Lopez is starting to act like the young ones. He is acting loco, like them. They go out to nightclubs, drive Bentleys, post pictures of themselves on the Web.

And they are dying in record numbers. If you just wait, they will all kill themselves. You won't even have to fight them."

"Is that true of Lopez, too?"

"Partially," she answered. "He is still careful, but not at the expense of a decadent life. Maybe he has just gotten in touch with his own mortality."

They heard the faint noise of a helicopter in the distance. "You said you know his habits," Kincaid said. "Tell me about them."

"For one, he loves gourmet food. He started asking me to find the most elegant restaurants in Mexico. It didn't matter where. He would fly his entourage and me anywhere I could find a five-star restaurant. His bodyguards would walk in first and confiscate everyone's cell phones. They promised to return them at the end of the evening. Lopez would spend two or three hours eating and drinking. He would order the most expensive things on the menu, thank the other diners for being so patient, pick up the tab for everyone, and leave."

The helicopter arrived and was circling overhead, on its final approach. "It used to be random," she continued. "But now, he spends most of his time between Culiacan, Cabo San Lucas, and his yacht. That's where all his whores are." She shook her head in contempt. "You know what his biggest expense is these days? Most people would say his yacht. It's not his yacht. It's Viagra."

As they boarded the helicopter, she turned to Kincaid and yelled over the sound of the rotors, "Right this very minute, I'm pretty sure he is staying in Culiacan."

58

MONDAY
NAVAL SPECIAL
WARFARE COMMAND
CORONADO

Fuller, Johnson and Rosen were waiting for Kincaid and Delgado as they deplaned on North Island. As they cleared the aircraft's stairway, Fuller put up his hand for them to stop. When Lillianna Martinez, who was following them, also stopped, Fuller waved her forward, pointing to a waiting van on the tarmac.

"We've got a problem, Rob," Fuller said, turning back to Kincaid. "Laura Simpson's been kidnapped."

Kincaid stiffened. "Shit! When?"

"Happened yesterday around 1700. McGuire's wife and Simpson were shopping at a mall out near the ocean. Simpson excused herself to find a restroom. She never came back."

"Do we know who?"

"We have their communiqué with us. Let's get back on the plane. Thompson has arranged for it to take us back north."

Once airborne, the five huddled in the back of the aircraft. "Before you read their long-winded missive," Fuller said, "let me go over what we already know. First off, the women had to be followed from McGuire's house to the mall. There's no way they could have just found them there. This was carefully planned."

"How'd they know she was staying at McGuire's?" Kincaid asked.

"That's unanswered question number one," replied Fuller.

"That's actually an easy one," Delgado said. "Remember that gang-banger Gallegos? He knew where you lived. They've obviously staked out your house. Probably followed you over to Mac's."

"We've kept this away from the cops, Rob," Fuller said. "Wanted to talk to you first. McGuire knows, of course. But now that he's one of us, he's agreed to play by our rules."

"Let me see the communiqué," said Kincaid. Johnson handed it to him.

"It's long and rambling, Rob," said Fuller. "Mostly, it says they have the girl. They want to show you that no one near you is safe. They want you to cease and desist from trying to kill or capture Lopez. They don't want to have to kill her, but that will be strictly up to you. They want you to come and get her. Alone. They even tell you where she is being held. And how to get there. Nice of them, huh?

"Anyway, if you come alone, they will take it as your agreement to stop hunting Lopez. They warn they have a small army watching her. If you come with your own army, they will simply kill her and fade away. Then your friends will start disappearing, only to be found beheaded by some major roadway." He stopped, watching Kincaid as he neared the end of the letter.

"Where are these coordinates?" he asked.

"On the outskirts of Pescadero Creek State Park. In the Santa Cruz Mountains."

"They have a small army, huh?" Kincaid asked. "A small army won't cut it against Red Squadron."

"*Fuckin'-A* right!" said Johnson.

"Do you think they really expected you to come alone?" asked Fuller.

"No. They know we'll come for her. Not sure they know how many we'll bring. They'll figure they have every advantage. Probably have people on every trail we need to get to the cabin. I just hope Laura is all right by the time we get there. There's no advantage to them in keeping her alive."

"Perversity, Rob," Fuller said. "These guys have the same mentality as the Taliban. They want to see you suffer, mentally and physically, before they kill you. No, I'm betting they'll have her alive so that when we do come, they can kill her in front of you, and then kill us."

"They will be expecting us tonight." Kincaid said. "I'd like to oblige them, but we can't go in blind. We need a *Bird*. Can we get Thompson to supply us with one?"

"Already done, L-T." Rosen replied. "The first thing I did when I read that letter was call Thompson and request one. He had it delivered this morning. Along with communication gear and more ammunition for the 7s."

59

MONDAY
SANTA CRUZ MOUNTAINS
WOODSIDE, CALIFORNIA

"Time to call, Ernesto. Make it good."

The man nodded and picked up the phone from the table. It was a burner. Not high quality. Probably wouldn't go through. "Signal still spotty," he said looking at the cellular status on the display screen. "Damn phone is on a 3G network," he said shaking his head in disgust. "In these mountains, I may never get through."

As he was waiting, he thought of the preparations that had to be made for Kincaid's arrival. He had put the suicide vest together this morning. About eleven or so, he would put it on her, and then stake her out in the clearing that fronted the cabin. A reversal of roles. The lamb leading the wolf to slaughter. His fondest hope was that Kincaid would try to sneak in and rescue her. He'd be on the hill fronting the cabin with the remote. As soon as Kincaid wrapped his arms around the girl to carry her away, he'd blow them both to dust. Kincaid had killed his friend from the Magic Kitty, Jesus, at this puta's house. And now it was payback time.

The only regret he had was having to kill Simpson before he had gotten his fill of her. She was a real looker. He would have much preferred to take her back to Mexico with him. That was just a fantasy, but it would have been nice to have her once more. When he took her this morning, she had been so doped up that she had hardly responded. He wanted to see the light of recognition in her eyes the next time he took her. *Ernesto ... from the Magic Kitty*. The stuck up bitch, she had never let him close. Kincaid and her ... double payback. He couldn't wait. It was going to be a good night.

There were ten of them in this small cabin, including the girl and the two gringos. The cabin was in a secluded section of Pescadero Creek State Park in the Santa Cruz Mountains. The two gringos had brought the girl here after kidnapping her from the mall. They had used it before and found it a perfect hideaway. The densely wooded terrain gave it a wild, remote feel that kept most casual hikers away.

The cabin itself had been built by a hippie commune in the late sixties. This was one of five or six cabins they had built in the general area. The commune had lived in them for ten years before the state finally evicted them. After a few years, the cabins literally fell apart. The two gringos had been told of this cabin five years before by park rangers. It was the only one of the original cabins still standing. The gringos, who had introduced themselves as *Cal* and *Stan,* after the two Bay Area college football teams, California and Stanford, had rehabbed the house and used it many times in the intervening years.

Ernesto held up his hand for quiet. The connection was going through.

"Señor Kincaid? Just wanted to let you know we have your girlfriend. She is a beautiful young woman. We are having mucho fun with her. Too bad we can't take her back with us to Mexico. We could sell her for mucho dinero. You can have her back. Just come alone. She will be waiting for you. If you don't follow instructions, though, my boss, Señor Lopez, told me to tell you he will pay for her burial. But only if they find enough to bury." He laughed and hung up.

"Time to go over the plan one more time," said *Stan*, the taller of the two gringos. "Can't have any slip-ups."

It grated on Ernesto and Lopez' other men to take orders from these two. But that had been the explicit instructions of Señor Palma. So they listened.

They each had been given an area to control. Primarily the ones with the trails most likely to be used by the two or three men expected to be with Kincaid. The gringos had them positioned in a staggered fashion with explicit orders not to engage them as they came through their areas.

They were told to text every fifteen minutes via their cell phones as to what was happening in their area. Unfortunately coverage was spotty so that instruction turned out to be "*try* to text every fifteen minutes." In any case, they were to allow them to pass through their area and then fall in behind them, essentially shepherding them into the kill zone.

"It'll probably take them two hours to drive down here from San Francisco," *Cal* said. "It's really slow driving the windy roads if you're not used to them. And it gets dark in these mountains early. Even if sunset is around nine, it will be dark in the forest here by eight-fifteen or so. Then they have to hike through the woods. Like us, they'll only be able to see through their rifle's night scope. Very awkward having to walk and look through the scope at the same time. You'll hear them coming a mile away. It's four o'clock now. I'm thinking they should all be dead right about midnight."

60

Kincaid hung up the phone and gave the thumbs-up to his team. They were all sitting in his kitchen having a beer, hoping for a call from the bad guys. "Perfect," he said. "Just what we expected. They knew we were going to come tonight. They just wanted to make sure by baiting us. They're also thinking they have some time before we get there. These poor bastards are wrong on all counts."

"And they have no idea who they are facing and what is in store for them," said Johnson getting up from his chair. "Let's go get these assholes."

They were dressed in full battle gear, including their Molle Plate chest rigs. They liked the Molle because their plates were positioned such that their vital organs were covered front and back.

After getting off the plane in Oakland, they had stopped at the same rental car agency they had used before and rented another black Chevy Suburban. Not the same one, though. This one had four-wheel drive. The clerk had asked if they were going to use it for a vacation. Rosen nodded and said, "We're going hunting."

In silence, the four men made sure their weapons were locked and loaded, placed them in the back of the

SUV along with the "bird", and took off. By 1730, they were on Highway Two Eighty, going south.

Chris Fuller sat with his tablet in the last row of seats, following the NSA supplied GPS coordinates to where Laura's iPhone was. With commuter traffic, it took the Suburban an hour to get to the Woodside exit, and then another hour to navigate the narrow, winding mountain roads. It was almost 2000 hours before they reached the entrance to Pescadero Creek State Park. The Park was closed, as they knew it would be, so they drove another hundred yards until they found a place where they could pull off the road far enough so the SUV could be hidden by a few well placed tree limbs.

"Final check," said Kincaid. "The GPS coordinates show her phone to be three point four miles west and south of our current position. Chris, the satellite pass JSOC did for us? What did that show?"

Fuller passed the device forward to Kincaid. "Take a look. These guys picked a good spot. This is one big-ass forest. Can't see much through the foliage." Kincaid looked and then held it up for all to see. "I've superimposed on the screen where the phone is," Fuller continued. "Scroll down and you can see the photos where the satellite tried to penetrate the tree cover over the GPS coordinates. Not successfully."

"Since we're not sure how many people we'll be facing," said Kincaid, "and since it's too light to send up the *Bird*, let's wait an hour or so."

"Let me try something out on you, L-T." Johnson said sitting down next to him with Fuller's tablet. "We read that this place used to be owned by a timber company, right?" Kincaid nodded. "Like a hundred years ago. But it's so overgrown now with trees that even the satellite's cameras can't penetrate the canopy."

"And your point is?"

"I'm getting to that, hold on." He put the tablet on his lap. "We're here, and the phone's GPS coordinates are over here." He spread out his thumb and index finger to cover the distance. "Three and a half miles. A lot of distance to map out with the *Bird* when it can only pick up thermal images." He held the device upright. "What do you think this is? This little tiny ribbon there on the satellite photo?"

"I'm not sure," Kincaid said. "You tell me."

"I'm thinking it's an old logging road that hasn't yet become entirely overgrown."

Kincaid pulled the tablet close. "Damn," he said. "Hey, guys, come here. Look at this. I think JJ just found something."

They would have to do a cross country walk of about five miles to get to the road, but their travel would take them away from the direct route to the cabin that Lopez' *small army* would expect them to travel. Since the old road still had less of a canopy, the *Bird* would be much more effective picking out any hostiles along the route. But best of all, the road, at its nearest point to the cabin, was only three quarters of a mile. Red Squadron would be coming at them from a direction they would never have expected. And even if the *Bird* had to fly above the canopy, over that short a distance it could more reliably pick up the heat signatures of anyone waiting for them near the cabin.

"Let's put in the Cateyes and get walking."

61

"Time to dress her, Ernesto," *Stan* said. It was ten-forty.

Simpson was tied to the bed, under a blanket. He pulled the blanket off her naked body and untied her. She made an effort to cover herself, but her movements were still sluggish, and her speech impaired. The drugs she had been given to keep her in a twilight sleep hadn't completely worn off.

"I'll take care of her," said Ernesto. "Maybe it's about time for all of you to go take up your positions, eh? Unless of course, you want to watch." He looked over at Simpson and laughed, pleased with his joke.

"*Cal* and I are getting really sick of you, Ernesto," *Stan* said. He had been sighting his rifle through the window, but now he brought it slowly back around until it was aimed directly at the Mexican's face. "You keep thinking about poontang, you dumb son-of-a-bitch, you're going to get us all killed. Just leave her alone, okay? We will be fighting at least one former US Navy SEAL. Probably two or three. If you don't treat them with respect, they'll eat you for lunch. Not cool. We've got a job to do."

Ernesto stared blankly into the barrel of the rifle, then reached down and pulled her in a sitting position so he could put her arms through the vest. Once secured, he connected two wires. The green light on his remote blinked, confirming the connection was made. Then he slipped the serape over her head, covering the four pounds of explosives and two pounds of ball bearings sewed into the front and back of the vest. He stepped back to admire his handiwork. "The lamb," he said, patting her head paternally. "The wolf will not be able to help himself." He took her by the arms, lifted her to a standing position and walked her out the cabin door. "Madre de Dios," he swore. "She is a beauty. A shame."

The rest of the men followed Ernesto out the door and into the clearing. "Do you all know where you are supposed to go?" *Cal* asked. The men nodded. "Time to take your positions. You'll probably have to wait an hour or so before they come. Don't fall asleep." He laughed. "And remember, just let them pass. We don't want individual gun battles going on. *Stan* and I will be at the nine and three o'clock positions on the hill there." He pointed. "Ernesto will be in the cabin playing with his explosives." Some of the men chuckled. "Better that we herd them all into the clearing where we can take them all out together."

The two men let the others disperse, then walked back to the cabin and waited for Ernesto to finish tying up Simpson. "We need to talk for a minute," said *Stan* as Ernesto returned and sat on the chair next to the bed where Simpson had been held. "Just want to go over again the plans for tonight.

"Tonight is about killing Kincaid and anyone he brought with him. But primarily, Kincaid. I know you want to test out your suicide vest. I would, too, in your shoes. But if any of us get a shot at Kincaid, free and clear, we are gonna take it. If that does happen, if we do get Kincaid, you can test your handiwork by blowing up your girlfriend out there.

"I don't care how horny you are, keeping her alive is not an option. She betrayed Lopez' operation in San Diego, and you know how Señor Lopez deals with people who betray him. If *you* don't do what he wants, you will have betrayed him, too. If we shoot Kincaid, you be sure to push that remote in your hand. Understood?" Ernesto was clearly not happy, but he nodded anyway.

"My partner and I will be about half-way up that hill out there. We'll have enough separation between us to have two interlocking fields of fire. If one of us happens to miss the shot, the other will make it." He stepped out the door and motioned for Ernesto to follow. "Kincaid will be coming from that direction, we think." He pointed east. "He may have people with him, too. He'll be cautious. After he finds the cabin, he might just go to ground for an hour or so to see if one of us gets twitchy and makes a noise." He walked to the corner of the cabin and pointed with one finger. "He'll come up behind the cabin here. We won't have a clear shot at him until he clears the back of the cabin on the other side. We'll probably wait until he gets around front, here by the window." He walked back to the front door. "You'll hear him, Ernesto. Don't get spooked. Just stay real quiet. This guy is a professional. You make a mistake with him, and he'll eat you for breakfast." Ernesto smirked. "We know what we are talking about. Just do what we say and you'll live to rape other defenseless women."

The two men left and started their hike into the tree line. "Let's not get too far up," *Cal* said. "These night scopes you got aren't the latest issue. Too bad you couldn't have just requisitioned night goggles."

"Couldn't take the chance that people would ask me to fill out paperwork. I ended up going the Internet route. Even on the Internet, the high tech stuff leaves too much of a fingerprint. That's why I bought these. Second generation, Viet Nam-era scopes. Russian-made. No infrared capabilities, only ambient light. But I figured, what the hell. If it was good enough for the Russkies back then, it should be good enough for us now. As long as he stays directly in front of us, we'll be ok."

"Let's hope. And after we get Kincaid? First thing I'm gonna do is shoot that son-of-a-bitch Ernesto. Put him and what's left of that woman in a shallow grave somewhere in these mountains and be done with it."

"I'm with you, partner."

62

The man known as *Cal* was way off in his calculations as to when Kincaid would arrive. As Lopez' men were leaving the cabin, Red Squadron was already preparing to launch the *Bird* from a position three-quarters of a mile to their rear.

"We're still going to have to fly her above the canopy, Rob. Too forested here. The infrared will pick out anything warm, though. That's all we'll need."

"Go for it," Kincaid said.

The *Raven* was launched though a small hole in the forest canopy and leveled out fifteen feet above the tree line. Fuller guided it southwest toward the target. Three minutes later the first red image showed up on the tablet. The *Bird* had found the cabin. Its outline was clear because it had retained the heat from the bodies that had occupied it during the day. They could even tell where the door and windows were by the heat signature that was escaping though them. They could identify ten individual bodies in the cabin.

They watched like voyeurs as Ernesto dragged Laura Simpson out the cabin door, tether her to a small tree in the clearing, and then walk back into the cabin. They watched as six men took different paths back toward the general area where Kincaid and his men had just come from. Finally, they watched the last two men walk away together up what looked like a hill fronting the clearing where Simpson was tethered.

"Our friends are in for a big surprise," Fuller said.

"It's unfair fighting such fuckin' amateurs," said Johnson. "But I'm not complaining."

Fuller ran the *Raven* in concentric circles from the cabin outward. It didn't take long to find one of the shooters who had been seen leaving the cabin about fifty yards to the west, lying prone on the hill, head pointed toward the clearing. On the next circle, the *Raven* picked up the second man on the same latitude, directly to the east, and about thirty yards from his friend.

Fuller circled the *Raven* another half hour before finding the other six shooters stationed at various places along the route they would now be traveling if they had not found the logging road. "Just so you know," Fuller said to Johnson, "these guys are not amateurs. We were just lucky you found this road. Otherwise we would have been walking into their trap right about now."

Another twenty minutes of circling by the *Bird* found nothing but a bobcat and two coyotes. He started to bring her home.

"All bandits accounted for, Rob," said Fuller. "We got one guy still in the cabin. The rest are scattered."

"Before she gets here," Kincaid said, "could you make one more pass over the cabin? Something I saw there has my danger meter twitching."

"Sure thing," he answered. The cabin became outlined on the screen along with the heat signature of what they supposed was Laura Simpson in the clearing.

"We're assuming that's her, right?" said Kincaid.

"Looks that way," Fuller said. "No one else it could be."

"Anything strike you as odd about her heat signature?"

Fuller tried refining the tablet's resolution. "You're right, Rob. Her signature is just a little brighter than the others. What would account for that?"

"We saw the same signature in Iraq, remember? The pile of dog shit on the road glowing bright red? An IED."

"Shit, Rob. You think they wired her?"

"Don't know, but better safe than dead."

"Here's what we are looking at," Kincaid said as the men gathered around him. "As you saw from the *Raven*, we have nine shooters scattered around with nothing else on their minds but to kill us. If it were just them, this op would be a piece of cake. But they have the girl, and it looks like they have her wired."

"That means one of the nine has the *kill* switch," Delgado said.

"Right, Vinnie," Fuller said. "Has to be the guy in the cabin."

"That's what I'm thinking, too," Kincaid replied. "Otherwise no use for him to be there. A wasted soldier."

"Probably because they have a pretty unsophisticated detonator," Rosen said. "Not much range."

"My thought, exactly," Kincaid said. "So, he's the guy we have to make sure we get. And storming the cabin ain't going to get it done. He'd hit that switch as the last act of his worthless life."

"Fragging him would present the same problem," Rosen said. "Lobbing a grenade through the window would still offer him a second to hit the switch."

"Even a death twitch would be all it would take, so we don't have a lot of options," Kincaid said. "The best one as far as I can determine is Johnson and his 417. To get the detonator dude to show himself, I'm going to walk slowly across the clearing toward Simpson. I'm hoping the guy in the cabin will come closer to the window to see what I'm up to. One shot, JJ. You'd get one shot. It's got to be an instant kill. Can you do that?"

"Not only can, L-T, but will."

"I have every confidence in you," Kincaid said. "But as a back-up, in case the guy doesn't present you with a shot, I want Vinnie down by the cabin. Depending on what kind of shrapnel they have the vest packed with, by the time I get halfway across the clearing, it if goes off, I'm toast anyway. But just in case. Vinnie, if I get halfway across the clearing and JJ has not taken out the prick yet, drop a frag on him. I'm counting on you to hold on to that puppy as long as you can before lobbing it in." Kincaid smiled and put out his hands, palms up. "The longer you can hold it, the longer Simpson and I might live."

"Good thing I like you, Kincaid," Delgado said, returning the smile. "For most people I would only hold it two, maybe three seconds. For you, I'll count to four. Consider yourself lucky."

"Whew. You had me worried there for a minute," he said. Then, turning to the others, he said, "JJ, before you get to blow off the cabin dude's head, I want you and Wolfman to take out the six who are waiting for us on the far paths. You want Chris to send the *Raven* back up so you can have real time intel on where they are located?"

"I'm fine with what we saw, L-T," Rosen said. "They shouldn't be hard to find and even easier to take out. We have the surprise factor. They won't be expecting us to come at them from behind." Johnson nodded his consent.

"JJ, I'll switch weapons with you for this part of the op," Kincaid, said. "The MP is a lot quieter than what you're carrying. You can pick up the *beast* when you return." Johnson nodded and made the switch. "Vinnie, you and Chris will take out the shooters on that ridge line above the clearing. They have the best vantage point, so they will be the top gunslingers. Be careful."

"Roger that, Rob," Fuller answered.

"Commo check," Kincaid said. "Microphone and ear buds." He whispered into his microphone and looked around. They all gave him thumbs up. "For each bad guy you bring down, one click on channel two. Once we count eight clicks, form up around the cabin. Especially you, Vinnie. I'll be on the east side of the cabin, but back in the brush. I'll be expecting you. Then we'll get serious about taking out the guy in the cabin.

"Questions?" There were none. "Then let's move out."

63

Kincaid made his way to a spot at the edge of the clearing, about thirty yards east of the cabin. He had moved deeper into the woods, making sure he was invisible to the shooters on the ridge.

From his spot, he could clearly see Laura. She was on her knees, sitting on her heels. Almost like she was praying. The pose reminded him of a picture his mom had shown him when he was a child of a pilgrim woman kneeling at the shrine of Our Lady of Fatima, a holy place in Portugal, where the Blessed Mother had supposedly appeared to three children in the early nineteen hundreds. The difference in the two poses, however, was *this* pilgrim had her arms tied behind her back and a rope around her neck fastened to a tree behind her, and wearing an explosive vest.

He heard a click in his ear. Then another. *Not much longer, Laura,* he thought, *Hang in there.*

In the next ten minutes, he heard four more clicks. Five minutes after hearing the last click, Johnson and Rosen were crouched at his side.

"Any problems?" Kincaid whispered.

For the sake of silence, Johnson held up six fingers. Rosen gave the thumb down.

Kincaid bumped their fists, and then directed Johnson's attention to a point across the clearing almost opposite their current position. "Anywhere along there," he whispered. "As long as you can get a clear shot into the cabin window. But take it slow getting there. The two guys on the hill are still in play." Just as he said that, they heard a click. Kincaid smiled. "Take that back. One in play."

Kincaid gave Johnson his 417. Taking it almost lovingly in his hands, Johnson checked the slide and sighted through the EOTech scope. He circled his thumb and index finger together. He was good to go.

"As soon as you hear me start talking to Simpson, get ready. I will have already broken cover. If you don't get him by the time I'm halfway across that clearing, Vinnie will frag him through the window and we'll hope for the best." Johnson nodded and quietly slid out to the left.

Johnson had just reached his spot when Kincaid heard the eighth and final click. He breathed a sigh of relief. Waiting a few more minutes to make sure Johnson was in position, he stood up and moved into the clearing. "Laura," he called out.

Simpson jumped like someone had hit her with a taser. She started shaking her head and stumbled trying to stand.

"Laura. Be still. Stay right where you are. Don't say a word. I'm coming to get you."

"No," she cried. "You can't. You don't understand. Don't!"

"Laura," he said soothingly. "I'm all by myself. They promised me if I came alone, they would let you go. I did come by myself. Now I expect them to let me take you home." He was talking louder making sure the guy in the cabin could hear what he was saying. "I've come here alone," he said again, even louder.

"No. Don't come any closer. I don't want to go with you. Don't you understand? Please. Just go away."

Kincaid kept walking. He noticed the serape. "I'm glad they gave you something warm to wear. That was nice of them. I know they probably gave you even warmer clothes to wear. To replace the ones you had on when they brought you here. These mountains can get quite chilly." He was trying to let her know that he knew she was wearing something under the serape, but he also knew she probably had no idea what he was talking about. It turned out it didn't matter.

The sound of the suppressed 417 spit out into the quiet night air. Five hearts in that clearing skipped a beat, but then ... nothing. A peaceful and welcome silence enveloped them.

Kincaid ran to Simpson. "It's all over, Laura," he said, holding her trembling body next to his. "We're here. You're safe." He slipped the rope from her neck, untied her hands, and got her to her feet. She was too wobbly to walk, so he picked her up.

Delgado had been the first to enter the cabin. He found Ernesto's body lying against the back wall. The suicide vest's detonator switch was laying ten feet to the right of the body. Johnson's shot had hit Ernesto below his right eye. As they had hoped, the switch had flown out of his hand the same moment the back of his head blew off. Delgado picked it up and laid it gingerly on the table.

Kincaid carried Simpson into the cabin and sat her on the bed. He lifted the serape. The suicide vest was definitely homemade, and not hard to disarm. He found the electrical connections and disabled them. He asked Vinnie to help him take the vest off.

Johnson and Rosen came in together and inspected the body. "Nice shooting," was the extent of their conversation.

Fuller was the last to arrive. "Rob, I think you better take a look at this," he said as he flipped two wallets on the table. "Got these off the bodies of our friends on the hill out there." Kincaid opened them. Staring back at him were the IDs of FBI Special Agent Michael Gray and FBI Special Agent Brian Jackson.

64

TUESDAY
SAN FRANCISCO

Kincaid pushed his way into Hartmann's office, threw the two wallets on his desk, and said, "What the fuck?"

After the battle, Kincaid's team spent two hours sanitizing the area as best they could. They picked up their spent MP7 shell casings, collected all the weapons and IDs from the dead bodies, and buried Gray and Jackson in shallow graves to keep the animals off them until their colleagues could retrieve them. Knowing Lopez wouldn't care about his men being buried, Red Squadron left them where they fell. After the forest animals had finished with them, they wouldn't be readily identifiable when found by the authorities.

Because she was still wobbly and hadn't yet completely shaken off the effects of the drugs she had been fed, Kincaid carried Laura Simpson the entire three and a half miles back to the car. On their drive back to the city, Kincaid called McGuire to tell him Simpson was safe. He left the same message for Admiral Thompson, adding that his people were ready to spend full time hunting Lopez. Thompson asked if he could be at NSWC tomorrow. Kincaid told him they could be there that night if he could get them a place to stay. Thompson chuckled and told him that he thought that would be no problem. That they would plan on meeting tomorrow in his office at 0830. Kincaid had purposely not told either man the news about Gray and Hamilton.

They arrived home just as the sun was rising over the East Bay hills. Kincaid set his internal clock to wake in six and a half hours and went to bed. Seven hours later, he was standing in front of Hartmann's desk demanding answers.

"What is this?" Hartmann said, staring down at the wallets. "And what gives you the right to barge into my office like this?"

Kincaid pointed to the wallets. "These do. Open them, asshole."

Hartmann reached down and flipped one open, did a double take, and opened the second one. "Were do you get these?" he demanded.

"Don't play dumb with me, you son-of-bitch," Kincaid uttered through clenched teeth. "I'll come across this desk and rip your arms out. These were the men you sent to kill me after you kidnapped Laura Simpson."

"I don't know what the fuck you are talking about," Hartmann said angrily. "I sent those men to San Diego two days ago to help Agent Garcia interrogate that Mexican lawyer you guys met in Borrego Springs."

"You're a lying sack of shit, Hartmann. How do you think I got these?" He slammed the wallets with his hand. "The two men who fit those IDs, *your men*, are lying in side-by-side graves next to a cabin in the Santa Cruz Mountains."

"I don't know where you got them, but I aim to find out. Why don't you just calm down a minute. Let me make a few phone calls. Please sit down." Kincaid remained standing. "Suit yourself," Hartmann said, picking up the phone and dialing a number.

He waited patiently for the call to be answered. When it wasn't, he hung up and dialed another number. After a few minutes, he hung up again. "Neither answers. Let me call Garcia.

"Hi, Pete. It's Bill. I'm here in my office with Rob Kincaid. Are Brian and Mike with you? I've been trying to reach them, but they don't pick up." From the look on his face, Kincaid could tell Hartmann didn't like the answer. "And you didn't call me?" Again, Garcia's answer obviously didn't please him. "You should have let me know. In any case, I want you back here today. Call me when you have an arrival time."

Hartmann hung up, stared at the badges and IDs for a long moment, then up at Kincaid with a bewildered look. "I..." he stammered. "... I don't know what to say. Apparently, Jackson and Gray never went to San Diego. They told Garcia that I had changed my mind and assigned them to another project. That he was to take over Palma's interrogation by himself." Hartmann shook his head. "I don't understand any of this. You said a cabin in the Santa Cruz Mountains?" Kincaid nodded. "In Pescadero Park?" Hartmann asked. Kincaid nodded again. "I know that cabin. It's one of ours. I honestly don't understand any of this."

"You were one of my father's long time friends," Kincaid said, putting his hands, palms down, on Hartmann's desk and leaning forward. "Did you have him murdered?"

Hartmann pushed back in his chair. "Now wait just a minute before you go accusing me of something I had nothing to do with. You have to understand. I loved your father. I would never have hurt him. And I know this mess here ...." he pointed at the wallets "...I know this looks bad. I can see it from your standpoint. But I'm telling you the truth about this."

"We'll see," said Kincaid.

"If it means anything to you, I plead guilty to not being savvy enough, or on top of it enough, to see those Agents were dirty. It was my responsibility, and I failed. I'm ashamed of myself for the failure in leadership. But you have to believe me when I tell you I am innocent of any complicity in their actions."

"We'll see," Kincaid said.

"If there is a silver lining in all this," Hartmann continued, "we now know that the leaks came out of this office and know who were the cause of them."

"We'll see," said Kincaid. He turned and walked out of the office. Before he reached his car, his attention had already shifted to getting Lopez.

65

TUESDAY
CULIACAN, MEXICO

"**I**t just goes to show you, Rinaldo, we are slipping," Lopez said, swiveling in his chair at the sound of the patio door sliding open. He smiled as the dark-haired woman entered his office from the pool, water droplets still trailing down her half-naked body. He had put a pool in his modest house on the flat outskirts of Culiacan for this very reason. He put the receiver to his chest and snapped his fingers at her, pointing to the humidor sitting on the ornate black walnut credenza to her left. Pulling one out, she seductively walked toward him, rolling the tip of the cigar on her bikini bottom where it disappeared between her thighs. "I'll call you back, Rinaldo," Lopez said, replacing the receiver in its carriage and pulling the girl to him.

"Where were we, my friend?" Lopez said into the phone. He had already instructed his chauffeur to take the girl back to wherever she had come from and used the tunnel system he had built to get back to the haci-enda on the hill. Settling into the comfortable leather sofa in the hacienda's sunroom, he called Palma back. It was two hours later.

"I think you said to me that we were slipping," Palma answered. "And then you slipped. With whoever you had there."

"I didn't slip," Lopez snapped back. "Just having a little recreation. It's none of your fucking business what I do."

"It is *my* fucking business what you are doing to o*ur* fucking business. And it's not a matter of slipping; it's a matter of becoming *soft*. You are living the good life too much, *Ahn-hel*. You have to start paying more attention to the business, and less attention to pussy."

Lopez yawned. From where he now sat, he could see the city stretched out before him two miles in the distance. Most people knew he owned the modest dwelling on the outskirts of Culiacan, and because he was in the city more frequently now to sample its good restaurants and nightclubs, they thought he had taken up residence there. But that wasn't the case. Even though cartel money dominated Culiacan, security was still an issue. Only Palma and a few of his most trusted soldiers knew he owned this hacienda in the mountains high above the city, and only Palma and even fewer trusted soldiers knew of the tunnel that connected the small house to the hacienda. The tunnel meant that Lopez could live relatively undetected in the luxury provided by the hacienda, while at the same time safely frequenting the epicurean and sexual delights Culiacan offered.

He knew Palma was right, though. Time to get back to business. But he couldn't let Palma get to him so quickly. A sign of weakness.

"I remember my friend getting the nickname *El Rhino* for activity that had nothing to do with *business*. Maybe that person should not be lecturing me at this moment."

"That person grew up, *Ahn-hel*. Unlike the person I am now *lecturing*." He let that sit for a minute, then continued, "But enough of this bantering back and forth. It doesn't get us anywhere. We have to stop the bleeding."

"I made some mistakes, Rinaldo. True enough. But my big mistake was I became too nice. Like with that puta Lillianna. When she turned on me, I should have killed her outright. But no ... I let her live so I could make her suffer a little by first killing her grandmother and whoever else was in the house that night."

"Speaking of Lillianna," Palma said, "what happened to her. How did we lose her?"

"Whoever they sent to get her was good," Lopez replied. "I had three of my best men grab her. They staked her out like a lamb ... enticing the wolf into a trap. The wolf took the bait, but in this case, the wolf won."

"Not the only case, Ahn-hel. We staked out that puta from the strip club in San Diego the same way. To entice the wolf. This Kincaid. Ernesto texted me that he had the wolf in sight. That was last night. I haven't heard from him since. He had six men with him, *Ahn-hel*. Good men. And two of the gringos, too. No word from any of them. I met this wolf at Borrego. He and his men are a different kind of enemy, *Ahn-hel*. And they are coming after us."

"Let them come," he spit. "I've had one-half of Mexico after me for the last thirty years. I've beaten them, and I'll beat these gringos."

66

TUESDAY
SAN FRANCISCO

After leaving Hartmann's office, Kincaid called McGuire to tell him that he was on his way to Mexico to kill or seriously degrade Lopez operation and to ask if Laura could stay with them again. Mac told him to bring her over as soon as he could, and plan on staying for dinner. Next, Kincaid called Delgado and told him to have the team ready to move south. They'd be leaving tonight on the last commercial flight out of SFO, and could be gone for a week or more. He also told Vinnie to tell Laura to pack for a week's stay at Mac's house.

It was a little after four by the time Kincaid and Simpson reached McGuire's house. Michele met them at the door. Taking Laura's suitcase, she said, "Let me help you unpack and then we can eat."

Kincaid took the opportunity to bring Mac up to speed on what happened the night before, and his confrontation with Hartmann that afternoon.

"What's your gut feeling tell you about him?" McGuire asked. "I've always felt the guy was slimy."

"I'm hoping he's clean, Uncle Mac. But I'm going to be wary of him from now on until he can prove to me he had nothing to do with my dad's death or sending those Agents to kidnap Laura and kill me. I do have to give him props, though. He looked genuinely sorry for what happened. Took full responsibility. Had an answer for everything that had occurred. He even went so far as using this episode with Gray and Jackson to clear up the problem as to who might have leaked to Lopez the time of my dad's flight."

McGuire nodded, and then changed the subject. "Terrible thing that happened to Laura. These are the kinds of things that can leave scars. I don't expect they will with her because she strikes me as a pretty tough lady. But you never know."

"Take good care of her, Uncle Mac."

"That I will, my boy. You can count on me."

They all made pleasurable small talk over dinner, and then retired into the living room where McGuire successfully embarrassed Rob by telling stories about him as a kid. Laura was next to him on the couch, thoroughly enjoying the tales.

"Memory book material," she said.

Kincaid smiled at her, and then looked at his watch. "I hate to break this *Rob bashing* party up, Uncle Mac, but I really do have to get going. Not only do I have a plane to catch at nine-thirty, but still have a few things at home to pack."

"I think we should let these two have a few minutes alone together," Michele said, tugging on McGuire's arm. He looked over at Rob with a *don't blame me* look, and departed with her.

"Isn't that cute," Kincaid said with a smile. "Mom and dad leaving us alone after our prom date."

She laughed, then said, "I know you have to leave, but I wanted to thank you again for last night. *All* of last night." She paused and put her head on his shoulder. "Especially for risking your life to save me. I'll never forget it."

Kincaid stood. "Best thing you could do *is* to forget it. Chalk it up as a nightmare. Fewer scars that way."

As he opened the door, she took his arm. He turned into her. She put her arms around his neck and said, "Remember when I told you in San Diego that you weren't anything like your dad? I was wrong." Then she kissed him. He felt himself kissing her back. "Take good care of yourself down there," she whispered in his ear. "I want you to come back to me."

67

WEDNESDAY
NAVAL SPECIAL
WARFARE COMMAND
CORONADO

At 0830, Kincaid and his team were seated at a large oval table in a meeting room attached to Thompson's office at NSWC. Also present was Lillianna Martinez.

"Glad you men could make it on such short notice," Thompson began. "Just wanted to fill you in on what is happening in our nation's capital. As you know, not everyone in D.C. is in favor of going after the cartels. But the president is still one hundred percent behind us. I've talked to him about this. For him, what's going on in Mexico has wider national security implications than just the drug violence. There is evidence that the cartels have started to help the Hezbollah groups coming into our hemisphere via Venezuela make connections with local insurgents in the various Latin American countries. We know for a fact that those Hezbollah groups are trying to find ways to smuggle nuclear material into the United States to assemble a dirty bomb. Some of the cartels, and that includes our friends in the *Tormenta* cartel, are allowing them free passage into America via their drug highways.

"The border with Mexico is almost two thousand miles long. Even it we were able to militarize it all, we still wouldn't be able stop all the smugglers. It would only take one with fissionable material to cause untold damage to this country. The president's overall strategic objective, therefore, is for us to so cripple the cartels that they won't be capable of supporting groups like Hezbollah. And that's why we are talking today. You have been given the responsibility of eliminating, or at least seriously degrading, the structure of the *Tormenta* cartel. It's *Go* time."

"About damn time," said Delgado.

"Some of you have met Lillianna Martinez," Thompson continued. "She is the closet thing we have to somebody inside Lopez' organization. She has insights that are valuable. That's why I asked her here today." He gave her the floor.

"There are two ways to kill the cartels," she began. "The first is to simply kill their leaders. Like Victor Lopez. The problem with only focusing on the leaders is that other "leaders" will take the place of the ones you kill. They will be no better, and in some cases worse, than the ones you kill. The second way to kill the cartels is to show them as weak. Their power comes because the people are afraid of them. The cartels seem to be able to do anything they want. Neither the local or federal authorities seem capable of protecting the ordinary people from their violence.

"If you want to kill the cartels, start there. If you want to really destroy Victor Lopez, squeeze him. Show the people that he isn't to be feared. Take from him this possession, and that possession. Give him no place to run or hide. Then kill him. Because you've made them look so weak, the people will not fear them as much, and from that time forward, the *Tormenta*'s will be finished as a major force in Mexico."

"If it were you, how would you squeeze him?" Kincaid asked.

"Victor Lopez has a house in Culiacan, and a yacht in Manzanillo. Of all his myriad possessions, these two have the highest symbolic value. Personally, I would choose his yacht as my first target. It's the most visible sign of his power and wealth. And since he spends a lot of time there, he obviously thinks it's impregnable."

"Look at the computers in front of you," Thompson said. "We have pictures of both targets. We'll let you guys choose which one to take down first."

Thompson brought up the pictures of Culiacan. "As you can see, it's a big city. Has close to seven hundred thousand people."

"Yes, but his house is in the less populated area," said Martinez. "In the southeast. On Abedules Street." She gave the address.

Thompson entered the numbers and the house appeared on their screens. It was nothing special. A one story red brick with bars on all the windows. Fronting the house was an iron gate attached to what looked like a guardhouse.

"Can you tell us what the inside of the house looks like?"

"The front door opens into a living room, with a kitchen to the left," Martinez said. "A hallway takes you to the back of the house where there are two bedrooms. But everything that happens in that house happens in the basement. The stairs to the basement run off the hallway. Lopez calls it his *playground*. It has lots of mattresses scattered around the floor, and features a full bathroom. It's his pride and joy. He spent a year building it."

"Must not have very good workers, then," Fuller said. "A year for what is essentially a big room with a bathroom?"

Martinez shrugged. "He didn't come there that often in those years, I guess."

"How much of a guard does he have at that house, Ms. Martinez?" asked Rosen.

"When I was there, very few, sir," she answered. "Two. Maybe three at the most. But many people know he lives there now. Many more than when I was with him. I'd expect, then, he'll have more guards now."

"We're positioning an RQ 185 *Big Bird* over Mexico," Thompson said. "We'll have updated pictures by tonight."

"What's Lopez' pattern when he is at the house?" Johnson asked. "Does he get up late? And if so, about what time? Are his bodyguards well armed? Pistols? Rifles? What? And where does Lopez usually sleep when he is there?"

"It all depends, Señor, on what time he comes in the night before and who he comes in with." She stopped, closed her eyes and let out a big sigh. "When he was with me, he slept until about eleven. Then was on the phone for a few hours. Took another nap until five or six, then started getting ready for the night."

"Bodyguards?" Johnson pressed.

"Two or three. All carry pistols. There are some rifles in the front closet. Maybe three or four. I'm sorry, that's all I can tell you. I don't know rifles that well."

"You told me and Rob that you think he is there this very minute."

"Yes. I'm sure of it. He likes it there because he can blow off steam at the nightclubs."

The room remained silent for a few moments, and then Kincaid said, "Let's move to the yacht."

Thompson brought up the pictures of the central Mexican coastline. He used the cursor to highlight a section of oceanfront property on what was essentially a peninsula between Manzanillo and the small town of Cuyutlan, thirty miles to the south.

"This is Lopez' villa," he said, using the cursor to circle a defined area. "Approximately one hundred acres. Nice digs."

"But he never stays there," said Martinez. "When in the area, he's on his yacht. You can see that here." Thompson hovered the cursor over it. "It sits moored three hundred meters from land. Only accessible by boat from the dock."

"Obviously for security reasons," said Delgado. "Since we will be coming at him from the sea, it makes little difference to us."

"If we followed Lillianna's preference to take the yacht out first, when would our first window of opportunity be?" Kincaid asked.

"Already arranged. At 1330 hours tomorrow, a *Seahawk* will pick you up from San Clemente, take you fifty miles off the coast and deposit you on the deck of the *USS California*, a DDS-capable submarine." Thompson looked over at Delgado. "In case they didn't have them in your day, a DDS is a Dry Deck Shelter for launching our Mark-11 SDVs."

"Sir," interrupted Kincaid. "No need to explain the language. We'll be training tonight and will get our dumb colleague here up to speed on all our new fancy toys." He looked over at Delgado. "SDV, by the way, means SEAL Delivery Vehicle, in case you didn't know."

Delgado gave him the middle finger salute.

"Any idea how many guards will be on the yacht?" asked Rosen.

"Not as of this moment, we don't. Like I said before, we'll have the *Big Bird* overhead. Her cameras will pick up any movement on the yacht. You'll have a number before you deploy tomorrow night. We won't know where they will be on the boat when you board, however. You'll have to find them yourselves. But at least you'll know how many you have to account for."

"Are we good to go for tomorrow?" Kincaid asked his team.

"Let's get it done," Fuller said, nodding to Kincaid.

"Sounds good, gentlemen," Thompson said. "I'll tell the *Seahawk* you are a *Go* and let the captain of the

California know you are coming. See you back here in two days."

As they were walking out, Kincaid turned to Delgado and said, ""Don't know how long it's been since you've had your flippers on, but better get used to them again. We'll be going out to San Clemente tonight to practice close quarter drills. Tomorrow we'll spend some time in the ocean. We've changed technologically and tactically since you were last in the water with us."

"But the drill is the same as I remember, right?" Delgado said. "Meaning if I can't cut it, I'm dropped."

"Pretty much."

"Thanks for the opportunity, Rob. I'll cut it. I'm back to breaking things and killing people. It doesn't get any better than this." He laughed.

68

THURSDAY
SAN CLEMENTE ISLAND,
CALIFORNIA

The consensus of the team was to go over to San Clemente Island as soon as they could. None of Red Squadron had been on the island for at least two years. They needed to get familiar with the new surroundings.

San Clemente is the southernmost of the Channel Islands, a chain of eight islands stretching from Santa Barbara in the north to San Diego in the south. The Navy has owned San Clemente since nineteen thirty-seven. It is home to the last of the Navy's live firing ranges. Consequently, SEALs spent a lot of time there training on a whole range of weapon systems, from artillery to pistols to constructing their own IEDs.

The thirty-five minute helo trip from NSWC to San Clemente Island gave Kincaid and his squad time to discuss their downrange weapon requirements. The important factor was what they needed to carry as a group. Being in sync was critical. This was not going to be a test run. This was serious. There was no margin for error. They would make out a list and have the armory fill it before the helicopter came to get them at 1330 tomorrow.

The gear they needed for the night's operation had been delivered to them from the NSWC armory at 0800. They each would carry the suppressed MP7 with laser sights, the standard Sig P226, and Cateyes. The submarine would provide all the underwater gear they would need.

They had spent the preceding two hours frolicking in *Mother Ocean*, as the SEAL community affectionately called the sea. Kincaid had studied the expected tides and weather in and around the Manzanillo coastline and had determined their most stealthy choice of entry would be to park the SDV eight hundred meters from the yacht and swim the rest of the way. Swimming eight hundred meters was a piece of cake, but Kincaid worried about how well Delgado would hold up. If he were going to be a hindrance, then they would leave him on the submarine. On a mission, there was no room for error. Hence the two-hour *Mother Ocean* frolic this morning. Delgado passed their test. They were ready.

The Sea Hawk lifted them off the island at exactly 1330 hours.

69

THURSDAY
ABOARD USS CALIFORNIA
OFF THE COAST OF
MEXICO

Fifty-two miles west of San Clemente, Kincaid's squad fast roped from the hovering *Seahawk* to the deck of the *USS California*. Ten minutes later they were sitting in the *California*'s galley eating grilled cheese sandwiches and drinking coffee.

"Good duty, huh?" Johnson said. "Probably could live like this for six months a year."

"Good duty until you're sitting on the ocean floor listening to the ping of the missile searching for you," Fuller replied. "Me? Given the choice? I'd rather be cold and miserable but have more control over how I die than sitting in one of these cans hoping not to be tracked down by a missile."

An orderly walked over to them and said, "The Skipper wants to invite you to his quarters as soon as you are through eating."

"Glad to have you men on board," said Captain Ron Turner, as Kincaid and his men took a seat around a small table in Turner's cabin. "As distinguished guests, I want you to know that my crew and I are here at your disposal."

"Thank you, Captain. That's kind of you," said Kincaid. He proceeded to introduce his team. "You know of our mission."

"I do. We're receiving communication already from the *Bird* they have hovering over the coast. You can look at the commo here or we can go to the con."

"If you wouldn't mind, Captain, we'd rather stay here for a while," said Kincaid. "It would give us a chance to look at the data coming from the *Bird*. We still have some planning to do."

"No problem," Turner said. He called to the control room and had the communication from *Big Bird* downloaded into the submarine's internal system. "You can stay here as long as you like. I've got to get forward." He went to his closet and pulled out two Tablets and placed them on the table. "Your incoming commo will be directed to channel three, a secure, password-protected connection. The Tablets are pre-programmed. Just turn them on." He gave them the password. "See you in an hour or so."

70

"**W**elcome to the Mark-11, our newest SEAL Delivery Vehicle," Kincaid said to Delgado as he showed him around the twenty-one-foot long submersible. Launch time was in two hours.

"Son-of-a-bitch, Rob," Delgado exclaimed. "Pretty damn cool. Got to admit you've come a long way since I left. And hell, that was just five years ago."

"Yeah. Everyone except the driver lies down on these racks. The driver sits here at the controls. We are all breathing from our scuba gear, though for longer missions we can tap into the SDV's compressed air supply. We get to the target, park this puppy on the bottom and swim to the yacht."

They had stayed in the captain's cabin for over two hours pouring over the pictures sent to them through the *Big Bird*. They all knew and appreciated the fact that one thousand, five hundred and twenty-one miles due north of their present location, an operator sat in an air-conditioned bunker on the outskirts of Cheyenne, Wyoming and pointed the RQ 185 cameras at a yacht in Manzanillo, Mexico, and sent the pictures electronically to a submarine sitting two hundred feet below the ocean's surface sixty-two miles off the Mexican coast.

Their mission sounded relatively simple. Get to the yacht. Plant four limpet mines at strategic places along the hull, arm them, get on board, neutralize the guards, find Lopez and kill him. If he wasn't there, they were to return to the submarine and send the signal for the mines to explode.

Sounding simple and being simple were two different animals. First of all, there was that pesky problem of the guards. *Big Bird* had sent, among other things, over two hundred photos of the yacht, taken at five-minute intervals over the past twenty-four hours. Kincaid and his squad were most interested in the ones that showed people.

They identified twenty-one unique individuals. None were Lopez, but that didn't mean he wasn't there. Just that he hadn't come on deck in the past twenty-four hours.

Twenty-one guards. They matched photos with times and saw the pattern. There were three watches. Seven guards each watch. They memorized faces and assigned numbers to each. One through seven had the midnight to eight watch. They would die first. If they were stealthy enough, they wouldn't even wake the other guards. They would die when the yacht exploded.

While the photos couldn't show the inside of the yacht, it did show all the entrances and exits as well as the outside corners and angles of the outer decks. Kincaid's squad committed those to memory as well. If a battle did break out, these were the places the bad guys would use as firing platforms.

By comparing those photos with the manufac-turer's specs of the inside of the Delta Marine yacht, also courtesy of the *Big Bird* operators, they could put together a detailed picture of the internal route they would take to Lopez' cabin.

At the thirty-minute mark, the squad met under the Dry Deck Shelter hatch to go over the attack plan one more time. They were fully clothed for the mission, complete with scuba tanks and masks and weapons. All that weight made swimming even tougher. Kincaid made a note to himself to watch Delgado carefully. With the predicted tide, this swim was not going to be as easy as it looked.

"You're the driver, Chief," said Kincaid. "Coming and going."

"Roger that, Rob," Fuller responded.

"We'll go to ground eight hundred meters from the yacht." Kincaid continued. "Captain Turner said lunar illumination was nil, so we won't have to worry about being seen from above. Should be a fifteen-minute swim to the boat. The Wolfman and Jim will place the limpets while the rest of us secure our gear to the aft starboard anchor chain." Everyone nodded. "Any questions about the boarding procedures?" The pictures from the *Bird* showed a thirty-foot swim platform extending from the stern. The manufacture's specs told them that platform could be raised and folded back into the stern when desired. They were prepared for both. When no one responded, Kincaid said, "Then let's rock and roll."

They launched at exactly 0230. The ride in took forty minutes. They grounded the SDV on the ocean floor about a third of a mile from the yacht. The swim took fifteen minutes. So far, so good. It was 0325. A few of the starboard portholes showed light, but the deck was completely dark and quiet.

While Rosen and Johnson went to attach the mines, Kincaid led the others to the stern where they stowed their masks, snorkels, fins and tanks in specially made container bags and tied them to the aft anchor chain. The swim platform was down. Guard number one was sitting on it smoking a cigarette, not paying any attention. Two faint clicks from Kincaid's MP7 sent the guard slumping backward in his chair, the tip of his cigarette starting to burn a hole in his shirt. He wouldn't feel it burn. One down, six to go.

When Rosen and Johnson returned, all climbed aboard. They had specific assignments, and all carried them out. Every now and then Kincaid could hear the sound of shell casings hitting the deck. He was with Delgado looking for Lopez' cabin. It was empty. No surprise, but he was disappointed nonetheless. He had fantasized about what meeting Lopez in person would be like. *Another day*, he thought.

He and Delgado rifled quickly through Lopez' desk and dresser drawers looking for anything of intelligence value. There wasn't much, but Delgado did snag an unopened bottle of Dalmore forty year old single malt scotch whiskey. He figured selling it would net him about two months rent. He saw Kincaid looking at him. "Tell no one," he mouthed. Kincaid just shook his head in amusement.

It turned out to be the perfect mission. Accomplishing what they came to do without even once being shot at is out of the ordinary. They collected their gear from the anchor chains, redressed, swam back to the SDV, and docked on the *California* at 0540. Before opening the hatch, Kincaid hit the control button that triggered the mines. Even at this distance, they felt a slight shock wave roll over the submarine a minute later.

71

FRIDAY
CULIACAN, MEXICO

In a related story, a spectacular explosion rocked Manzanillo early this morning as the yacht of reputed cartel leader, Victor Lopez, blew up and sank at its mooring half a mile off Mr. Lopez' villa. No word on the cause of the explosion or if there were any casualties, but late reports say that Mr. Lopez was definitely not on board.

Lopez was reading a book, but looked up at the television when he heard his name. On the screen was a picture of what looked like the remains of his yacht smoldering in its berth. He grabbed the remote and hit rewind.

His loud scream and the sound of a glass shattering against the wall brought in his two bodyguards, guns drawn.

"Patrón. What is it? Are you all right?" one said as the other checked the closet and the outside patio.

"No," he yelled, his body trembling. "I'm not alright. Get me Palma on the phone. Right now. Fuck the cutouts. I can't waste the time. Call him directly."

"Are you sure, Patrón? No intermediary? What if the federales are tickling your wires? They will know where you are."

"Don't argue with me, Jaime. I don't give a shit what they do. I'll shoot them all down like dogs. I need Palma, now."

"Si, Patrón." Both guards left the room to make the call. As soon as Lopez' door was closed, one turned to the other and circled his temple with his forefinger. "Going loco," he said. The other guard nodded his head in agreement.

"You have to calm down, *Ahn-hel*," Palma said. "This is not the end of the world. They are just showing you their strength. Playing with you. Two heavyweights sparing in the ring. It means nothing."

"The snake is being torn apart, Rinaldo."

"What the hell does that mean," Palma said. "Speak sense, will you?"

"I am speaking sense. The man in my dream. The giant. He came again last night. This time he held the snake high above him, like holding a trophy."

"You told me that before, *Ahn-hel*. You have nothing to worry about."

"Let me finish," Lopez said, becoming quieter now. "He is holding the snake above his head and then he starts to pull it apart. Piece-by-piece. My dream. Don't you see, Rinaldo? It is coming true."

"Nonsense, *Ahn-hel*. You should have listened to the shrink instead of killing her or whatever you did."

"Cut out her tongue," Lopez said, grinning at the remembrance.

"Well, never mind about her. Calling me directly like this was stupid. You know that. You keep doing stupid things like this, and they *will* tear you apart."

Lopez remained silent for a few moments. "You're right. As always. Call me back using normal channels," he said, and disconnected.

Five minutes later, Lopez' phone rang. "Sorry, Rinaldo. That was stupid on my part. I get so angry. Not calm like you. That's why we are such a good team, eh? The beauty and the beast."

Palma laughed. "I wouldn't go that far, but, yes, we are a good team."

"Where do you think they will come after me next?"

"They have Lillianna Martinez. Think about what she knows about you. Your habits. Your hangouts."

Lopez thought about that for a moment, then said, "She knows about my house here in Culiacan. Not this one, but the one in the flats."

"Then that is where they will come. I would prepare a big surprise for them, *Ahn-hel*."

72

FRIDAY
NAVAL SPECIAL
WARFARE COMMAND
CORONADO

Lopez' guard was right. They were *tickling his wire.* Thirty minutes after Lopez called Palma, Bill Rogers, the DD of Signals Intelligence in the National Security Agency, was on the phone with Roy Thompson.

"We got a hit we think you should know about," he said. "Ever since you picked up that attorney Rinaldo Palma in Borrego Springs, we've been monitoring his activities closely. Some of this information is sensitive in that none of it would be useable in a court of law. All Palma would have to say is the calls were to actual and or potential clients, and therefore fall under his attorney-client privilege. No judge on earth would allow in it as evidence."

"The hell with judges and courts of law, Bill," Thompson said. "We aren't going to take this guy Palma to court." He paused, then said, "And if you are recording this damn conversation, you can take what I just said about Palma any way you want. Tell me what you've got."

"He's been talking to someone in San Francisco. Not a lot, but some. We don't know who it is because that person uses burner phones. One time use, then destroyed. No record of ownership. But at least you know he's been talking to someone up there. Thought it might be useful to you."

"That's great, Bill. But that can't be all you called me about. There's got to be more, right?"

"There is more, Roy. I've just saved the best for last. Palma received a call about an hour ago from Victor Lopez' private phone. We know he has one, though we've never traced any direct calls either to or from that phone, until now. The feeling here is he always routes calls through untraceable cut-outs. Why he didn't use the cut-outs this time is a mystery.

"Anyway, they talked for about a minute and a half. The conversation came out garbled on our end, but we are working on it. What we do know is the call was placed from Culiacan, Mexico."

Thompson let out a big sigh. "Bill, big thanks to you and your crew. We had Culiacan on our radar from another source, but knowing he is there now means we can act on this immediately. When you decipher the conversation, let me know, okay?"

"Will do," he said. "Good hunting."

73

Kincaid's squad was back at NSWC by 1400 hours. At 1430, they found themselves in the Blockhouse with Thompson and Vaughn.

"You're going back in tonight," Vaughn said. "When we break here, I want you to go to the armory and stock up on gear needed for a house breach."

He showed them updated *Big Bird* photos of Lopez' house in Culiacan on one of the flat-paneled television screens hanging on the opposite wall. "We've had the techs go over these and there are no substantive differences in the house or its surroundings from the last photos you saw." He replaced the pictures of the house with drawings of what they thought the inside of the house looked like. "These are from Lillianna Martinez' recollections. No guarantees, but I think she's playing square with us."

He turned on the television. "One more thing," he said. "You will be in a city, tonight. A very big city. Our Marine friends in Hermosillo have agreed that you can use their base as a staging area. They will even supply a chopper to get you to Culiacan. Except for them, no one can know you are in Mexico. Their strategy, whenever they are in populated areas, is to always wear a mask or hood to cover their faces. For them, it's a way to prevent the cartels from recognizing them and going after their families."

"It's going to be nice to eliminate those animals," Fuller said. "I can't wait."

"Agreed," Vaughn said. "Back in two thousand nine, a young marine officer was killed in a shoot out with one of the cartels. After being buried with full military honors, gunmen charged into the home where his family had gathered to mourn, and murdered his mother and brothers and sisters. Since then, their marines go to extremes not to be identified.

"Because we are Americans, we don't want to be identified, either. So remember that when you are at the armory. Face masks for everyone."

"What about the neighbors, sir?" Kincaid asked. "We are going to draw a crowd if things get noisy. Remember what happened in Pakistan when we were taking down bin Laden. Half the freaking town came out for a look-see."

"We've thought of that, Rob. That's why we are sending Lillianna Martinez with you. She won't be wearing a hood. She'll already be known by some of the neighbors because of her former involvement with Lopez, and she can talk to them in their own language, which none of you can."

"How much time do we have before going downrange?" Kincaid asked.

"You will leave here at 2000 hours. It's a two-hour trip, but with the time change you will arrive at 2300 hours. You will immediately be flown by helicopter to Culiacan. At 0100 hours, you will be set down in a mountain meadow two klicks from your target. Far enough away they won't hear the sound. You will ex-fil at 0600.

"I suggest you go to the armory now, and then get some sleep. It will be a long night. Good luck, gentlemen. Come home with Lopez' scalp."

"Let's make a list of what we need," Kincaid said as they returned to the barracks. "It will help us analyze what we think we'll be facing tonight."

"Good idea," Fuller replied. "First thing I think of is... it's a house. We have to get in. Break down a door or two."

"In Mexico?" Delgado chimed in. "I'll bet all we'd have to do is huff and puff and the door will just fall down."

"You can huff and puff all you want," Fuller said. "We'll leave your dead-ass carcass on the doorstep. I'm guessing heavy wood or maybe even steel. This is a guy who doesn't want visitors."

"Breaching tubes, then," Kincaid said. "How many?"

"Three max, L-T," said the Rosen. "No use loading ourselves down with stuff we won't use."

"It'll be dark in there," Fuller said. "We all should be wearing ChemLights."

"Good thought," Kincaid said, marking them down on a pad he had in front of him. "We'll wear them on our vests front and back. So none of us will get shot by Delgado."

"Very funny," Delgado said.

"Grenades?" asked Kincaid. "For indoor ops we should all carry at least two frags and a flash-bang. Agreed?" Nods around. "And I want everyone wearing their Molle. Just like Pescadero Creek. A life saver. JJ will carry his beloved 417 and we'll all have our trusty 7's. Objections?" No one spoke. "We all have our Sigs, right?" Nods around. "Then let's take this show on the road." He paused. "And don't forget the balaclavas."

74

FRIDAY
CULIACAN, MEXICO

While Kincaid's squad was in the armory picking out their gear for the raid that night, another small army was also preparing for battle.

In the basement of the house on Abedules Street in Culiacan, Mexico, Victor Lopez was addressing nine of his most experienced bodyguards. "I'm positive they will come tonight," he said. "You've all had military training. You've even done battle with our own marines in the streets of this city. Tonight you will battle soldiers of the US military." Someone in the back row spat. "Exactly," Lopez said, acknowledging the gesture.

"I'm not sure how many will come, but it won't be any more than we have here in this room. The one thing they cannot afford is publicity. A company of American troops invading Mexico would not play out well on their six o'clock news. No, they will come in quiet and stealthy. So be wary."

"Why don't we just ambush them outside the house, Patrón? As they come trooping down the street?"

"You are way ahead of me, Miguel," Lopez replied, smiling. "I want you to take two men and occupy the house across the street. When they approach the door, you'll have a clear shot.

"Then why so many of us, Patrón," asked one of the men, "if they all die before they reach the front door?"

"Si, Patrón. We want to have some fun, too," another said from the side.

"I've been successful in business for thirty years," Lopez said, "precisely because I take nothing for granted. My track record is perfect because of redundancy. Always have more than your enemy at the point of attack. Overpower them. Beat them down. That is why you are here. Redundancy. To beat them down, *just in case*."

"There will be no *just in case*, Patrón," said Miguel. "We won't fail you. They won't even reach the front door."

"*Just in case*, men," Lopez replied, "I want the rest of you in the tunnels.

"If they succeed in getting into the house, they will finally end up here in the basement. If they do get this far, I want them to find the tunnel entrance in the bathroom. And, if they get into the tunnels, I want them buried there."

He looked over the men. "Miguel has his men. You six come with me. I will show you where I want you."

75

"Rob? Mac. I was hoping I'd find you. How are things going on your hunt?"

"Heating up, Uncle Mac. If you had called any later, I wouldn't have answered."

"I won't keep you, then. Saw the news this morning about that mysterious explosion that destroyed some yacht in Manzanillo, Mexico," McGuire said. "Thought you might have been busy." He laughed.

"Can't say anything in particular, but I can tell you some of my buddies and I had a great swim last night." McGuire chuckled. "By the way," Kincaid continued, "I've been out of the loop for a while. How's the anthrax thing going? Slowed down?"

"Deaths are slowing down dramatically, as you'd expect when word got out that it was anthrax powder in the drugs that were causing the deaths. Funny thing, huh? You hear you could drown in your own phlegm if you so much as sniffed a line of coke, and guess what? You stop sniffing.

"With that being said, over four thousand people have died so far. As far away as New York and Boston."

"Son-of-a-bitch. And no one is asking why the cartels would be doing this? Killing, in a literal sense, their own business?"

"Lots of people, Rob," McGuire said. "But there is no one else they can think of to blame. There are the usual conspiracy nuts on both sides of the aisle. Some contending it's our own government doing this. Others saying it's Russia, or China or, I don't know, maybe even Bangladesh. They're all nut cases, as far as I can tell.

"The consensus of the talking heads is still that it's a power struggle inside the various cartels in Mexico. I've heard on independent authority that there are some cartels moving away from drugs and into more lucrative, and more violent, job opportunities. I know that seems odd, but makes a kind of quirky sense to me."

"Don't know, Uncle Mac. I'm still having trouble seeing the logic on this one. But mine is not to reason why, I guess."

"Well, all this is a way of leading up to why I really called you. Wanted to give you a heads up that early tomorrow morning ... like around two in the morning ... Hartmann and seemingly every cop in every major city, including yours truly, along with the FBI, DEA, and every other government alphabet agency, is going to raid and close down every known drug dealer, drug distributor, drug house, ... you name it, even legal medical marijuana stores... in the country. This is so big, so all encompassing, it wouldn't surprise me to hear that Pfizer and Bayer will also be raided."

"Shit," was all Kincaid could think to say.

"Amen to that," McGuire said. "They'll be going after Fly, too. I'm gonna call him and let him know what's coming down. I owe him that. I'll tell him to destroy every single damn warehouse where he has drugs stashed; every receipt; every single piece of paper that would connect him with running a drug operation. He's going to end up doing some time, but not as much as he could if he doesn't do what I tell him."

"Don't you get in trouble helping some guy like that, though," Kincaid said. "Watch yourself." He paused, and then said, "I'll be tied up tonight pretty much. I guess I'll have to read about your adventure in the paper."

"Whatever you're doing or about to do, be careful," McGuire said. "Don't want to be reading about *you* in the paper."

"Would never get in the newspapers, Uncle Mac. We are not even here, remember?"

76

SATURDAY
CULIACAN, MEXICO

The helo was on the ground for only twenty-three seconds before it headed back to Hermosillo. Kincaid's squad sprinted to the side of the clearing and knelt down to stay out of sight the best they could. They had put on their balaclavas, and clipped the ChemLights to their Molle vests, front and back, on the ride in. The ChemLights were only visible to night vision systems. Now there was no way they would mistake one of their own for a bad guy.

"I was thinking on the way down," Kincaid said. "We all saw the pictures of the house we'll be attacking. But it wasn't the house that got me. It was the street. We were all in Iraq. Even Vinnie. I don't know about any of you, but this street reminded me a lot of the streets in Fallujah. Long and narrow. Streets that favored the ambusher and not the ambushee. A hellhole where we lost a lot of good people because we weren't careful enough.

"So we are going to take it very slow from now on. Vinnie, you stay with Lillianna. I'm not saying anyone is waiting for us, but let's just pretend they are. That way, we have a good chance of seeing sun-up."

They walked a mile through fields before they came to pavement and Abedules Street. They were three long blocks from the target house. Kincaid signaled a halt. He walked back to Lillianna Martinez and whispered, "You come up behind me." He motioned to Delgado to follow her. "You know these streets better than any of us. We need your eyes. If you see or hear anything out of the ordinary, you pull on my shirt, okay?" She nodded. Kincaid was impressed. He saw no sign of fear in her eyes. He was even more impressed when he saw the bulge of pistol she carried in the waistband of her pants.

The squad walked single-file on the side of the street opposite the target. When they were within two houses from the target, Martinez pulled Kincaid's shirt. He signaled the squad to stop, and knelt down facing Martinez. She knelt with him and whispered, "I smelled smoke, did you?"

Kincaid raised his head and sniffed. "Faintly," he said.

"It is coming from that house in front of us," she said. "The one directly across the street from house we are going to. I saw a slight wisp of smoke coming from an open window."

"Could it be just the owner of the house taking a late night cigarette break?" Kincaid asked.

"No, sir. The owner of that house is Vincent Lopez. Nobody lives there."

Kincaid signaled them to pull back. They found a vacant lot and all squatted.

"If they have people stationed there, we have to eliminate them before we take the main house," Kincaid whispered.

"If that is true, then I am the only one who can find out," Martinez said. "I can walk down the middle of the street. A woman. They wouldn't expect that. I will stop in front of my old house and start rambling on about something or other. A thorough nuisance. I will either be shot or told to leave. We'll find out one way or the other."

"Don't like it, Rob," said Fuller. "Too dangerous for her."

"Have a better idea?" Kincaid asked.

"No."

"I do," Delgado said. "I'll strip off all this gear and go with her. We'll be a couple having an argument. Since I don't speak the language, it will be a one-sided argument. Like most marriages." He grinned. "If she's loud enough, they will come out to tell us to leave."

"And then what?" Rosen asked.

"I'll be belligerent. He'll come over to get me. He'll leave the door open. You guys will just walk in and blast everyone. I'll have my Sig. I'll take the guy who comes for me."

"A risky melodrama," said Rosen, "but it's crazy enough it just might work. And if it doesn't, all we'll lose is Delgado."

"I'll remember you said that," he replied with a smile.

It happened just as Delgado had predicted. Lillianna made an impressive enough fed-up wife that one of the guards opened the door and whispered loudly to shut up and move on. When the couple made no sign they were going to leave, he stomped out towards them. As he was moving, so were Kincaid and his team. By the time the guard reached Delgado, Kincaid and Fuller had walked into the house and shot the two unsuspecting gunman. At the same time, they heard a slight *pop*, signaling that Delgado had dispatched the guard on the street. All three bodies were piled on one another in the living room of the house. Rosen did a quick recon, whispered an all clear and the six of them walked quickly and quietly over to Lopez' front door.

77

Fuller checked the front door for booby-traps. "Clear, Rob. The door is reinforced steel. Looked like he didn't want visitors."

"Lillianna, take the street," Kincaid said. "This blast is going to wake everyone. If they come out of their houses, be firm. Tell them there is nothing here for them. Tell them Mr. Lopez is just doing some repairs to his house. He's sorry he disturbed them. Tell them they don't want to piss off the Angel of Death." She nodded, smiled and left.

"We'll use two charges," Kincaid said. He affixed one around the door handle and one by the upper door hinge, and set the timer. "Going hot," he said. "Eight seconds." Even though the charge would blow the door inward, he was warning his team to take cover. The backblast could carry shrapnel.

The explosion blew shards of steel twenty feet into the room. In the small space, the overpressure from the blast also blew out every window. If anyone had been waiting in ambush for them, they would have either been torn apart by shrapnel, or had their head explode from the pressure of the blast.

Before the dust had settled, the team stormed into the house and took up defensive positions. They noticed the remnants of surveillance cameras everywhere, but there was nobody on this level. Kincaid motioned to the stairs leading to the basement. They knew that any bad guy waiting for them down there would be badly concussed, but nonetheless they were still cautious on the descent.

No one was on the basement level, either. They discovered the reason for that in the bathroom.

"L-T. You might want to come take a look at this," said Johnson. When Kincaid came into the room, Johnson was on his knees looking under a bathtub that had been raised four feet from its base by hydraulic lifts. He pushed himself back and stood, revealing a large hole in the floor. He pointed. "Stairs, L-T. Shit, there's a fucking tunnel under this place."

The squad huddled together to form a plan of action.

"Could be that Lopez was here when we breached and took off," Delgado said. "We could be just a few minutes behind him. I'm for not wasting any more time. Let's get after the son-of-a-bitch."

"On the other hand, this could all be a set-up and he and his guys could be sitting down there just waiting for us," said Rosen.

"I'm more inclined to be with Wolfman on this one," Kincaid said. "I don't think Lopez, or anybody for that matter, could have withstood the blast, raised the bathtub and escaped into that tunnel before we got down here. I think he had this set up and wants us to come after him."

"Looks that way to me, too, Rob," said Fuller. "But that doesn't mean we shouldn't oblige him."

They all knew that a tunnel, especially a tunnel you had no familiarity with, was a very dangerous environment for a gunfight. Especially if you were the one stalking. The pursued wouldn't even have to have a clear shot. Just fire in the general direction of the pursuer and hope the ricocheting bullets would find a mark.

"You guys all laughed at my insistence on bagging an EOTech from the armory," JJ said. "Well, who's laughing now? This baby is thermal." He lovingly patted the top of the sight. "With this, we can see the bad guys' heat signatures way before they see us."

"Good point. Gives me an idea," Kincaid said. "Who wants to go first?" Delgado raised his hand. "Good, Vinnie. We're gonna drop a flashbang down the stairs. Soon as it goes off, you'll go down. Anyone waiting close by will be so disoriented that you can waste him easily."

"Then me, L-T," said Johnson.

"Exactly," replied Kincaid. "You'll be our eyes."

"Then let's do it," Delgado said walking over to the stairs while pulling out the grenade. "Ready?" he asked. When everybody nodded, he dropped the flashbang into the tunnel. "Flash out," he yelled. Everyone closed their eyes and put their hands over their ears.

The noise and intense flash of light caused by a flashbang grenade was sufficient to cause immediate blindness and loss of hearing. Anyone within twenty yards of detonation experiences disorientation, confusion and loss of coordination. As soon as it went off, Delgado rushed down the stairs. His team waited for the all clear, but instead heard a rhythmic click, click, click of the MP7 being fired.

"You good?" Kincaid yelled down.

"We got light bulbs strung out down here, Rob," said Delgado. "But not anymore. We're clear."

Immediately Johnson hit the stairs. Seconds later he yelled "clear" and the rest followed him into the tunnel.

78

They huddled at the base of the stairs to get their bearings. "The whole tunnel was lit up like Grand Central Station," Delgado said. "This is a well used path."

"And constructed by someone who knew what he was doing," said Fuller. "It's ventilated. You can tell. I used to work the mines when I was a teenager in Pennsylvania."

"Thank God for Cateyes, huh?" Rosen said with a smile. "Advantage *us*."

"We're clear ahead, L-T," said Johnson looking through the EOTech. "Can we take off these damn masks? Sweat is pouring into my eyes. Hard to see."

"Do it," Kincaid said. "Then let's move out."

The tunnel was cylindrical, but tight, forcing them to walk single-file. Johnson led the way. About one hundred yards in, they came to a fork. Ahead of them was a small portal about the size of the door on an apartment-sized refrigerator. To their left, the tunnel looked like an extension of the one they were in now.

"Can you see anything to your left?" Kincaid whispered to Johnson.

Johnson nodded, knelt and swung the HK around the corner. "Nothing here, L-T," he said.

"Check the tunnel in front."

Johnson crawled forward and scoped through the small opening. He lifted his hand and pointed his thumb to the ground. Nothing.

Kincaid motioned for the squad to get as close together as they could in the confined space so he wouldn't have to talk too loud. "I'm going to take the Chief with me to explore the tunnel to our front," he said. "Everyone else, stay here. We'll see where that one leads, then come back.

"We aren't in a hurry. If Lopez was trying to escape, he'd be long gone by now, anyway. If not, we'll still meet him in one of these tunnels. If you hear us in a firefight, come quick."

Kincaid and Fuller crawled through the small opening. The tunnel was about five feet high. Once through, they were able to stand, though not without stooping. They walked on, and soon were splashing through dirty, shallow water. The smell was horrific.

"Shit," Fuller said. "This is the freaking city sewer system."

"Gee, how'd you guess?" Kincaid said, laughing. "I'm thinking this must have been the original way out of that house. Just think, if you were being chased, wouldn't you want to come out here? In this shit? Dogs would lose your scent. Pursuers would slow down on account of what they were sloshing through, and you'd have an infinite number of manholes through which to escape. Perfect, if you ask me."

"Makes you wonder where that other tunnel goes, doesn't it?"

"That it does. Let's get back and see."

They had just turned back when they heard the HK engage. Two shots in rapid succession, then a solitary one a moment later. They broke into a dead run.

79

It was two forty-five in the morning. Victor Lopez had been waiting for word that Kincaid had been shot and killed in the damn tunnel. But he had dozed, and the dream had come again. His nightshirt was soaked. He called Carlos Valazquez, his chief of staff, wanting to be told that Kincaid had been killed, though he knew that was not the case. His dream had told him Kincaid was alive.

"An update, Carlos."

Valazquez gulped and cleared his throat, knowing what the outcome of this conversation would be. "We haven't heard from the three shooters in the house. We must assume they have been neutralized."

"And the tunnels?"

"Three have been killed, Patrón, we have three left." That Lopez wasn't ranting and raving by now, threatening to cut off the hands and feet of those who haven't served him well, had Valazquez worried. For his own safety.

Lopez took a seat at his desk. He mentally traced the tunnel from his house in the flats to where he now sat, in his casa looking out at the city of Culiacan. He wondered how close Kincaid was. *The giant in my dream*, he thought. *Tearing me apart piece by piece.*

"How many soldiers do we have, Carlos?"

"One hundred and twenty-two, Patrón."

"All loyal?"

"Of course, Patrón."

"But some more loyal that others, eh?"

"Si. That will always be the case no matter how many you have."

"How many are in the hacienda now?" Lopez asked.

"Not many, Patrón. No matter how loyal the soldiers are, only a few can be really trusted. There are only ten left who know about the hacienda. They are here in the casa."

"I want you to take them and pick forty others, Carlos. The best you have. And move them to El Mesa Cocoyole. You know where. They cannot tell anyone. Even their families. I will need their loyalty for six months. We will house them in tents. No construction can take place. I will double their pay and reward their families while they are gone. This applies to you, too, Carlos. Can you see to that?"

"Si. When do you want this move to be made, Patrón?"

"Immediately. I am leaving tonight." He paused. "I want you to prepare the airplane."

"Patrón, are you sure?"

"We have discussed this many times, have we not?"

"Si."

"Then do it. The plane will leave in exactly one hour. You know what to do, right?"

"Si, Patrón."

"And one more thing. Bring me the three soldiers who were in the tunnel."

80

When they got back to the portal, they pressed themselves flat on either side of the opening.

"It's us. You guys okay? What's happening?'

"I got two heat signatures, L-T," said Johnson. "Popped them both. We were waiting for you to get back before we went forward."

"Is it safe for Chris and I to come through?"

"Come ahead. We got nothing in front of us."

Kincaid and Fuller slithered through the opening, trying to keep as low a profile as possible.

"You guys smell like shit," Delgado said.

"We do? We didn't notice," Fuller replied.

"What happened, JJ?" Kincaid asked.

"I was keeping an eye on the tunnel, Rob. It goes straight for about fifty yards, then it looks like it ends. Obviously it had a passage off to either its right or left. Turns out it was the right.

"Anyway, these two guys come around the corner. Casual as hell. Both armed, both oblivious to the fact that we are here and that I can see them. I took them both out."

"You fired three times."

"Second guy I had to shoot twice, sorry."

"Let's go see the effect of bad shooting," Kincaid said with a laugh.

They moved out, still in single file. As they got closer to the bodies, the tunnel widened out enough for two to walk abreast.

"Move the bodies out of the way," Kincaid said. "I'm going to peek around the corner with Johnson. See what we are facing."

What they were facing was another three hundred yards of unobstructed tunnel; the only obstacle was being an uphill slope all the way.

"I wonder if this tunnel is connecting a Lopez house up there with the Lopez house back where we came from?" Kincaid asked. "Who has the SAT phone?"

"Wolfman, I think," Johnson replied.

"Hey, Wolfman," Kincaid said loud enough to cause an echo. Rosen looked up and Kincaid waved for him to come forward. "You have the phone?" Rosen nodded and pulled it off his vest. "Reception in here?"

"I don't know, L-T. Haven't tried it yet."

"See if you can reach Thompson, okay? I have a question for him." He looked at his watch. 0300. "Dammit." Rather than shouting again, he crawled back to where Delgado was. "Vinnie, we have to be at the LZ at 0500. I need you to get back to the other house and collect the Martinez woman."

"On my way, Rob. Wouldn't want to leave her behind." He smiled and started to leave.

"And don't forget to wear your damn face mask," Kincaid said, clapping him on the back as he passed.

"We are going to take this slow." Kincaid told his team as they started their walk up the last leg of the tunnel. "Just too damn inviting. Look for wires. Just like these bastards to put trip wires out."

As they got closer to the end, two things happened. The first was they saw a set of steps built into the side of the tunnel wall leading to a round wooden hatch cover. The second thing that happened was that as they got closer to ground level, Rosen's SAT phone was able to make connection with Admiral Thompson at NSWC.

"Admiral, I need a favor," Kincaid said. "We need *Big Bird* to get a camera on the house we are about to come up under or near. It's another house Lopez owns in the foothills of Culiacan. He's living there now. Can *Big Bird* pick up my location via the satellite?"

"Let me check. Hold on." He was away from the phone for two minutes, just enough time for Fuller to quietly remove the hatch cover from the top of the cave.

"Rob, he says he already has you."

"Tell him we need him to fix the house we are near. This is where Lopez is. We don't have the people, or the time, to get him tonight. He may try to run. They have to keep track of everybody that comes and goes to this place."

"Got it Rob. Good going. He has no place to run, no place to hide. He's done."

It was 0315 when they came up from the tunnel. They were approximately a quarter mile from the villa. All the lights where blazing and you could see lots of movement through the windows.

"Damn," said Johnson. "How many people does he have working for him? Glad we didn't have to face that army tonight." He took the HK from his shoulder and sighted through the EOTech at the upstairs windows. "Give me permission, L-T," he said, "and I'll finish this hunt tonight."

"Wish I could, Jim, but a gun battle here and we'd have the local militia all over us. Besides, we have to get back to the LZ. Extractions at 0500. We haven't got much time left."

Just then they heard three shots coming from the upstairs room with the picture window. "Pistol," said Rosen. "What the fuck would someone be shooting at this time of night in their bedroom or den?"

"Can't worry about that now," Kincaid said. "We gotta move or we'll be stuck here."

They were still within a mile of the villa when they heard the noise of an airplane revving its motors. They all turned back to see a single engine Cessna TT take off from behind the house.

"Shit," Kincaid said, "the son-of-a-bitch has got a landing strip back there, and now is getting away."

"I can probably bring the plane down with a few well-placed shots from this, Rob," Johnson said, bringing the HK up to eye level and flipping the selector switch to full auto.

"No, let *Big Bird* track it to its destination. We've come this far. Let's at least get the pleasure of taking him up close and personal."

Big Bird was tracking it. But not very far. The plane's *destination* was just a short four miles from the villa. It was at that point the Cessna blew apart in the night sky, scattering fiery pieces of itself onto the rocky terrain below.

Three of the SEALS watched with a mixture of anger, joy and unfulfilled ambitions. Not Rob though. All Rob could see was his dad smiling.

81

SATURDAY
NAVAL SPECIAL
WARFARE COMMAND
CORONADO

**MASSIVE NATIONWIDE
DRUG SWEEP**
FEDS RAID PRODUCTION AND
DISTRIBUTION CENTERS IN
SIXTEEN CITIES OVERNIGHT.
THOUSANDS ARRESTED!

was the headline of the NY Times that was slapped into Kincaid's hands by Admiral Thompson when they landed at North Island. "Bad news, guys," Kincaid said as he held up the paper for his team to see. "Your suppliers have all been shut down."

After Lopez' plane went down, Kincaid and the rest of the team met Delgado and Martinez at the LZ. They were picked up at 0500 and, after transferring planes at Hermosillo, had arrived at NSWC an hour ago, and were now sitting in Thompson's office.

Lillianna Martinez had already been taken off base to a safe house where arrangements were being made to fast track her for citizenship. The DEA had already offered her employment.

"As soon as we wrap up the After Action Report," Thompson said, "I'll let you guys get some rest. You must be dog-tired."

"We'll be okay, sir," Kincaid replied. "Most of us got some sleep on the plane inbound."

Thompson took out some papers from the top drawer of his desk. "We received this report just about an hour ago that SEMAR, a Special Forces unit of the Mexican Marines, raided the 'house on the hill' as they are now calling it. No doubt that Lopez had lived there, but also no question that he was closing up operations. The place had been sanitized."

"That accounts for all the activity we saw through the windows," Fuller said.

"The report says they found three bodies in one of the bedrooms," Thompson continued. "Shot through the head. Execution style."

"With all due respect, sir," Kincaid said, "I don't think any of us care about those details. What about the plane? Was Lopez on it?"

"They think so, but aren't one hundred percent sure. It makes sense that he was. With the house compromised, he'd want to get out quick. This was probably a contingency plan made when he first moved in."

"But no body was found."

"Not yet. A small plane like that? It's going to take weeks just to comb the countryside. My honest guess is that the Mexican government will not put a lot of resources into this. They'd just as soon close the book on Victor Lopez."

"And if he turns up later?"

"They'll deal with it then."

Kincaid went to the barracks and promptly fell into a fitful sleep, haunted by dreams of planes exploding in the sky. He was actually happy when Delgado shook him awake. "Thompson wants to see you in his office," was all he said.

"How long have I been asleep?"

"Three hours," Delgado said.

"Take a seat, Rob," Thompson said. "Remember when I said the Mexican government would just as soon close the book on Victor Lopez?" Kincaid nodded. "Well, they may feel that way, but *we* just reopened it."

82

"**R**emember I told you about my friend Bill Rogers, the DD of SIGINT. He was the one who tracked Lopez' call to Rinaldo Palma. It was that call that gave us the confirmation that Lopez was in Culiacan."

"I remember, sir," Kincaid said, feeling the excitement building.

"He just called twenty minutes ago. Guess what? That dumb shit Lopez just called Palma again on an unsecured phone. Palma cut him off immediately, but not before Rogers' people tracked the signal back to the source."

Kincaid leaned forward. "Tell me."

"Your boy Victor Lopez is alive and well in a nowhere place called Cocoyole."

"The airplane was just a diversion, then. Pretty convincing contingency plan."

"Would have worked, too, if he could have kept himself from gloating to Palma."

"So, Cocoyole is where?"

"Hard to find. Can't ask anyone in Mexico. Soon as we do, Lopez would know within an hour that we know he is not only alive, but where he is hiding. We had to use a satellite. It's in the Sierra Madre Occidental range.

It's nothing more than a very small valley between some very steep and very jagged peaks. As the crow flies, it's about two hundred and sixty klicks northeast of Culiacan. And I mean *as the crow flies.* The roads in are nothing more than dirt tracks."

"Anybody live there?"

"Lopez now. Before him? It was used at one time, years back, as an ostrich farm. Probably some business venture of Lopez'."

"Is the *Bird* on him?"

"As of ten minutes ago."

"Have they seen anyone with him, or is he alone?"

"First report is he has fifty armed guards." Thompson paused, and then added, "This is going to cause us a problem, Rob. The mountains around there are not suitable for helicopter insert, and landing a helo on top of them would be a no-no to the Mexican government. Got any ideas?"

"We are going to get that prick, sir. Once and for all. The five of us will HAHO in."

83

HAHO is a paratrooper acronym for a High Altitude, High Opening parachute jump. It's a tricky maneuver. You have to get it right, or bad things usually happen. Getting it right was what Kincaid's team and Admiral Thompson were discussing in his office later that afternoon.

"You're going to be jumping at an altitude of thirty thousand feet, forty miles from the target," Thompson said. "In the middle of Mexico. I'm going to have trouble getting permission from the Mexican government for this."

"Why not just do it and ask for forgiveness later," said Fuller.

"That's not the way things work in international circles," Thompson responded. "Especially with an unidentified aircraft flying over your country."

"We'll be going early in the morning," Johnson said. "On the map, this place looks to be about seven hundred clicks from the Arizona border."

"Six hundred and seventy-two, to be exact," said Thompson.

"Even better," replied Johnson. "That's only an hour in and an hour out for the plane dropping us. Couldn't we claim pilot error?" He laughed.

"I don't find any of that amusing, mister," Thompson said with an edge to his voice. "One thing we *could* do, however, is fly the plane under the radar. When it's twenty miles from the drop zone, it could pull up to thirty thousand feet, drop you guys and then slide back down under the radar. That maneuver could be done in less than twenty minutes. We just might get away with it. I'll confer with my Air Force friends to see if they have the assets to pull it off.

"But before I do that," he continued. "I'll see if I can get permission to use the *Bird* on this. I'll have to go higher in the chain of command, but it would be perfect. The *Bird* has radar-masking capability. As you know, we were in Pakistan killing bin Laden for just over forty minutes, and their air force never saw us."

He wrote himself a note and placed it by his phone. "Okay. Now to something more important. Let me give you a quick briefing on what's going on in Washington. The drug raids a few days ago caught flack from certain of our liberal friends in the press. Now, some of our elected representatives are getting squirrely about pushing the drug issue any further. They are saying we've hurt the cartels enough. That they have been crippled. I'm going to put this request for air force assets to go after Lopez through, but I just want you to know I can't be one hundred percent certain that it will be approved."

"And the president?" Delgado asked. "Where does he sit on this?"

"He just wants it to go away."

"What if we presented him with the best of both worlds?" Kincaid said. "Every since I saw that plane explode with Lopez supposedly on it, I've been thinking. Americans love to win, right?" Thompson shook his head in the affirmative. "What if the president could claim that American has won, or is winning, the war on drugs" He's be a hero. His second term would be assured."

"I'll give you that, but I don't see where this is going," Thompson said.

"I'm going to Lopez, sir. The president being given a captured and jailed Victor Lopez would signal to the world that America has put a dagger in the drug business coming out of Mexico. He's in jail and most of his operation in this country was rolled up last night.

"I'm not tracking where you are going with this, Rob."

"We've come up with a plan, sir. Contingent, of course, on whether or not you can get the powers that be to bite. After we HAHO in, I'm going to walk into their camp to arrest Lopez. The team will stay in the hills."

"You've been sniffing glue, right?" Thompson said. "What if just kills you right then and there."

"Well, I guess that would mean I wasn't successful. But I will be successful because I'm going to make him an offer he would be a fool to reject."

"And that would be?"

"I will promise to pull the US military off him. He would no longer be a target. We'd want him to go to jail for a few years, of course, for the purpose of salving Americans' sense of justice."

"You think he'll go for that?"

"An offer he can't refuse, sir. He knows that with his wealth, he'll own that jail and everyone in it within a week. He'll have his own suite of cells. Parties every night with girls and drugs. He'd be living large. Wouldn't you go for something like this?"

"I might, but he may not. The *Angel de la Muerta* may want to live up to his reputation and shoot you, instead."

"Well, that's when the other part of the offer comes into play. I will tell him that if my team hears a gunshot, and I don't immediately call Chief Fuller, he alerts *Big Bird* who will rain down Hellfire missiles on the entire camp, killing Lopez and everyone else in it."

"I'm surprised that you are letting Lopez off so easily, Rob. Given that he killed your father, I thought the revenge factor would dictate the Hellfires would come first."

"Seeing the plane explode last night, sir, when I thought he was on it," Kincaid said, "gave me no joy. I just want to see all this killing stopped. This is as good a way as any."

"I'm impressed, Rob. You're showing a surprising amount of maturity. This will go on my AAR on the effectiveness and efficiency of using firms like yours. I promise."

"Thank you sir. I appreciate it."

"Let's meet again here at 0900," Thompson said. "I'm thinking I can unilaterally send you in as long as I get the assets. I'll see what I can do."

"We appreciate that, sir. I'll look forward to you resolving any of the issues that stand in our way."

As they were walking back to the barracks, Fuller said, "You did it, Rob. Congrats."

"Thanks," Kincaid replied. "Hated to do it to Thompson. He's a good man. But I couldn't take the chance that he would allow someone to pull the plug on our going in. It looked like he bought that bullshit story hook, line and sinker."

84

SUNDAY
COCOYOLE, MEXICO

One of the many things SEALs learn in their initial HAHO training exercises are the health risks associated with jumping out of an aircraft at forty thousand feet. For one, there is a lot less oxygen pressure at that altitude. For two, it's damn cold up there.

By the time the aircraft door opened at their predetermined stand-off distance from the target, Kincaid's warmly clothed assault team had just finished thirty minutes of breathing one hundred percent oxygen from the tanks the air force had provided. They had their oxygen bottles attached to their vests and the breathing tubes in their mouths. They were ready.

It would be dawn in an hour. They wanted to be on the ground at first light. To ensure their glide slope for the fifty-two mile journey was as uniform as possible, the gear the team carried had to be apportioned so that the team members more or less weighed the same. Since Delgado was the smallest member of the team, he carried most of their gear, including most of their weaponry. He was the first one out the door. They all carried altimeters and GPS systems on their wrists so they could stay close to each other as they glided downrange. Four seconds after leaving the plane, Delgado deployed his chute. The others followed his lead.

Two hours later they were on the ground, gathering their gear and distributing the weapons. The eastern sky had just turned a golden orange. They all carried the HK 417 with the twenty-inch barrel, and the Sig Sauer p226 9mm. Standard SEAL fare.

They were on a peak six hundred feet above and behind the camp. They counted twelve four-man tents in a semi-circle around a larger tent designed for eight men. They took bets that only one man occupied that tent. Off to the side was what looked like an old commissary tent. Next to it was a homemade washbasin with running water. The cooks were already running around preparing for breakfast. They saw men come out of their tents and walk into the brush on the far side of the clearing to do their morning duty."

"Glad I won't have to wade through the latrine to get back to you guys," Kincaid said with a grin.

Just then, three generators in back of the commissary tent kicked into action, a signal that breakfast was about to be served.

"No sentries, Rob," whispered Rosen who was lying next to him in the sparse brush that protruded up through the rocky base of the hill.

"I noticed," he replied. "They think no one knows where they are. Aren't they going to be surprised?"

On Kincaid's hand signal, they all backed away from the ridge and gathered out of sight behind a large rock outcropping. "How do I get down there? Has anyone seen one of the so-called *dirt paths* around here?"

"The only thing I've noticed," Johnson said, "are some rocky trails that probably were used by the ostriches back in the day. Down the far side over there." He pointed to where the water was.

"Okay. That's where I'm going, too. I'll come out of the tree line by the food tent and running water. Get myself a drink. Real deliberate. Let them discover me."

"Once you're done with Lopez, how do you expect to get back here?" Delgado asked.

"Quickly, Vinnie, quickly," he replied with a laugh. "Chris will be on the radio with the *Bird* operators to tell them to release as soon as the first shot is heard. I'm hoping the gunfire will catch the guards by surprise and give me time to get past them and into the tree line. You will be laying down suppressive fire. All you have to do is keep them pinned down until I'm clear and the Hellfires arrive." He stood and started down the back side of the mountain. "Wish me luck."

It took a few moments before anyone noticed Kincaid standing by the sink helping himself to some water. Once the shout went up, however, it was just a matter of seconds before he had ten guys surrounding him, screaming and yelling. He was hit in the back of the head by the butt of a rifle, and went to all fours, stunned. The blood running into his eyes from the head wound kept his vision blurry. He sensed, rather than saw, the men surrounding him clear a way. When he tilted his head up, he was looking into the face of Victor Lopez.

At Lopez' command, they searched him. Finding nothing, they roughly dragged him into the large tent and threw him on the dirt floor. "Fortune has shined on me once again, Señor Kincaid. Having you show up in my camp like this." Kincaid sat back on his heels. "You come to my camp unarmed. You must have a death wish, no?" Without waiting for an answer, he walked over, lifted the flaps on the tent and dismissed all his guards. "You stay here with me, Carlos. Your gun, please." Lopez thought of his dream. *This couldn't be the giant*, he thought. *I have him a prisoner. He can't harm me.*

"I do not have a death wish, Mr. Lopez. I've always wanted to meet you. Ever since you killed my father."

"Ah, that. A mistake, my friend. I didn't even know your father. But I was warned about him. That he wanted to put me out of business. Ironically, it was his death that *has* put me out of business, at least temporarily. He caused me all this trouble." He swung his hand, palm up, in a wide arc. "Living here, for example, when I could be living in luxury in any of a dozen Mexican towns. I wish I had never heard of your father. And now you. I tell you, it's always the relatives that cause the worst problems. I tried to kill you twice now, did you know that?" Kincaid nodded. "You have proved tougher than most to kill, Señor."

"You can kill me now, Mr. Lopez. But my friends will finally get you and rip you apart. You will have ten of me after you. There is no way you can beat them. But enough of this talk of killing. I've come here to offer you a way to live. To offer you a way to return to the life you had before. Good food. Women. Luxury."

"And what do I have to do to receive these gifts?"

"Surrender to me."

Lopez laughed long and hard. Carlos followed his lead. "You must have eaten the loco weed, Señor Kincaid. I have the gun. I have fifty soldiers. You are alone. You will die soon."

"I came here to die with you, or to rescue you, Mr. Lopez. It is your choice. I am not alone. I have an entire platoon of US Navy SEALs in the hills surrounding your camp. I also have a drone two hundred or so miles from here loaded with Hellfire missiles. At the first sound of gunfire, those missiles will launch, and three minutes later this valley and everything in it will be nothing but clods of dirt and blood. That includes you, Mr. Lopez." He paused. "Do you have some water? I'm very thirsty."

Lopez nodded to Carlos to bring some water. "You don't have anyone here. You are lying."

Kincaid reached under his shirt and found the small radio mic. "Chris? Tell Mr. Lopez what you see." Kincaid handed Lopez his ear bud. "Mr. Lopez, I can see your tent. There were twelve men standing guard in front of it just a few minutes ago. They have all gone back to their tents. There is another twenty or so still eating breakfast. We have all of them in our sights. Anything happens to my friend in there, you will all die."

Lopez waited a moment and handed Kincaid back the ear bud. "What is your proposition?"

For the half hour, Kincaid laid out what surrender would look like. "The bottom line," he said, "is that the US military will leave you alone. You can become the new Señor Guzman. Go to jail for a few years. Live in relative luxury at a jail of your choosing. And, most importantly, you won't die today."

"And if I accept this, what happens now?"

"You will give me the gun. You will tell your guards to retire to their tents until you instruct them differently. I will walk you out of here, not as a prisoner, but as a friend."

"What do you think, Carlos?" Lopez asked.

"I don't trust him, Patrón. I wouldn't do it."

"You just don't want to lose a job." He laughed. "I will take care of all of you for as long as I am in jail." He turned to Kincaid and gave him the gun. "I accept."

"Now tell your guards to go to their tents. After you do that, I want to talk to you awhile. I have some questions I need answered."

When Kincaid was sure the guards were gone, he sat in a camp chair across from Lopez. Carlos stood behind his boss. They talked for thirty-five minutes. Kincaid had all his questions answered, and felt as if a great weight had been lifted off him.

He pulled the mic from his shirt. "Go hot with the lasers, and tell the *Bird* to release," he said. In Wyoming, the operator maneuvered the RQ 185 into position. Fourteen miles above the Pacific Ocean and four miles west of Culiacan, Mexico, its electronics making it invisible, the cameras in the *Big Bird* saw the city of Culiacan in the distance. It saw its hotels, and taxicabs, its bars and nightclubs, it even saw Lopez' casa high on the hill. But the cameras by-passed all those sights. They were looking for something special. Red laser beams. They found four of them in a mountainous region two hundred and some miles to the north and east of Culiacan. The operator armed four AGM 114M Hellfire missiles. When he saw the cameras had identified the laser beams, he pressed a button and the four missiles dropped from two of *Big Bird*'s outboard pylons. Four seconds after being released, their engines ignited. They quickly went supersonic, traveling faster than the roar made by their rocket engines.

"Time for me to go," Kincaid said, standing.

"Let me get my jacket," said Lopez.

"Don't bother. You aren't coming."

"I told you, Patrón. I told you," Carlos yelled. "The gringo was lying to you." He tried to pull Lopez back. Kincaid shot him once in the face.

"Wait," shouted Lopez, putting his hand up in front of Kincaid's gun. "You don't have to kill me. I can make it worth your while. I can reward you handsomely."

"I'm sorry, My Lopez," Kincaid replied. "You've been a big help telling me all who were involved in my father's death. But all I can see is you in a Mexican jail for the next two years living the good life while my father and hundreds, maybe even thousands, of people you have butchered in your life, lie rotting in the ground."

At that moment, the only thing going through Lopez' mind was the vision of the snake and the giant tearing him to pieces. That, and a second later, a bullet.

Kincaid looked down at the body. *For you, dad,* he thought, while knowing he had more to do before his dad could completely rest in peace.

SIX MONTHS LATER

MENDOCINO COUNTY, CALIFORNIA

It was early evening when they turned off Highway One and onto the paved road that the car's GPS said led to their destination. A quarter mile in, they came to an electronic gate and pushed the red button as the sign instructed. A short moment later the gate retracted silently on its steel runners. Before them, across a vast highland meadow, the sun dipped below a series of dark clouds that speckled the horizon. The ocean had turned a blue black, topped with tiny whitecaps as far as the eye could see. The car's occupants were thankful for the mild weather, unusual for this part of the Mendocino coastline in the dead of winter.

The road bent slightly right, and they could see the modern, medium-sized house with an attached garage sitting on a rocky outcrop high above the churning surf. Motion sensor lights came on as they came to a stop in front of the stone pathway leading to the front door.

"Hope he's not waiting inside the door with a gun," Vinnie Delgado said. "The long road in, coupled with motion sensors, are designed to keep him from being surprised by guests."

"Vinnie's right, Rob," Tom McGuire said as he put the car in *park*. "You sure you don't want us to come with you?"

"No, but thanks. I've got to take care of this myself. I've waited long enough." He disengaged his hand from Laura Simpson's sitting next to him in the back seat, put on a pair of latex gloves, kissed her, exited the car and walked to the front door. Before he could ring the bell, the door opened.

"Rob Kincaid," said Bill Hartmann with no surprise in his voice. He looked out at the three people in the car parked in his driveway. He shrugged, as if resigned to his fate. "I've been expecting you. Please come in."

The last time Kincaid had seen Special Agent William Hartmann was three months ago on television. His retirement from the Federal Bureau of Investigation was national news. He was awarded the prestigious Homeland Security Medal by the president himself.

He had aged noticeably since then. His black hair was now generously speckled with gray, and the stomach that spilled over his belt attested to the fact that he had given up both the gym and Weight Watchers.

Hartmann led him through the living room to a large, freshly painted kitchen with walls lined with leaded glass cabinets filled with dishes and pottery of every kind. An antique four-legged green stove stood proudly in the far corner. Off to the right was a small breakfast nook. Hartmann guided Kincaid to it, and offered him a seat at an old-fashioned yellow Formica-topped table.

"Coffee?" he asked.

Kincaid nodded. "Black."

Hartmann disappeared around the corner and came back with two mugs of coffee. He sat down opposite Kincaid, his back to the kitchen's outer wall. "Like the gloves. Nice touch." He took a deliberate sip, swallowed and then said, "I've been following your adventures the last few months. Through the obituaries. I knew you'd show up here sooner or later."

"You are the last," Kincaid said.

The team had stayed on the peak above the Cocoyole valley just long enough to see the encampment obliterated by the Hellfire missiles. They then radioed their position to Thompson and two hours later were picked up by helicopter and taken to the Mexican Marine base at Hermosillo.

Back at NSWC, Kincaid shook Admiral Thompson's hand and thanked him for the opportunity to personally confront Lopez. For his part, Admiral Thompson said the country owed Red Squadron a debt of gratitude for their service.

"How did you find out about my involvement?" Hartmann asked. "The word was Lopez and his people were killed by air-to-surface missiles ordered up by Mexican Special Forces. I knew that probably wasn't the case. I suspected it was you and your people. Did you get to talk to Lopez?"

"I did. It's a long story that I won't bore you with. Let it suffice to say I was sitting in Lopez' tent and he had just handed me his *chief of staff's* weapon. Carlos was the guy's name. Did you ever get a chance to meet him?" Hartmann's face remained impassive. "Just wondering was all. Nice guy but overly suspicious," Kincaid said, toying with him. "But a nice weapon. An HK P7. I dropped the mag and saw it had a full complement of S&W .40 cartridges. *Nice gun*, I remember thinking."

"Stop being so condescending, please. Just tell me how you found out."

"Sorry. You asked so I'm just telling you," Kincaid said. "Let's see. Where was I?" He paused. "Oh, yeah. Well, I had the gun and I asked if I could just talk to him for a while. He agreed.

"I asked him how he knew my dad's flight number. He said right off it came from you." Hartmann stiffened ever so slightly. Kincaid took full notice of the twitch, and smiled inwardly.

"Lopez told me that Palma had received a phone call from you out of the blue. He said neither of them knew who the heck you were. He said they were very skeptical so Palma called a few people in Northern California to check you out. Lopez told me you told Palma about Operation *Snow Plow* and gave him my dad's flight information.

"When I got back from Mexico, I checked. The flight arrangements were made out of the FBI's office in San Francisco, so everyone there knew the airline, flight number and time. Including you. And you told Palma and the *Tormentas*."

"Actually, it was Mike Gray that talked to Palma. He and Brian. I never spoke to the man personally."

"But you ordered him."

Hartmann sat up straight, and looked directly into Kincaid's eyes. Silently unapologetic.

"When I heard you were back and the mission was successful," he said, "I had a hunch you may have extracted some information from Lopez. I knew for sure you had when I started reading the obituaries.

"If I remember correctly," said Hartmann, "the first deaths were the baggage handlers, correct? The ones who planted the bomb?"

Kincaid didn't answer.

"Being in the business I'm in ... or was in ... I had access to a gazillion reports. It was through those reports I followed your path to my door. I don't know if you killed the baggage handlers personally, but if you did I give you a lot of credit. Their deaths are still listed, at least as of about three months ago, as robberies gone awry. No clues. No suspects."

"There are still no clues or suspects," Kincaid said.

"Then that female in San Jose. Everyone knew she had ties to the cartels. Truth was, she actually played both ways. We were using her, too. Lupe Mendoza. She was the one who sent that gang-banger up to San Francisco to kill you. The press reported she was drowned."

"In her bathtub under suspicious circumstances was the official report," Kincaid said. "And don't forget about Agent Garcia."

"Ah, yes. Poor Pete. He was the rational one. The other two were so volatile. They really got worked up over *Snow Plow*. Remember when Gray went after you in our office that first day, and Garcia came to your defense?" Hartmann smiled sadly and shook his head. "But, like the others, he wanted it to succeed so badly that he'd do just about anything to assure it."

"Including killing my father," Kincaid said.

"Including killing your father, yes. He actually was against it at first. But finally succumbed to the pressure from the other two."

"Did you send Hamilton and Gray out to kidnap Laura Simpson?" Kincaid asked. "And hold her until I came for her?"

"The way things operated in our Task Force was by consent. I didn't really order anyone to do anything. They would come and tell me what they had in mind, but it was generally never my plan. The kidnapping was really Gray's doing. He was the one who thought you were the fly in the ointment, and had to be eliminated. Turned out he was right."

Kincaid remained silent.

"And two weeks ago ... Palma," Hartmann said.

Kincaid reached into the small of his back and pulled out a Glock 19. He laid it on the table in front of him. The Glock was given to him by McGuire. Untraceable. Kincaid took pleasure in seeing the fear in Hartmann's eyes. A small payback in and of itself.

"Yes, Mr. Palma," he said, tracing the Glock with his index finger. "Almost as bad as the Angel of Death himself. Lopez told me a lot about Palma. They were childhood friends. Amazing huh?"

Hartmann sat silently for a few moments, then said, "That was a bloody one. Did you kill Palma, or was it the guy in the car outside? In any case, it was bloody. That's why I remembered it so vividly. He was found outside a warehouse on our side of the border, as I remember. Right hand cut off and his throat slit. The official report was gang warfare. But we both know the gangs don't slit throats. Cartels maybe, but not the gangs. Gangs use guns. Much faster and quicker. So it wasn't hard for me to see Palma was your kill."

Kincaid remained silent.

"And now you have come for me. Is that it?"

"Why did you have my father killed?"

"I know this is hard on you, Rob. It was hard on me, too. I liked your dad. We had worked together for years, and worked closely on *Snow Plow*. While not my best friend, he was a good friend. Like a brother in a lot of ways. You have to understand, none of what happened was personal. Walt was brilliant. *Snow Plow* was brilliant. It was his baby. But Walt started to have reservations about the ethics of the operation. It was his operation. He got everyone excited about it, and then decided it was unethical? Come on."

"You killed him because he was having second thoughts?"

"No. The real reason was the president wasn't going to sign the order to send SEALs into Mexico. He was backing out on his commitment to your father. He needed his backboned stiffened. The only thing, in my estimation, that would give him the courage he needed would be the perception that Walt had been murdered by the cartels. If we had asked Walt, he would have thought it was a good idea. Means to an end."

"Did you ask him?"

"No. And I know whatever I say cannot take away your pain, but I hope you can see from all the good that has come from *Snow Plow*, that Walt's death was not in vain."

"Did my dad know about the anthrax?"

"Hell yes. This was *his* plan, Rob, through and through. That's what I meant about his death not being in vain. He knew we were at war, and in war civilian casualties were inevitable. When he conceived the plan he was willing to sacrifice thousands of people in order to win that war, but then as it got closer to being put into operation, he started having second thoughts."

"I have a few questions about the anthrax part of this."

"Ask away."

"At the beginning, you presented it as an attack by Al Qaeda, right? That's how you wanted it seen?"

"Of course. Wouldn't have made any sense otherwise. That's what the common folk would have expected. And *Snow Plow* gave it to them. A terrorist attack. Using anthrax. Got everyone's attention. The public was demanding action."

"And how were you able to switch it from Al Qaeda to the cartels?"

"Well, that was the tricky part. It was testimony to your dad's real genius. Obviously, Task Force 64 couldn't just come out one day and say, 'Oops. We made a mistake. It's not Al Qaeda. It's the cartels.' That would not have flown.

"So your dad came up with a way to let the discovery that the anthrax had been seeded in the drug supply evolve naturally. Your dad obviously couldn't have foreseen you would be involved in any of this. He knew that once the data started coming in, people would see the inconsistency and finally discover the drug angle. We had to doctor the data a little, to highlight the ambiguities. But that wasn't hard."

"How did you get the anthrax?"

"Your dad took TF 64 to New Orleans. I stayed here to run the shop. They contracted with some street gang there to steal the anthrax from a local university lab. The gangbangers never knew what they were stealing."

"And seeding it? How'd you get the amount of drugs needed?"

"Come now. Don't be naïve. Law enforcement warehouses hold enough drugs to rival the cartels. All we did was mix it and get it out on the streets. Once it was out, it had a life of its own. How some made it to the East Coast I'll never know."

In a perverse way, Kincaid was proud of his father. The complexity of *Snow Plow*, all the moving parts, was stunning.

"Your dad did this country a hell of a favor," Hartmann continued. "Through his sacrifice, we accomplished what American society and American politicians have been trying to do since president Reagan's time. To get America off drugs. 'Just Say No,' right? Drugs are a cancer in society. Most of the violence in this country is a direct consequence of drug use. And that violence manifested itself most especially in our inner cities.

"Have you seen the stats lately? Inner city crime is down thirty-eight percent in the last six months. Virtually the entire decline is being attributed to the fact that the demand for drugs in those neighborhoods is down."

Kincaid said nothing.

"You've seen the latest polls, right? Since we put *Snow Plow* into play, drug use in this country has dropped almost sixty-six percent. Just roll that number off your tongue. Sixty-six percent. And since the demand in this country is going down, what's happening in Mexico?

"The cartels are not as rich as they once were, and therefore losing some of the juice they had. Some of the cartels are even branching out. Diversifying. Taking up extortion and human trafficking. More old time Mafioso stuff. Easier for us to monitor and control.

"The violent death rate in Mexico has dropped by fifty percent since *Snow Plow* went operational. Your dad would have willingly given his life for those kinds of numbers. He did a great thing for this country. You have to agree with that, right?"

"It certainly wasn't a great thing for him," Kincaid answered. "It cost him his life. As for the country? I'm not sure about that, either. If I could have been here to talk to him before this got put on paper, I think I would have successfully argued him out of it. On moral grounds, if nothing else.

"Too many people died. But that's just me. There will be others who think differently, of course." Kincaid picked up the Glock. "I'm not smart enough to be the moral arbiter about whether what he did, what Task Force 64 did, was good or bad. I'll let history sort that one out. But I can be the moral arbiter about you. You killed my father and you are now being brought to justice for that murder."

"Is this where you shoot me?" Hartmann asked, looking directly at Kincaid.

"No. I'm going to give you the same chance I gave to Victor Lopez. Well, maybe not the *same* chance, but close. I'm going to give you three choices.

"I will leave here and go directly to the press. I will lay out exactly what you did. Exactly what *Snow Plow* was about. That you had a direct hand in killing over four thousand Americans. I'll get the exact figure before I approach them. I'm sure there are many more. And their only offense? They took drugs."

"They died because of choices *they* made," Hartmann said. "I didn't force them to break the law and take drugs."

"I think most people in this country would say you became responsible when you seeded the anthrax powder into the drug supply."

"I'll take my chances," Hartmann replied. "For most people, I'll be a hero."

"I doubt it, but, again, that's beyond my pay grade. What I do know for sure, Agent Hartmann, is that you would be convicted for killing my father and one hundred and eighteen people on that airplane."

"You have no proof of that. It would be my word against yours."

"How can you be so sure?" Kincaid asked.

Hartmann didn't respond. Just looked down at his hands.

"You would be stripped of your honors. People around the country would look at you as a horrible monster. You'd be put away for life. For a former law enforcement officer, your living conditions in prison would be ... well, let's say ... difficult?"

Hartmann continued to look at his hands. The muscles in his cheeks reflected his clenched teeth.

"Okay," Kincaid said. "Here's your second choice. I'm going to give you a chance to retain your dignity. I'll leave the gun here on the table. It has one bullet in it. The gun has no history so it can't be traced. You can do the honorable thing. The manly thing. It's a chance you didn't give my father. I'll give you time to write a note of explanation."

"And my third option?" he asked.

"I'll shoot you myself."

It was an hour later as Kincaid, Simpson, McGuire and Delgado stood on a bluff a half-mile from the house watching the sun settle into the sea that they heard the shot.

They returned to the house and found Hartmann sitting on the glass enclosed back porch that faced the Pacific Ocean. A typed and signed letter, more of an *apologia* than a confession, was found on his desk in the study. He had used his own weapon to kill himself. McGuire retrieved the Glock. They made one last pass through the house, locked the front door and exited through the garage. At a payphone in a small fishing marina three miles down the main highway, they called the local police and reported hearing a gunshot. They gave the location, and hung up.

Special Agent in Charge William Hartmann was laid to rest with full law enforcement honors. The Deputy Director of the FBI, John Dunnigan, was flown in to give the eulogy. He began by saying that no one can ever understand the personal demons that make a person take their life, but even if Hartmann had lived, the debt the country owed to him could never be repaid. He praised Bill Hartmann as the brilliant leader of *Snow Plow*, the operation that single-handedly won America's War on Drugs, the longest active war in the nation's history. The letter Hartmann wrote was left unmentioned, as were the four thousand Americans who died of anthrax poisoning.

Walter Kincaid was posthumously awarded the FBI Medal of Valor for his part in designing *Snow Plow*, now used as the blueprint for dealing with drugs and drug trafficking.

Rob Kincaid, Laura Simpson, Tom McGuire and Vinnie Delgado were present at both ceremonies, and ultimately satisfied. All the players in the drama known as Operation *Snow Plow* had paid the ultimate price for their participation. It was time to move on.

In January of the next year, Rob Kincaid presided over the opening of Red Squadron Security Agency's new headquarters in San Francisco. At the opening, Laura Simpson was introduced as the firm's new general manager. After purchasing Giants season tickets next to the McGuires', they all went to Arizona to watch the Giants in spring training. A week before the season opened, Rob proposed to Laura. She accepted.

Business was booming. The Giants looked like Series contenders. Kincaid was home and about to become a married man. Life was good.

=

DENNIS KOLLER is the author of *The Oath,* a *Tom McGuire* mystery novel, also set in San Francisco. He came late to novel writing, spending the first 20 years of his career life in marketing. In those years, his creative urges were assuaged by writing articles for trade journals and by writing direct response appeal letters for non-profits, mostly in the higher education space. His company, Pen Communication, specialized in hand-written direct response pieces used by many PBS stations around the country to raise funds. It now publishes his novels. Mr. Koller is a voracious reader and has been following the drug wars in Mexico for the past ten years. He lives in the San Francisco Bay Area. Learn more about his work at www.denniskoller.com.